CAPTIVE OF WOLVES

EVA CHASE

BOUND TO THE FAE

BOOK

1

Captive of Wolves

Book 1 in the Bound to the Fae series

First Digital Edition, 2020

Copyright © 2020 Eva Chase

Cover design: Yocla Book Cover Design

Ebook ISBN: 978-1-989096-82-6

Paperback ISBN: 978-1-989096-83-3

Talia

I can always tell when they've come to steal my blood. It's only those times that my captors arrive all together, the three hulking men-who-aren't-men marching into the room that holds my cage.

When they enter on their own to shove food and water through the bars or to change my toilet bucket, they have a curt, preoccupied air as if paying me any attention bores them. The group effort gets them excited. They always come in chuckling and giving each other hearty smacks on the shoulders, congratulating themselves on a job well done before they've even done it.

Or maybe it's mostly done already. I have no idea what they want my blood for or how large a part of those activities it is.

All I know is that while my entire existence here is awful, these days are the worst.

The second I hear their merry voices on the other side

of the door, my fingers clench around the scratchy fabric of my wool blanket. Every nerve in my body clangs to propel myself away from the threat. But the farthest I can go is the corners of my cage, which isn't anywhere at all.

It'll be over faster the more cooperative I am. And my one chance at ever getting *out* of this awful existence depends on me tamping down on my dread enough to focus all my attention on listening.

As my captors walk in, my fingers keep clutching the blanket. It's the only protection I have against their harsh gazes and sneers. They can't be bothered to go to the trouble of clothing me, but they don't want me coming down with a chill either. I'm valuable enough to be kept alive but not remotely comfortable.

The man at the head of the bunch gazes down at me where I'm crouched on the hard metal floor of the cage, his nose wrinkling in undisguised revulsion. It must stink in here—*I* must stink, considering I can't remember the last time they bothered to even hose me off. I've lived in filth for so many years I can't tell anymore.

As far as I've been able to tell, that man—the one with hair as brilliantly yellow as the petals of a sunflower and ears that rise to inhuman points—is the leader. Yellow doesn't do much other than watch and order the others around. But he's the one who unlocks my cage. I have to concentrate on him.

The second of my captors, the one with the rotund belly and heavy feet, goes to the plain cupboard that's the room's only other furnishing. I think of him as Cutter because of his role in this ritual. He gets out the little ivory-handled knife and a glass vial. My skin twitches in anxious anticipation.

The third of the men bends down beside the cage until he's almost at my level. His lips curl into a grin that looks cut into his ruddy face. He isn't burly like the other two but all sharp angles, from the tips of his ears to the toes of his narrow boots to the tufts of his blueish white hair that poke from his scalp like icicles.

I'm uncomfortably familiar with Ice's angles. Occasionally he gets bored enough with whatever else his life consists of to saunter in here and "play" with me. He'll poke and prod until he forces out a gasp of pain.

They have a rule about injuring me—I've heard them talk about it. Nothing that could jeopardize my life is allowed. Ice has made a hobby out of discovering all the ways he can torment my body without causing any tangible damage.

Not surprisingly, he's always the one who volunteers to pin me down.

I could make it even easier for them. I could sprawl out on my belly the way they'll want me positioned so he has no reason to shove me down. But he'll push me around anyway, and whatever small fragment of pride I've somehow held onto balks at the thought of prostrating myself quite that willingly.

Yellow leans forward. Black tattoos in unfamiliar symbols mark all of their bodies, but he has the most, several on his arms and neck, one poking from his hairline at his temple. A twisting line from one stretches across his chin all the way to his lips.

He's going to say the word—the word that spills from

his mouth with a resonance that prickles down my spine. The word that opens the door.

The word I have to learn.

He rests his hand on the latch. His lips part, and the sounds slip out fast and sibilant, one blending into the next. "*Fee-doom-ace-own.*"

That's what it sounds like to my pricked ears, anyway. That's what it's sounded like since I realized some kind of magic holds my cage closed and that the word is the key, although it took several attempts before I was sure of each of the syllables. I replay everything I've heard my captors say over and over in my head, searching for meanings beyond the obvious that might offer a helpful clue to ending my torment, but that word is the one I've returned to the most.

I'm still not *really* sure of it, or I'd be able to say it properly, wouldn't I? Just how much does his voice lilt upwards with the "ace" bit? How long does he stretch out the "o" in "own"?

What am I missing?

I might be missing the capacity to work any kind of magic word at all, no matter how well I say it. In the back of my head, I know that, not any flaw in my concentration, could be the problem. Because these *aren't* really men, and they have powers beyond anything I understood before they threw me in this cage. He says the word quietly and quickly, but I don't think he's all that worried about me overhearing it.

He doesn't think I could use it. But it's all I have.

He unhooks the latch. The hinges squeak as the door swings open.

The cage is barely big enough for me. When I'm sitting, I can touch the bars overhead without raising my arm completely. Standing is out of the question. But the doorway is large enough for Ice to squeeze through. There's just enough space for him to grab me by the back of my neck and slam my face against the floor.

Pain radiates through my skull. He clambers on top of me with his pointy knees digging into my calves and the spikes of his elbows jabbing my ribs. His weight bears down on my back, squashing most of the air from my lungs until I'm on the verge of suffocating. He grinds one of those elbows into the tender spot just below my shoulder blade, and I catch my lower lip between my teeth.

I hate the whimper that slips out of me anyway. I hate his fingers burrowing into the hollow between my cheek and my jaw to press my face even harder against the grubby metal. I hate that he knows exactly how to take me from discomfort to agony in the space of a breath.

I hate the jagged snicker that tells me how much he loves it. There are easier ways they could position me, but this one is more fun for them.

A jolt of adrenaline shoots through my veins, more panic than anything else, and I have to clamp down hard to smother the urge to thrash against Ice's hold. There is no escaping him. I know that. And the one time I tried, when I didn't know very much yet, the man on top of me repaid me in spades for the one kick I landed to his gut. He grasped my foot and twisted his hands, and the bones snapped in an explosion of pain.

That pain has never quite gone away. They didn't let

the fractures heal right—a little extra security against me running away. I can't really walk in this cage, but any time I put weight on that foot, a dull ache spreads through it. Extra security and a constant reminder of the consequences of fighting back.

I have other ways of defying them that they can't see. I pull all the way back into my mind, into the depths where the pain is only a distant buzzing, into an imagined vision of the world they wrenched me from. It isn't a part of that world I ever experienced in real life, but one I dreamed about traveling to someday back when I could have dreams that large.

Before me lies a broad pool of turquoise water surrounded by weather-sculpted rock. Brilliant sun beams down to glitter off the ripples. I would drift in that pool, embraced by gentle warmth, gazing up at the clear blue sky...

Cutter lets out a raspy sound of amusement. "Can we have her arm already?"

Ice leans his weight onto his left elbow in a way that nearly dislocates my shoulder. The spike of pain shatters the illusion I've formed in my head. As he yanks my other arm toward the open door, I grit my teeth, but a little cry seeps out anyway. He snickers again. I squeeze my eyes shut, tears leaking out despite my best efforts.

Cutter doesn't revel in the process, but he doesn't appear to have any objection to his companion's antics. Without another word, he slices the knife into my wrist.

It's a shallow stinging, mostly drowned out by the cacophony of hurts already coursing through my body. From the glimpses I've gotten of the vial, they only take a few teaspoons. He pinches the flesh and then ties a thin bandage over the wound with a perfunctory tug to fix it in place.

Cutter straightens up. Ice pushes off me, knocking my head against the metal floor once more for good measure. When he's clambered out, Yellow shuts the cage door and voices his magic to lock it.

Normally, this is when they'd leave. Instead, Ice peers down at me, folding his arms over his chest. The light glittering off the pale, spiky tufts on his head turns them even chillier-looking.

"She barely responds anymore," he says. "It makes this rather tiresome."

Cutter shakes his head. "Only you would wish for a fight."

"I'm only saying that while we have her, we might as well make use of her for some entertainment in between more vital matters."

"What did you have in mind?" Yellow asks as if he doesn't really care about the answer. He's eyeing the vial rather than me, with a triumphant gleam in his eyes.

Ice rubs his jaw, showing the tattoo that spears across his knuckles. "We could give her the run of the castle. Make it more of a chase."

Hope flickers to life in my chest despite the throbbing of my ribs. I might not even need to make the magic work to get my chance. If I could get that much closer to—

His sneering voice cuts through my thoughts. "Of course, I'd break her other ankle to ensure she can't get far without our say so. She can crawl around the place like the vermin she is."

My blood freezes, a wave of despair dousing the flare of hope in an instant. *No.* Fleeing this place with one unsteady leg would be hard enough. Escaping without the use of either... They might as well cage me within my body and swallow the key.

"Let me think on it," Yellow says in the same distracted tone. "It is something of a waste putting her to use so infrequently. Perhaps she could polish the floors while she's down there."

He's really considering it. I bite back the scream that's trying to bubble up my throat.

"Sleep well, dung-body!" Ice calls over his shoulder to me, and they all laugh as they head out.

A shiver runs through my limbs. Within moments, I'm shaking so hard I can't get a hold of myself. I roll onto my side and pull my knees up to my chest, gulping air and groping for control.

I can't let it happen. I can't. I can't. I'd rather be dead.

But they won't let me take that escape either.

Listen. I have to listen to that magic word again. Listen and then try, oh please, oh please...

I close my eyes and reach back to the turquoise pool I pasted into my scrapbook of wonderful places years ago, when I was still a kid. I can't quite conjure up the warble of the breeze over the water or its warm caress against my face, but gradually, my shudders peter out.

Over time, I've built an extensive imaginary world inside my head. Along with the exotic locations from my scrapbook, I summon up scenes from favorite movies: mine, sweeping fantasy epics of heroic adventures, and the ones Mom always loved, comedies where everyone speaks in arch remarks and often with British accents. In the long stretches of when I'm left alone, I fantasize about stepping into those stories, joining conversations with comments that sound just as valiant or smart. It stops my brain from turning into mush with boredom.

If it weren't for that pretend world, this existence would probably have reduced me to a mess of vague thoughts, shudders, and pain by now. I run my fingers down my side to my right hipbone, to the tiny mottling of scars there. One for each year I've been able to mark, digging my ragged fingernail into my skin until it bled. Eight altogether.

How many more years lie ahead if they shackle me to a ruined body and set me to work? Will I even be able to drift away inside my head in between the worst parts, or will I lose even that make-believe escape?

Another shiver ripples through me. I force myself to breathe slow and steady. The chance isn't gone yet. I have to focus on that and not on the terrors that might lie ahead.

As I uncurl myself, I reach toward the ceiling of my cage. I might not be able to walk in here, but I've kept myself strong however I can. Gripping the bars, I heft myself up and down, over and over, until a different sort of ache burns through my muscles.

It isn't comfortable, but there's something satisfying about knowing I still have some small say over what my body is put through. It helps that the exertion makes it hard to think about my future, now even more precarious than before.

I'm bicycling my legs in an attempt to work those

muscles too when the sound I've been waiting for reaches my ears. The muffled but audible thud of what I assume is the building's front door carries all the way to this room.

I flip into a crouched position, keeping most of my weight on my good foot. My captors never say much around me, but from the snippets I've gathered over the years, I've gotten the impression they have to leave this place to complete their plans. I don't know who else might live in the building other than the three of them, but to the best of my knowledge, no one else here has ever seen me. Even if I run into another inhabitant, they might not realize I'm meant to be a prisoner.

If I want to regain my freedom, this is my best opportunity. Possibly the last opportunity I'm ever going to get.

I just have to say that strange word right.

I tip so close to the cage door that my forehead brushes the bars. Fixing my eyes on the latch, I dredge up my memory of my captor's lilting pronunciation. My voice comes out in a whisper. "Fee-doom-ace-own."

When I reach through the bars to rattle the latch, it doesn't budge. I'm *sure* I said it exactly the same way Yellow did. But then, I've felt that way dozens of times before.

"Fee-doom-ace-own," I say at the latch, letting my voice rise, shifting my inflection. "Fee-doom-ace-own. Fee-*doom*-ace-own. Fee-doom-ace-*own*! Come on!"

My heart is pounding. I grasp the bars and gather my composure. It's not just being trapped in here that I'm scared of. I'm also scared of what will happen if I *do* get out. What I might face beyond this room. What my captors will do to me if they catch me. Every time I've tried this, that terror lurks right behind my resolve.

I can't let the fear stop me. I *can't*. Nothing could be worse than what I'll face if the sharp-edged man gets his way.

Thinking about dragging myself around this place with its bone-white floors and walls, scrubbing them clean, enduring jabs and kicks all day long, my soul recoils. That tropical pool I dream about is out there somewhere. Even if it feels like a fantasy now, it's a place as real as this one. Wouldn't it be worth anything to get there?

I'll scream at the lock until I'm hoarse if that's what it takes. I can do this. I have to.

I train my gaze on the lock and pull all my determination into my lungs. "Fee-doom-ace-own. *Fee*-doom-ace-own. Fee-*doom*-ace-*own*. *Fee-doom-ace-own!*"

The final incantation crackles over my tongue like an electric shock. The hairs on my arms jump to attention, my mouth goes abruptly dry—and the latch twists beneath my desperate fingers.

I'm so startled I nearly choke on the little saliva I have left. Breath held, I apply more pressure, and the latch turns all the way. The door squeaks open at my nudge. The way is clear.

I'm *free*. Of the cage, at least. Oh my god.

In that first moment, my body locks in place. I clench my jaw and tug the scratchy fabric of my blanket around me in a makeshift cloak. I ease out through the opening, first my head and shoulders, then a shuffling step—

A thump and a shattering sound reverberates through the room's ceiling, and I flinch. Panic seizes me.

They've come back. They've come back early, and they're angry.

The thought has barely passed through my head before voices filter through the door. Terror blanks my mind. On pure instinct, I yank the cage's door closed and throw myself to the back of the space, huddling under the blanket in case something in my expression or my pose will give away what I've accomplished.

There's a scuffling noise outside, which isn't what I'd expect. Then footsteps tramp in, accompanied by those voices—but now that I can hear them more clearly, I don't recognize the speakers.

"Phew. Whatever they were keeping in that cage, they obviously didn't believe in cleaning up after it." That voice is buoyant with more warmth than I've ever heard any of my captors express. He must take me for just a heap of blanket, nothing living in here right now. I will my body to stay utterly still.

It doesn't sound as if he's *bothered* by the fact that my captors would have been keeping something in this cage. Even if he seems friendlier than them, that doesn't mean he's any kinder. Who are these people? What are they doing here?

"This doesn't look like a room where they'd be keeping their notes stashed," he goes on. "Or… how did Sylas put it? 'Apparatus'?"

The voice that answers is dryly melodic but equally male. "If only Aerik and his cadre had been kind enough to leave detailed instructions posted in their front hall. It appears they're just as irritating in this as they are in every other way."

"I suppose it *is* their big secret."

"Let's not have any sympathy for the devils, now. Come on, we may as well have a look in this cabinet while we're here."

I'm still tensed, motionless, under the blanket, but the fabric has fallen so that one fold gives me a sliver of a view into the room. A man strides into view, tall with ample brawn filling out his simple tee, dark auburn hair sprouting above his broad, boyish face. As he inspects the cabinet, his eyes gleam so avidly I assume the first voice was his.

He doesn't look menacing, despite all that powerful bulk, and his ears are smoothly rounded at the top, but my gaze catches on the black symbols inked on his skin. One follows the curve of his bicep; another partly encircles his wrist. Symbols like the tattoos all three of my captors display.

My body goes even more rigid than it already was. Whoever he is, he must be one of them. A man-who's-not-a-man. A monster in human-like skin.

The other man saunters up beside him: even taller and equally brawny in his high-collared shirt, his tawny hair rumpled into artful disarray. Where the first man gives off an eager, youthful energy, this one is all languid, muscular poise. With the angle of his face, I can only see the corner of his smile—and an ear with a low but obvious point at its peak.

"Well, now we know where they keep some of their empty glassware and linens. No papers in there?"

The boyish one leans in to paw through the contents. "Doesn't look like it." He sighs and swivels on his heel with no diminishing of his upbeat energy. "So much for that. Let's see what else they've stashed down here in the basement."

The poised one holds up his hand. The edge of a tattoo spirals up across the heel to his palm. "Just a moment. There's something..." He inhales audibly and turns —toward me.

I stop breathing completely. I am a rock. A bundle of rags. A lump of nothingness that should be of no interest to anyone.

My silent pleas have no effect. The man's nostrils flare, and he stalks toward my cage with a purposefulness that turns my gut to water.

2

Talia

With the intruder standing right in front of my cage, I can only make out one leg in trim midnight-blue slacks through the small gap in the folds of my blanket. My body screams out for me to sink into the hard metal floor, away from him—as if I wouldn't have done that years ago if I could.

Please, no. I was so close. Just leave, leave me alone, let me flee.

My heart is thudding so hard it nearly drowns out his dry voice.

"With all the foul smells in here I almost missed it. Take a good, deep breath, little brother, and tell me what your nose tells you."

The other one sucks in a breath. My own breath quivers over my lips, as shallow as I can keep it.

"There's a hint—like the tonic." The boyish one's voice

vibrates with excitement. "And… human." Another breath. "Female?"

Oh, no. What do I do now? The cage door—it isn't even locked. I released the magic on the latch. Horror crawls through me with a betraying twitch of my arm.

"Human, female, and awake, though in what state beyond that I can hardly guess. It would appear this cage is still in use after all." There's a rustle of fabric as the poised man drops into a crouch. "Get our glorious leader. He should be here for this."

Footsteps thump as the other one dashes away. An ache has formed at the top of my throat. It's taking all my strength to hold my body in place, frantic tension clutching every muscle.

The way these men have talked, I don't think they like my captors very much. What does that mean for me? What are they going to do to me?

They could be better than the monsters who stole me… or they could be worse. And even *better* wouldn't necessarily mean *good*. Right now, all I'm sure of is they're cutting off my last chance at escape.

The man speaks in a lower, smoother tone. "Hello in there. Why don't you come out and let us have a look at you? Can you even understand me?"

As long as he thinks I can't, I have an excuse not to respond. I stay where I am.

More footsteps thump into the room—at least a few sets. How many of these intruders are there?

A rich baritone resonates through the room with a note of total authority. "What's the fuss about, Whitt? We can't be sidetracked by Aerik's vulgar hobbies."

"I don't think this is a sidetrack—I think this is *the* track, straight to our goal. Perhaps they have this servant assist them in making the tonic. There's a whiff of it in here."

"All the whiffs I'm catching are putrid," a fourth voice says, this one sharp and grating. It reminds me so strongly of the man who pinned me down less than an hour ago that I flinch.

There's a pause, and then I sense someone else crouching by the cage. "No, Whitt's right. Can she speak?"

"I don't know," says the poised one who's apparently named Whitt. "This is all we've gotten out of her so far: a very adept impression of a crumpled blanket."

"Well, we don't have time to wait for her to warm up to us. Let's see what we've got in here."

The latch clicks; the hinges squeak. My body clenches up, my fingers digging into the coarse fabric, but of course that doesn't stop him. A powerful tug on the blanket pulls it partway off me, exposing my bare back and legs to the room's cool air.

It's too much. Panic flashes through me, and without any conscious intention, I'm snatching at the blanket, wrenching it toward me, kicking out with my legs. My good foot smacks a solid arm. I jerk back against the bars of the cage, my pulse hammering—oh god, am I going to have my ankle shattered by *these* monsters?

The man with the resonant voice just... laughs. Not my captors' jeering snickers, but a deep guffaw as if he's a little impressed along with his amusement. "We've got a fighter," he says. "Pitiful thing. Come on now, we just need to talk."

And I'm supposed to believe that? I let the fabric tumble away from my face so I can see what I'm fighting against and find myself staring into a pair of mismatched eyes set in brown skin.

The man who's leaning through the cage door looms even larger and brawnier than the first two, like a grizzly among lesser bears. He carries a mark of at least one violent battle. His right eye, fixed on me, is a dark brown as rich as his voice. The other shines milky white, bisected by a pale, jagged scar that cuts from his hairline across the eyelid to halfway down his cheek.

Thick waves of coffee-brown hair fall to his massive shoulders, but don't quite obscure the steep points of his ears. Curving black lines of tattoos creep up his neck from under his shirt collar. More darken his forehead and the edges of his jaw. Every inch of his being emanates power.

The sense washes over me that if he wanted to, he could maul any of my captors to shreds without suffering more than a few scratches. Possibly all three of them at the same time.

I don't stand a chance.

"There we go," he says evenly. "Answer a few questions about your masters, and we'll leave you alone. We're not here to hurt you."

Someone behind him makes a rough noise. The boyish man-who's-not-a-man peers over the grizzly's shoulder. "Somehow I'm thinking Aerik and them don't have the same qualms."

"It's none of our concern," the sharp-voiced man says from somewhere beyond my view. "Let dung-bodies wallow in dung. We need to know about the tonic."

"Hush," the grizzly says without looking back, quiet but firm. His attention stays on me. "What do they have you do for them, little scrap? Something like cooking? Can you tell us about it?"

My voice stays locked at the back of my mouth. I don't want to tell them anything, but I'm not sure I could even if I did want to. There's a lump as big and hard as a fist lodged in my throat.

"It appears she's dumb in more ways than one," the sharp voice says. "Drag her out and make her show us."

I can see just enough of the poised one—Whitt's—face to watch him roll his pale eyes. "Right. Fantastic plan. Take the creature that's already terrified mute and terrify her more. That'll definitely open her up."

"There are other ways we could open her up," the other snaps.

The grizzly slashes his broad hand through the air, its back dappled with another tattoo. "Enough." As the others fall silent, his gaze roves over me. Even with the blanket, even though he only has one eye to inspect me with, I feel utterly exposed.

"Ignore them," he says to me. "This is just between you and me. Your masters let you out sometimes, don't they? They bring you to another room—somewhere they're mixing things or bottling things? I only need to know where, and then we're gone. We'll see that you forget we were ever even here."

I do want them gone. Gone so I can scramble out of here before those "masters" return. But I have no idea what he's talking about. My captors never let me out, and I've never heard them talk about cooking anything.

My throat is still closed, but I manage to shake my head, willing him to understand. Willing him not to be angry. I don't have what they want. I can't help them with whatever they're searching for.

"No?" He frowns, which turns his already intimidating face fierce. My pulse lurches. "Do they bring something in here for you to help them with?"

I shake my head again, not quite restraining a shiver at the same time, and the blanket slips over my arm. The grizzly glances down at my wrist, and even though he was crouching there unmoving before, somehow he goes even more still.

Before I can react, his hand shoots out to grab my arm just below the bandage. He yanks it toward him. A yelp jolts out of me.

I try to scramble backward, but there's nowhere to go, and his fingers grip me tightly. He pulls my wrist level with his nose. His eyes widen.

"Please," I say, my voice stretching so thin on its way up my constricted throat that it's barely a whisper.

He doesn't seem to hear. Still clutching my arm, he turns toward his companions.

"She doesn't smell like the tonic because they put her to work on it. She smells like it because she *is* it."

The one called Whitt guffaws. "She *is* the tonic? She hardly looks fit to be bottled."

The grizzly glowers at him and jerks my arm up higher. "They bled her today. The scent is clear as anything. *This* is their wretched secret ingredient."

Through the panic and my scattered thoughts, the pieces click together. What they're searching for is the same as the reason the other monsters take my blood. They aren't going to leave me alone. They're here for *me*.

What fresh hell will they drag me into?

The moment that question crosses my mind, my body is already reacting. I flail and thrash, hitting out with every limb, a piercing wail wrenching out of me. *No, no, no. No more. Not when I was so close.*

"Shut her up!" one of them says.

The grizzly is already heaving me toward him, blanket and all. His powerful arms squeeze me against him, trapping my arms. The smacking of my knees against his thighs doesn't make him so much as blink. His hand claps over my mouth, and a scent like earth and woodsmoke fills my nose with my next frantic breath.

As I squirm and kick, voices volley around us.

"This isn't what we planned for. We weren't supposed to be taking prisoners."

"If she's what we need, then she's our new guest of honor. Let's get her out of here fast, before she makes such a stir the neighbors catch on."

"Snap her neck—that would do the trick."

Panic blares through me with a shriller edge. I struggle twice as hard, as hopeless as it feels. The grizzly hefts me up in his arms like I'm weightless, one arm dropping to catch my legs, and then I'm bundled tight against him, barely able to move. I swing back my head, one of the few parts of me not clamped in place, and my skull slams into my kidnapper's jaw.

He lets out the faintest of grunts, his grip not loosening in the slightest. "Kill her, and there goes the supply. We'll take her—now. But we need her pliant to get her out of here unnoticed. August, the blanking grip."

"But—"

The next word is a snarl. "*Now.*"

I wriggle in his hold like a fish wrapped in a net, my head whipping back and forth, but it's not enough. The man with the warm, boyish face steps up beside the grizzly and presses his hand to the crook of my neck. As he says a quiet but emphatic word, his thumb and forefinger pinch and squeeze—and my awareness snuffs out into blackness.

3

Sylas

The moon is on the rise. Even with it hidden beyond the oaks and pines around us, I'm aware of every fraction of its journey to scale the horizon. The prickling energy of its full-faced state carries on the warm evening breeze alongside the green and musky scents of the forest and the beasts that live in it. Once, the ghostly impressions beyond regular sight that sometimes seep through my deadened eye show a glimpse of it like a translucent afterimage superimposed against the shadows.

Far too soon, that round white circle will be completely exposed in the darkening sky. With every passing minute, its energy niggles deeper into my bones.

I don't like it. I don't like the turn our mission took or how much time we had to spend departing Aerik's fortress with our unexpected cargo. I thought we'd be hurrying off with a sheaf of papers or a notebook or two, ideally after downing a vial of the tonic. We'd have moved faster and had more advantage of stealth in our wolfish forms. We wouldn't have needed to worry about that moon.

But there were no vials remaining in the fortress. Aerik and his pack must have taken this month's entire batch to distribute. And while our cargo isn't much more than a slip of a creature, she's still significantly more unwieldly than a book.

Aerik and his cadre will know someone broke in. The pottery Kellan smashed—accidentally, he said, but the bastard can be fastidiously careful when it suits *him*—would have told the story well enough even if we weren't absconding with an entire human girl they were keeping locked away. The last thing I want is to add our names to that story. No one can know it was Sylas and his cadre who stole the secret of the tonic, not until we've decided exactly how we're going to leverage that secret in our favor.

So, we had to make awkward use of one of the faded pack member's wheelbarrows and some hasty concealment spells, and now we're tramping through the forest an hour later than we were meant to be returning to our carriage. Which means we're an hour closer to the moment when the full moon's energy overwhelms us completely.

There's no telling what we might do then. Whether we'd spare the girl or savage her or misplace her in the woods. Whether we'd rage deeper into the woods or back out into the open fields where Aerik's pack might spot us on their return. If we don't make it away from this foray in time, we'll manage to fall even farther in standing than we already have, and that catastrophe will be on my shoulders too.

August is carrying the girl now, slung over his

shoulder, still limp from his magic-enhanced touch. With her ratty blanket wrapped around most of her scrawny form, she bears an uncomfortable resemblance to a sack of bones—and a half-empty one at that. The pink ridges of scarring that mottle one of her knobby shoulders bear testament to a more brutal savaging than the cut on her wrist some time in her past—a savaging that appears to have come with a gouging of wolfish fangs.

This is the key to Aerik's surge in prestige, to all the favor he's curried in the past several years, and he's treated her with less dignity than I'd subject my worst enemy to. Starved, hunched, and filthy, mute with fear at the very sight of us…

I can't shake the image of my first glimpse of her eyes, the pale green of newly budded leaves but bloomed wide with terror, so striking in her sallow, sunken face.

A rat would deserve better treatment, and humans are leagues closer to fae than any rodent. I'd amassed a great deal of disgust for Aerik's methods already, and I believe tonight has just doubled it in magnitude.

Not all of my companions would agree with me on the measure of humans compared to rodents, though. Kellan stalks behind August with his silvery gaze lingering on the slumped girl, his expression like that of a cat planning to pounce on a mouse. I've kept our home free of human servants to spare them from his inclinations, but clearly that's only given him plenty of time to stockpile his antagonism toward those who turn so quickly to dust.

He notices my gaze and gives me the bitterest of wolfish grins. "So much riding on a piece of dung. No wonder Aerik kept the secret so very quiet."

"I expect it had more to do with the fact that the blustering prick relished lording his mysterious cure over the rest of us," Whitt remarks in his careless way. He strides along with an air of total nonchalance, but I can scent a hint of stress from him.

I doubt it's the coming of the moon that worries him, though all of my cadre will be able to sense it as well as I can. He's never been overly concerned about the shifting of our natures—which I suppose makes sense, considering he earned the nickname "Wild Whitt" well before that wildness became inescapable. He has no shortage of pride, though. He won't like the idea of our raid being discovered and the disgrace that would follow any more than I do.

Even Kellan's chuckle manages to sound bitter. "Still, imagine having to keep this stinking creature around for years, having to handle the pathetic thing before every full moon, always needing to be so *careful* with it so as not to lose the rotting source of their claim to glory." His lip curls with disgust aimed in a very different direction from mine. "The only proper use for a dung-body—"

"The only proper use for your *mouth* right now would be to take in enough breath to pick up your pace," I interrupt, keeping the edge in my voice firm rather than acerbic. He *is* a member of my cadre, and I am his lord, and I will not swat him across the head as if he were a sulking whelp, as much as I might sometimes be tempted to.

I owe him more than that, and may I never forget it. He certainly never will.

Clearly I will have to keep an eye on him when it comes to the newest—if temporary—member of our household, though. So far, Kellan hasn't overtly disobeyed a direct order. He knows there'd be no room for leniency there. But he has appeared to enjoy finding ways to maneuver around my obvious intentions, increasingly so in the past few years.

In consideration of his circumstances and our history, I've allowed him all the patience I can, but there are limits. There may come a point when he'll regret trying me.

The bloated orb of the moon will be easing its thickest span above the horizon now. We have perhaps fifteen minutes before the change comes. As long as we're on our enchanted ride and away, it won't matter. The secure hold I conjured with the thing to ensure we didn't damage our bounty is large enough to hold the girl.

We must be almost upon the carriage. I'm running low on the landmarks I made note of to guide our way—

Whitt has sauntered farther ahead. He halts, his head jerking around to scan a small clearing—a clearing that's familiar and too empty for comfort. An annoyed breath hisses through his teeth.

"Our ride appears to have conveyed itself without us."

I curse under my breath. I know the true names of every family of tree in this wood and any other; I can talk a seed into a sapling; but while I've lived so far from the Heart of the Mists, my magic has dwindled. All it would take is for some other nearby fae with greater reserves calling for a vehicle, and my hold on the conjured carriage would falter.

August swings around, a shadow crossing his normally cheerful face. "How are we going to get back? We're still too close, and the moon—"

"I know." I swivel, taking in the forest. "I can fashion another carriage." It might take a minor sacrifice after all the power I've already expended this evening, but a bit of skin is nothing compared to the vengeance Aerik will want to rain down. "I just need to find a juniper."

None of that specific tart scent reaches my nose. There is nothing I can use close by. A fresh wave of the full moon's prickling energy washes through my body, making my thoughts twitch. Soon I'll lose my ability to control them—to control all of me—altogether. My jaw clenches.

"Let's move!" I bark, and lope through the trees at a faster pace, drawing lungfuls of air through my mouth. If I can catch even the slightest hint of juniper to direct my way... I train my dead eye as intently as my whole one, willing it to offer some fleeting image that might help, but all it catches on is a shimmering echo of the carriage racing away through the forest as it must have done not long ago.

A shiver runs through my body, nearly making me stumble. My muscles aren't just prickling now but coiling in anticipation. My skin tightens, and an ache runs through my gums where my fangs are on the verge of springing forth.

The change is coming on faster, stronger, than ever before. That's the story of our wretched lives, isn't it? Even if I slammed into a juniper right this instant, I'm not sure I could hold onto my awareness long enough to work the necessary spell.

A growl is building in my throat, and my shoulders are itching to bow. In a matter of moments, I'll be nothing but a mindless beast.

The wrongness of our malady stabs through me. I am Sylas once of Hearthshire, lord of my lands even if those lands aren't much better than a dung heap these days, and I succumb to no one.

No one except my own raging beast erupting out of me to meet the moon.

I wheel toward the others. August has stumbled with a ragged grunt. He bends, his back shuddering, the girl slipping from his grasp. Her bandaged wrist falls toward the ground, and one solid thought anchors me in the midst of the storm rising within.

I didn't want to do it this way. We don't even know what she is or how she is it. But none of that will matter if we lose ourselves to our beasts tonight.

With the last bit of conscious will I have in me, I throw myself to August's side, raise the girl's hand to my lips, and nick her forefinger on my sharpening teeth.

The merest bead of her blood seeps into my mouth, sharp and metallic with that odd glimmer of resin-y brightness that I recognized from Aerik's tonics. The second it touches my tongue, the furious clouds rolling through my mind dissipate. The contractions in my muscles release. My fangs retreat.

I am myself again—fully, gloriously myself, like stepping out of searing heat into the cool spray of a waterfall. I could roar with joy.

But I don't, because I have my cadre to think of. I grasp August's shoulder and press the girl's split fingertip into his mouth. His breath hitches halfway into a snarl. He gazes up at me with startled, awed understanding lighting in his face.

Whitt pitches forward, his body shaking. He lurches into a tree trunk. I scoop up the girl's horrifyingly meager weight and stride toward him. It takes a few seconds, his head thrashing from side to side as his skull stretches, for me to get a grip on his jaw tight enough to be sure he won't chomp her whole hand off. I maneuver the nicked finger between his lips.

With the taste of her blood, he sags onto the ground, his features reverting to their usual configuration. He takes a deep gulp of the night air and laughs with abandon.

Kellan has collapsed into the dirt, his limbs bending into their wolfish alignment, his face now fully canine. As I approach, he snaps at me, staggering up on four legs. His body isn't quite finished reshaping itself though, and his balance is off. I swipe a smear of the girl's blood across my own finger, catch his muzzle in mid-sway, and dab the miraculous substance on his tongue.

He finishes his shift, but with alert awareness in his darkening eyes. His wolf stretches and shakes out its body, and then he rears up to transform back into a man. He stands there staring at the girl in my arms with an expression that looks as revolted as it does elated.

Yes, I will definitely need to keep a tight leash on him around the human.

Whitt has picked himself up, brushing grit from his clothes. He's ogling the girl too, but in his case it's only open amazement.

"By all that is dust. To halt the change right in the middle of it—it barely took a second—" He shakes his head with another laugh. Then something in his face shutters again. "What *is* she? How in the lands did Aerik find this treasure?"

"I expect we'll get more answers from her back at the keep," I say. "We must get the entire measure of the situation before we decide how to proceed from here."

Kellan's lips curl into a grin that can only be described as vicious. "I don't give a rat's ass what she is. There's no way the arch-lords can dismiss a gift like this."

August's head jerks around. "Who says we're offering her to the arch-lords just like that?"

I tuck the girl's limp body over my shoulder much as he did before and raise my other hand. "We aren't doing any offering or gifting or anything else until we understand what we're dealing with. And for that, we need to get home. Whoever finds me a juniper first gets the last of yesterday's roast."

That both shuts them up and sets them stalking off in different directions. I adjust the girl in my grasp, the sap-like note of her scent teasing my nose again.

She's a treasure, all right—a prize beyond imagining, and a complication far more immense than I'd made any preparations for.

4

Talia

The first thing I'm aware of is the drape of a soft sheet over my shoulders. My head is nestled in a fluffy pillow. Fresh summer-sweet air grazes my cheek.

The sensations are so familiar and yet not that my mind jars to a halt around one thought: it was all a dream. No, a nightmare. An excruciating, seemingly endless nightmare that I've finally woken up from into my actual bed in my actual bedroom, and any second now Mom will rap on the doorframe and ask whether I want waffles or French toast for Saturday breakfast, and Jamie will leap onto the bed and insist I help him with some tricky level in his latest video game, and everything will be perfectly, blissfully *normal*.

Then I open my eyes.

I find myself gazing up at a ceiling that's nothing at all like my ceiling back home. It looks as if it's made out of the kind of vibrant, polished wood you'd expect from floors in some old but posh mansion, rings and whorls showing faintly in the chestnut-brown grain.

And it's not just the ceiling. I ease my head to the side and take in the rest of the room. The walls and, yes, the floor gleam with the same wood, other than a finely woven rug that covers a patch beside the bed.

I *am* lying in a bed, one with posts of a darker wood carved with intricate fern leaves, a spruce-green sheet covering me to my shoulders, a blanket in the same hue woven with silver embroidery folded at the foot. Matching curtains in a heavy fabric hang on either side of a window. Sunlight streams through it across the rug and one corner of the bed.

I blink and blink again, dizzy even though I've barely moved. I'm not home, but I'm not in my cage. Is *this* a dream? A startlingly real one that my captors will shock me out of at any moment with the clink of a glass of lukewarm water or a dish of jumbled food scraps hitting the floor? How—? Where—?

The memories of my last waking moments rush into my head in a flood. Opening the cage—the unexpected noises. The four unfamiliar men-who-aren't-men gathering around my cage, questioning me… threatening me. Dragging me out.

Did *they* bring me here? Why would they put me in a room like this? Why did they want me at all? They were looking for something—something about a "tonic." That must have been what my captors were putting my blood into. Why anyone wanted that tonic, especially enough to steal me away over it, I still have no idea.

The monsters who've kept me all this time won't be

happy about my disappearance. I remember how loud the leader yelled at the sharp-edged one the time early on when he wasn't so careful with his torments and I spent a day retching up everything in my stomach. *She's not here to be your toy. We need her alive. Find something else to play with before you destroy everything we've gained.*

I recovered from those injuries, and the sharp man resumed his playing after a short period of penance, but it was always clear: having me alive was important. *Having* me was important, period. And now they don't.

What will they do to steal me back?

Different images flash through my mind. Shudders of color and sounds blot out the room around me. Scarlet on dusky green, a scream, a fleshy tearing noise, the stars swaying overhead—

When I'm aware of my body again, it's trembling, my breath coming in short pants. My heart is racing as if I've just run a mile full tilt. I feel like I might vomit now.

I roll over and press my face into the pillow. It's real. A delicate lavender scent tickles into my nose. I send my mind off to another of the photos I printed off of a landscape I dreamed of visiting one day—a vibrant green landscape with little hills rising in whorls like miniature castles—until my breaths and my pulse even out. Then I dare to open my eyes again.

How can I think about the future when I don't even understand my present? The simple act of breathing bewilders me. When was the last time I tasted outside air rather than the stale, lifeless stuff in the room that held my cage?

At least eight years, by the scars on my hip. Eight years

since I breathed fresh air. Eight years since I felt sunlight. Eight years since I set eyes on anything outside.

I've accomplished the first of those things. A desperate urge grips me to achieve the other two before anyone can come and take them away from me all over again.

I push myself to the edge of the bed and discover in the process one more thing that's different: I'm wearing clothes for the first time in forever. A loose, sleeveless nightgown hangs on my emaciated frame, the fabric thin but smooth. When I swing my legs over the edge of the bed, the narrow band of lace at the hem gathers around my knees.

Someone put this on me, maybe one of the strangers who dragged me from my cage. It's hard to feel embarrassed about that when the alternative would have been lying here naked. Some person here cared enough to restore a bit of my modesty.

Out of nowhere, tears prick at the corners of my eyes. I blink hard and inhale deeply, my fingers curling around the edge of the mattress.

The bandage on my wrist is gone too. I study my arm for a moment without quite processing what I'm seeing before my thoughts catch up.

The cut where my captors took my blood—it's gone. The skin is sealed over, only a faint pink line where it used to be. How…?

There are too many questions I can't answer. I lift my gaze toward the window again. That one goal I can achieve on my own.

My skinny calves and feet jut from beneath the nightie's hem, the right foot with its unnatural crook in the middle. I haven't stood up in over eight years either. The thought of trying right now makes my pulse stutter. Thankfully, the window is close enough that I can reach the nearer curtain without leaving the bed.

I tug the heavy fabric farther from the frame. There are two panes of glass, one raised almost level with the other, letting the breeze whisper in. I lean forward to get a better view.

For the first several seconds, the sunlight is so dazzling it whites out my vision. It falls across my face and paints my skin with warmth. As my eyes adjust, my cheeks pinch with an unexpected movement of my mouth.

I'm smiling. How long has it been since I last did *that*?

Based on the view, I must be on at least the second floor of this strange wooden building. Beyond the window, fields mottled with green and a sicklier yellow stretch out toward a darker mass of trees. To my right, a dozen or so small structures dot the field. I'm not sure whether to call them houses, although I can make out doors and windows. The outer shells of the buildings look like massive stumps with the bark filed smooth, rising to a curving peak as if some immense giant came by and twisted off the rest of the tree.

The sun I found so bright is only just coming up. Its rays sear the forest's treetops.

East. That way must be east.

It'd be a lot more useful to know that if I had any idea which direction my real home lies in.

The sound of footsteps carries through the opposite wall of the bedroom. My heart bashes against my ribs, and

I shove myself all the way back onto the bed without thinking, propelled by a surge of panicked adrenaline.

My hands skitter across the sheet, but I can't see anything around that I could use to defend myself if I needed to. Other than the bed with its covers and the window, there's only a small table on the other side of the bed that holds an empty ebony bowl and a tall wardrobe too far away for me to reach in time.

A man opens the door and walks in, coming to a stop just inside. It's the one I thought of as a grizzly bear with the scar through his left eye. He somehow looks even bigger than before, his massive frame nearly as tall and broad as the doorway he passed through.

He's wearing similar clothes to those I've seen on my captors, his grass-green shirt showing a hint of chest and the snaking line of a tattoo behind the lacing at its V neck, the sleeves loose from the shoulders to partway down his forearms where they narrow to grip his wrists, his black slacks fitted to his muscular thighs and calves.

A leather sheath hangs from his belt, the glinting hilt of a dagger protruding from it. My fingers tense around the sheet instinctively, as if the weapon makes any difference when he could do more than enough damage with those fists and feet.

He shuts the door behind him with a nudge of his heel, his mismatched gaze trained on me. Even though his left eye is clouded over, I get the impression it's watching me just as much as the uninjured one. My shoulders hunch, my legs pulling closer to my body, as if I can shrink away from his scrutiny.

"We might as well start at the beginning," he says in the low, resonant voice I remember. "What is your name?"

I stare at him. In more than eight years, my captors never bothered to ask that question. It never mattered to them. Before, in my old life, I must have told people my name dozens of times, but I'm out of practice, and giving it up now feels somehow perilous. Why does he want it?

The man frowns. He walks to the end of the bed and rests his hand on one of the posts. The black lines of the tattoos that creep up from under his sleeve and up his neck across his jaw remind me that he's not really a man, no more than the ones who shoved me into their cage were.

"Do you understand me?" he asks, measuring out the words more slowly.

I nod automatically, just a brief dip of my head before I catch myself with another flicker of panic. Should I have acknowledged that? Was I better off if he thought I couldn't?

He takes another step, and my body cringes against the headboard. The man takes in the movement with his pensive gaze and stops where he is. He lowers himself so he's sitting on the edge of the bed right by the footboard, turned toward me, leaving a few feet between us.

He's only slightly less intimidating closer to my level.

"You're scared," he says—a statement, not a question.

A hysterical giggle claws at my throat. *Ya think?* Jamie would have said, with all his eight-year-old impertinence, if someone made a ridiculously obvious observation.

"Why don't I start then?" The man leans against the bedpost behind him with no hint of impatience. "I'm

Sylas, originally of Hearthshire, and this is my keep. You won't find yourself in a cage here. I just have some questions to ask to give me a better sense of your situation."

He could be lying. But if it matters enough to him, he could probably also find ways of forcing the answers out of me—ways much more unpleasant than this. A longing trickles up through my chest—a longing to clutch at this moment of relative peace and normalcy, however brief it might be.

I open my mouth. My tongue tangles. How long has it been since I last spoke—an actual conversation, not just a single word or a cry prodded out of me?

Finally, I work a fragment of my voice from my throat. It comes out in a raspy whisper. "Talia. My name. It's Talia."

As I say it, it no longer feels like giving up but reclaiming something my captors never quite managed to tear away from me. I am Talia McCarty. I'm a human being, not—not vermin, or whatever else the monsters called me. It's easier to hold onto that certainty here in actual clothes sitting on an actual bed with sunlight streaming past me.

"Talia," Sylas says, rolling the name off his tongue as if tasting each syllable. In his resonant baritone, it sounds lovelier than I ever thought of it before. Important. Like I'm not just a human being but a figure of acclaim. "Can you tell me how you ended up in that cage in Aerik's fortress, Talia?"

Fortress. Like *keep*, it sounds like a word from a fantasy movie, not the reality of my childhood. But then, the reality of my childhood didn't include men who could change into beasts or magically sealed locks, either.

How did I get into that cage? The icy splashes of memory flicker in the back of my mind, but I manage to stay focused on what's in front of me. I don't have to go back there to answer.

My voice still refuses to rise above a whisper, but I don't force it. "They attacked me. Bit my shoulder." Of its own accord, my hand rises to the ridges of scar tissue there. "I was out, walking in the woods, after my family had gone out for dinner. They looked—they looked like huge wolves, and then they didn't. They took me... like you did... and when I woke up I was in the cage."

"I apologize if our actions reminded you of that time. We had to make haste to ensure we weren't caught and forced to leave you there."

I'd appreciate the apology more if I knew what he and the other men he was with plan on doing with me. They talked about me too much like the ones who put me in that cage—like I was something they wanted to use.

And here comes the part where he gets at that purpose. He tips his head, the sunlight picking up a hint of deep purple in the thick, coffee-brown waves of his hair, and indicates my now-sealed wrist. "We healed your most obvious wounds as well as we could. They were taking your blood. How often?"

"I don't know. I think it was weeks apart. I lost track of time pretty quickly."

"Of course. And the rest of your days there? It doesn't appear they treated you all that well."

"No." My back stiffens. The words tumble out before I

can catch them. "Are they—are they going to know you took me? If they come here—"

Sylas holds up his hand. "They shouldn't know, but even if they figure it out, I have no intention of letting them throw you back in that wretched cage. Aerik is mostly talk and not much action. If he dares to try me, he'll regret it." He grins, baring fierce white teeth.

I don't know whether I should believe him, but he seems sure of himself. I suck my lower lip under my own teeth for a moment and realize I haven't answered his question. "The rest of the time, mostly they left me alone except to bring a little food and water. And to change the toilet bucket."

"Did they ever tell you what they wanted your blood for?"

I shake my head. "They didn't really talk to me."

"All right. What of your life before that? Were you already here, in the Mists, or did they take you from the human lands?"

My words fail me for a few heartbeats. "The Mists? What's that?"

I guess my confusion is answer enough. Sylas's mouth twists. "The land of the fae. Where you are now. You had no knowledge of us before the attack, I take it."

"No." *Fae.* Like faeries? My mind dredges up an image of Tinkerbell, but the man in front of me is about as far from that little pixie as I am from Batman. He doesn't have much in common with Santa's elves or the seven dwarves either.

"You had an ordinary human life, then?" he asks. "Parents, school, playing in the park, that sort of thing?"

He must be able to tell just looking at me that I'd have been taken as a child. If I've counted the years right, I'm barely out of my teens. "Yes," I murmur, too much anguish balling at the base of my throat just with that one word of acknowledgment.

"No experiences before your kidnapping that stand out as unusual?"

"I—I can't think of any."

My fingers are starting to ache where they're clutching the sheet. Maybe Sylas notices. He stands, smoothly but so swiftly my heart skips a beat.

"I think that's enough talk for now. We should get some food and drink into you before you waste away before my eyes."

My stomach pinches, but I've had enough experience since my kidnapping to clarify, "Nothing that... does funny things to my head or my body. Just normal food?"

Sylas's expression turns so perceptive I wonder if that mismatched gaze can pierce right into my mind and see the ways my captors chose to muddle me when it suited them. "Ordinary food only. And perhaps you'd like the use of a proper toilet as well."

Yes, that would be helpful if I don't want to soil these nice sheets—well, any more than my unwashed body already has.

He beckons for me to follow him. My limbs balk, but only for an instant. I'm not sure what's going on here, and I'm even less sure of where *here* is than I was before our conversation, but even if Sylas is like my captors in some ways, he's giving every indication of being gentler. And I know what state I'll end up in if I try to refuse to eat completely.

I ease off the bed and brace my feet against the floor. As I put my weight on them, a faint ache spreads through the warped one. Keeping more of my balance on my good side, I manage a few wobbly steps.

But it's been too long since I really walked. For all my attempts at keeping my strength up, there are muscles I didn't reach—muscles I need to hold me up.

Sylas is just opening the door when a tremor runs through my legs. I try to tense them, but it's too late. They give beneath me, sending me toppling onto my hands and knees. The twist of my foot with the fall sends a sharper needle of pain through my ankle.

I scramble to right myself, and Sylas is there, grasping my arm firmly but carefully to help me up. Having that huge, powerful frame so close to me is nearly overwhelming. I don't think it's just my unworked muscles to blame for my unsteadiness now.

His gaze has fallen to the floor. "Your foot. Is that from before, or did Aerik's men injure it?"

"It was them. So I—so it'd be harder for me to run away."

He makes a gruff sound that's unnervingly growly and reassuringly disgusted at the same time. Easing me around, he takes my hand and sets it on his elbow. "Put as much of your weight on me as you need to."

The muscles in his arm are even more solid than I expected, flexing as I adjust my grip. Heat floods my face. But what's he going to do if I refuse—sweep me up like he did from the cage and carry me to my meal? No, I can handle this.

As I limp beside him into the hall, a snicker carries from behind us. Sylas's head swings around at the sound.

Another man, one I didn't see last night, peers at me, his eyes glittering silver in his pale face. When he speaks, I recognize that sharp voice as the one who suggested they kill me rather than deal with my struggles.

"So the dung-body is a cripple as well. Wonderful."

"Move along, Kellan," Sylas commands.

The other man brushes past us without further comment, but his words linger. The icy fear that Sylas's calm presence started to melt solidifies in my gut all over again.

This place may be prettier and more luxurious than my cage, but who's to say it's any safer?

5

Talia

It turns out faeries have toilets. Or at least, these faeries do.

After Sylas helps me to the room he calls a "privy" and the heat of approximately a thousand suns has burned across my face with embarrassment, I manage to convince him that I can make my way to the porcelain throne without assistance. And I do, grasping the sink for balance as I leverage myself over.

Of course, neither the sink nor the toilet are actually made out of porcelain. They're more of a shell-like material with a pearly sheen on the inside. I can't see any pipes. Is there a fae sewer system, or will my pee be washed away by magic?

It's easier letting my mind puzzle over silly things like that rather than to dwell on the contempt in the silver-eyed man's voice when he talked about me.

This setup sure beats a bucket, even if the details are

odd. Rather than toilet paper, I find a wicker box full of leaves. I try to dampen one at the sink and give myself a bit of a wipe-down everywhere I can reach, though it doesn't feel all that effective. Then I splash more water on my face.

The room has no mirror, but maybe that's a good thing. If I could see how bedraggled I must look, I'd feel ten times more awkward walking back out.

Sylas leads me down a spiral staircase that's the same polished wood everything in this keep appears to be built out of. I cling to his elbow as little as possible, which is still quite a lot. He doesn't remark on my shakiness—or anything else, for that matter—but I catch him eyeing my feet in apparent contemplation. Do I even want to know *what* he's contemplating about them?

There is one question I can't hold back, as nervous as I am about the answer. When we reach the bottom of the stairs at one end of a wide, wood-lined hall, I glance up at him and gather my courage.

"Why did you bring me here? I mean, what—what are you going to do with me?"

Sylas considers my face now, his expression so unreadable I can't tell whether he's annoyed or amused by the question. "I was planning on getting you full of breakfast," he says. "We're almost at the dining room."

That isn't what I meant, as I'm sure he knows, but before I can figure out how to demand a proper response —and whether it's worth the risk that he'll turn those fierce white teeth on me rather than offering one— another of my rescuers-slash-kidnappers from yesterday pokes his head from a nearby doorway.

It's the man with the broad boyish face, which splits with an eager smile. Now that I've got a better look at him, I'm struck by his eyes. The sharp-voiced man, the one Sylas called Kellan, might have a silver sheen to his irises, but this guy's are pure gold, as radiant as that smile of his, both warm and utterly inhuman.

"You're up!" he says with the same buoyant energy I saw before. "Perfect. I was just about to serve the meal."

Then I notice the spatula he's brandishing and the apron draped over his muscular frame. Apparently he's also the one making our breakfast. Smells drift from the room behind him: creamy and meaty, buttery and doughy. My stomach gurgles loud enough that I suspect the whole keep can hear it.

The eerily gorgeous guy widens his grin. "And it sounds like you're ready for it."

My lips part, but I don't know what to say.

Sylas motions to me. "Her name is Talia. Talia, this is August of my cadre. I wouldn't typically have any of them working the kitchen, but we're in short supply of staff."

"And I like doing it." August twirls the spatula in his fingers and waves it at me. "If this isn't the best breakfast you've ever had, I'll keep trying until I get there."

It's guaranteed to be the best breakfast I've had in more than eight years, as long as Sylas was telling the truth about no funny business with the food. My throat's still closed up, but I tip my head in acknowledgment, and somehow August's smile grows even wider. It doesn't quite reach his eyes, though. They've crinkled at the corners with a shimmer of something almost sad…

It's probably pity. My face flushes again, but pity is

better than contempt, at least. "Thank you," I manage to say, though still in the whisper I'm having trouble breaking my rusty voice out of, so I'm not sure whether the attempt makes me seem less pathetic or more.

Maybe I should be encouraging these men to see me as pitiable if it means they keep offering me comfy beds and extravagant breakfasts. They want something from me just like my former captors did. If they think I'm strong enough to withhold it, who's to say they won't change their approach to something harsher?

Sylas guides me on down the hall, and August pauses partway through turning back toward the kitchen, taking in my limp. His gaze jerks to Sylas, the shine in his eyes flaring with fury so suddenly I flinch.

"Is she still hurt?" he demands, the muscles in his shoulders coiling.

"Her foot," Sylas says. "It's an old injury Aerik's people dealt, healed badly. And I expect she's simply become unused to walking, given the size of the cage they had her in."

"Mangy beasts," August mutters with a hint of a snarl.

Sylas claps a hand to his companion's shoulder. "They don't have her anymore. Settle yourself down, and let's have that breakfast."

Still muttering under his breath, August stomps off into the room. It appears that everyone takes Sylas's orders. He said this was *his* keep. And that August was part of his—

"What's a cadre?" I ask as we continue down the hall.

Sylas peers down at me from his great height as if bemused that anyone could be unaware. "All lords have a cadre—it's our inner circle, our closest advisors and comrades in arms. For now, mine will be the only folk you have for company. Better not to involve the rest of the pack when the matter involves some… discretion."

Because the more people who know I'm here, the more chance it'll get back to this Aerik—the one with the sunflower-yellow hair who commanded my other captors, I assume? But I'm more struck by another part of his wording. *Pack.*

My legs lock. My hand tightens on the silky fabric of Sylas's sleeve, wanting to both grip harder for balance and to shove myself away. I knew they weren't really men, but I didn't know for sure they were *that* much like the others.

My whisper comes out with an additional quaver. "You're wolves too."

Sylas has stopped next to me. I thought of him as a grizzly before, but his predatory, brawny self-assurance could fit one of those massive wolfish monsters just as well. Whose claws slashed through his one eye?

His other, dark eye holds my gaze. "We're fae. All of the Seelie can shift from man into wolf as it suits us." He touches his chest. "The animal belongs to us; it does not consume us. How much of a beast any of us becomes is a matter of personal choice."

I'm guessing he'd put himself above my captors on that scale. That doesn't mean there's nothing beastly about him at all. Just standing here with his attention focused on me makes the hairs on the back of my neck rise.

If he's a predator, there's no world where I wouldn't come across as prey.

An acidic voice that's quickly becoming familiar

reaches us from farther down the hall. "Except when it isn't."

Kellan is leaning against a doorframe, his silver gaze as cold as before. He isn't quite as beefy as the others, but his lean frame still exudes plenty of power—and animosity. It doesn't strike me as a good sign that he must be part of Sylas's "inner circle" too.

I've lost too much of the thread of the conversation to know what he's referring to, but Sylas's expression darkens. "Are you here to eat or to complain?" he asks.

The other man shrugs, swiping a hand over his sleek hair, which is a shade of orange so pale you'd think most of the color had been wrung out of it. He stalks into the room he was standing by, and, joy of all joys, we follow him.

The keep's dining room stretches long enough to hold a table for twenty under two chandeliers that look like coiled branches sprouting from the ceiling. They're not lit now, their jeweled leaves twinkling in the glow from the broad windows opposite us. Someone has already set out silverware, plates, and goblets for five around one end of the table.

Sylas takes the head of the table so automatically I can tell that's where he always sits. When he gestures for me to sit kitty-corner to him, Kellan's lips curl in disdain.

"We're to be faced with the dung-body through the whole meal? Not what I want to rest my gaze on if I'm going to keep my appetite. There are plenty of other seats, all of them grander than she should expect."

August barrels into the room then holding a platter on each hand and two more balanced on his bulging, tattooed arms. "If you're so concerned about the view, maybe you should head to the other end and spare her having to look at your ugly mug." He sets down the platters with a series of clinks.

Kellan bares his teeth. "I think you forget *your* position here, whelp."

August bristles with a flash of his eyes, and Sylas holds up both hands, one toward each of them. "Enough. I prefer that she sits near me. The rest of you can take a chair wherever you'd like in consideration of that." He shoots a pointed look at Kellan. "Ideally without any more commentary."

Kellan glares at his lord, but he sinks down at one of the places already set—thankfully the one that's farthest from me.

August grabs the seat beside me. "Where's Whitt? This is usually the one morning out of the month when he's up at a normal hour."

"Last night was hardly a typical night," Sylas says. "And I have no intention of waiting on his whims. Dig in."

I'm already ogling the dishes August laid out. Saliva pools in my mouth. If I'm not careful, in a second I'll be drooling.

One platter is heaped with flat, circular patties that look kind of like small hamburgers but smell like sausages. Another holds little boiled eggs that are robin-blue even without their shells, which give off a delicately appetizing zesty scent. The third offers a rainbow of cut fruit, much of which I can't recognize in colors as vibrant as gems, and the fourth ornate pastries twisted into five-pointed stars, the crisp dough so airily puffy I half expect them to start flaking under my gaze.

I don't know where to start. The men reach for the serving utensils and load their plates. When the long-tined fork is free, I take a sausage and then a scoop of fruit and a pastry that appears to have melted chocolate in the hollow at its center.

August motions toward my plate. "There's lots for everyone. Take as much as you want."

Just what I already have looks like a feast. As I look at it, my stomach knots. I'm not used to proper meals anymore—and I'm not exactly relaxed about this whole situation, either.

"I don't know how much I can manage when I got used to... not much," I murmur.

"Aerik's crew obviously didn't feed you right, but we'll fix that. After all that, you are a wee mite."

"We could even say a dust mite," says a breezy, melodic voice from behind me. The fourth of yesterday's men strolls into view and flops his well-built frame down in the chair across from me.

By daylight, Whitt's light brown hair looks sun-kissed, the rumpled strands veering upward at their varying angles as if to embrace the sky. Or maybe, given his attitude, to goad it.

His gaze barely flits over me, and then he's stabbing at the sausages, tossing several onto his plate with a few flicks of his wrist. His presence doesn't leave me as cold as Kellan's, but my muscles tense more all the same.

"She can't help how she is," August declares, and pats me on the arm. "Go ahead. Eat, even if it's only a little."

So much emphasis has been placed on how much food I consume that my stomach has clenched twice as tight as before. But I do need to eat before I get any more light-headed.

I cut off a chunk of one of the sausage patties and nibble at it tentatively. A savory flavor made richer by a subtle mixture of herbs seeps over my tongue, and my mouth starts watering again. It's delicious. I haven't tasted anything this good in ages. I haven't tasted anything that tasted like *food* in almost a decade.

No blurring or tingling effect muddles my senses. As Sylas promised, the herbs mustn't hold any magical properties. I stuff the rest of the bite into my mouth, and the next thing I know, the entire sausage has disappeared from my plate. My stomach still aches, but more of that is tension than hunger now.

August grins at me, obviously taking my speeding devouring as a compliment to his cooking, and glances around at the others. "So, I take it we haven't gotten any —" He cuts himself off and hesitates with a hint of chagrin. When he speaks again, I can tell he's changing the subject. "I was going to hunt before lunch. Any particular meat the rest of you are keen on today?"

Was the first thing he meant to say something he didn't want to mention around me?

Whitt waggles his fork. "Since you're taking requests, let's have a buffalo. Or elephant. I've always wondered what those taste like."

Sylas makes a dismissive sound at the joke—at least, I assume it's a joke. Who knows what animals roam around this place for fae men to hunt? "I wouldn't mind some venison," he says.

August nods, and the table lapses into a silence that doesn't feel totally comfortable. It could be they always sit here, awkwardly quiet, while they eat, but it seems more likely that my presence has thrown a wrench into their typical flow of conversation. What is there they'd want to talk about that it'd be a problem for me to know?

Not the kind of thing you can ask even in the best of circumstances.

Gradually, I swallow morsels of a melon-like fruit that tastes close to honeydew. The third is enough to transform the ache in my stomach into a sensation of fullness. I've already eaten twice as much as my former captors ever offered me in one meal. I sip from my goblet, which turns out to be full of a lightly bubbly liquid with a raspberry-esque flavor, and clasp my hands together in my lap beneath the table.

As deftly as Sylas dodged my question, I still need to know what's going on here. It doesn't matter how scared I am of the answer. Am I a guest, or am I a prisoner?

For a few minutes, I watch the food disappear from the fae men's plates, working up my courage. "Thank you for the meal and getting me away from the place with the cage and... everything," I say finally, willing my thready voice a little louder. "It's been years since they took me away. If I wanted to go home—"

Kellan interrupts me with a bark of a laugh. His voice is chilling. "Go home? You can wipe that idea out of your mind forever, pipsqueak."

"*Kellan*," Sylas says, his growl turning those two

syllables ominous. He turns his mismatched gaze on me. "We'll treat you as a guest, but you will stay here for now. It'll take some time to decide how to best handle the situation. I stand by my word that Aerik and his pack won't lay one more claw on you."

All right. It's not really a surprise, but his words still echo through me with an icy quiver. However generous any of these men might be with me, I've traded one set of captors for another.

I *am* better off, though, aren't I? I'm not locked in one corner of a room behind immoveable bars. This keep must have a door to the outer world somewhere, and the outer world, even if it's some sort of faerie realm, must have gateways to the world I came from. I just need to find out how to get there so I'm not wandering aimlessly at the mercy of whatever monsters come across me next, and then I can escape after all, better fed and rested than I'd have been fleeing from my previous captivity.

If I ask for any of the information I need now, I'll tip them off to what I'm thinking. Instead, I incline my head as if in acceptance and take another sip of my drink.

Kellan's silvery gaze lingers on me. Is that suspicion in his eyes? I have the urge to shrink inside my skin.

He wrinkles his nose. "If the sight of her wasn't bad enough, the stink alone should consign her to the upper reaches."

"Thankfully, that's solved easily enough." Sylas points his knife at Whitt. "You've demolished at least twice your share of breakfast already. Go run our guest a bath."

6

Whitt

Run our guest a bath. As I turn on the faucet, I repeat the command in my head in exactly the mocking tone I was tempted to toss it back in our glorious leader's face. Not a request but an order, as if I'm a servant and not cadre. Presumably this is August's fault. His frolicking around in the kitchen has convinced Sylas we should all play staff.

Water hisses from the tap. I drop a towel on the tiled floor next to the gleaming tub, since Heart help us if the mite could manage to find even that on her own. Where are the clothes Sylas dredged up for her from who in the lands knows where?

I'd rather not know. I prefer to think as little as possible of what relations our lord might or might not be having with beings of the female persuasion, human or otherwise.

That turn takes my mind in a darker direction than

my initial silent heckling. I find the bundle of human-made fabric, rougher even at its best than what the fae can spin but I suppose more familiar to our "guest," and leave it next to the towel. As I step back, I pull a flask out of one of my vest's many pockets.

It's important to always have lubrication on hand should one want to grease one's mood.

I toss back a shot's worth of faerie absinthe. It burns in the best way going down. Before it's even hit my stomach, the edges of my annoyance have smoothed with a tickling glow.

It's less the alcohol that provides the lube than the cloying fruit this beverage was made from. If that scrap of a human took one bite of the peach-like globes, she'd find herself attempting to walk on her hands and gulp grass for dinner without any idea she was behaving at all oddly.

My being relegated to a servant's task is Kellan's fault the most, really. Even when he was merely a visitor in Sylas's domain, you could always tell where he'd recently passed by from the terrorized glaze that came over the human servants' eyes even while under their enchantments —and the fact that one or two of them was liable to go missing if he was around long enough. A pity he wasn't Aerik's brother-by-marriage instead. They clearly share some inclinations.

But no, he's our problem. Here in our new abode with that mangy prick as a permanent fixture, it's no wonder Sylas has declared collecting servants from beyond the Mists to be "too much trouble." And with the pack so dwindled and beaten down, our benevolent benefactor hardly wants to add to their burden other than a few tasks here and there.

None of that bothers me overly so except when the burden falls on my shoulders instead.

The bath full, I shut off the water and wipe my hands of the chore. When I step into the hall, August is just helping the girl up the staircase. I turn on my heel away from them and take a deep inhalation, absorbing the lingering scents.

Sylas has come by too—on his way to his study, no doubt. He tends to go there when he'd rather not be disturbed, but disturbing people is a particular talent of mine.

I amble over and knock—as a courtesy, and because he is my lord and I'd rather keep my throat intact, thank you very much.

"Come," the rumbling voice says.

Sylas's study is one of the grandest rooms in the keep, naturally, since it's fit for a lord. I'll never say he doesn't have decent taste in décor. As I prowl in, I tamp down any envy I might otherwise feel over the expanse of that hawthorn-wood desk, twice as large as the one in my own office of sorts, or the liquor cabinet against the wall with its assortment of rare vintages left over from our great exodus.

Would keeping my dishonorable emotions in check be easier or harder if I didn't have to admit our lord has filled the role quite capably? It's impossible to say. As we all do, he has his weak points, but on the measure of things he's as tremendous a lord as anyone could ask for.

Sylas glances up at me from where he's sitting behind

the desk, a journal full of notations open in front of him. "What is it, Whitt?" He doesn't need to stand and show off his full height to convey the authority we both know he holds over me—over this entire place. Everything from the command in his tone to his imperious gaze gets the message across.

I prop myself against the bookcase next to the door and aim a smile at the oldest of my younger half-siblings: the only offspring who ever mattered to our father.

"I was merely wondering what the delay is about. It's not like you to dilly dally. We know how the girl can be used—we experienced the power of her blood ourselves last night. You've been waiting for a chance like this for decades. We invaded Aerik's domain specifically to *get* that chance. Why not turn her over to the arch-lords straight away and claim our reward?"

Sylas considers me thoughtfully, as if he thinks I should be able to put the pieces together on my own. Out of everything, this side of him, measured and penetrating, irks me the most.

My half-brother's passions can be as fiery as those of any of our summer kin, but he always keeps an even temper with me. It feels like a judgment—as though he's determined that I'm so volatile he can't afford to be anything but steady with me. As though I'm fragile along with that volatility, and the wrong word or gesture might send me spiraling beyond my control into some action that'll harm me more than him.

It would irk me less if there wasn't a tidbit of truth hidden in that assessment. But I do have enough awareness of the important lines not to cross them... most of the time.

"We've experienced it," he says. "The arch-lords haven't. They won't be able to test our claim until the next full moon. And given our circumstances, I'm not inclined to trust them to take our word for it."

He might have a point there. All the same— "I could smell the same essence as in the tonic from her small wound even through the stink in that room. We give her arm another little nick, and they can't miss it."

"It may not be enough. They know—"

Another knock on the door interrupts him. When Sylas calls out, it's both Kellan and August who peer in.

Kellan notes my presence with a narrowing of his eyes, as if he thinks I'm there on some untoward purpose. I wish that I *could* scheme with our lord against the jackass. The closest I've come—the closest Sylas would ever allow—was a series of stealthy discussions on the matter of whether, given the prick's clear and growing discontentment, it would be more generous or insulting if Sylas gave him full leave to seek a place in a different pack should he wish to.

The trouble is, as much as I suspect Kellan might wish to, there aren't likely to be any packs of anywhere near the standing he'd accept who'd accept *him*. His reputation is the most tarnished of all of us by virtue of proximity to the initial offense, as he no doubt realizes. And perhaps he wouldn't wish to anyway, since he must know there's no lord other than the kin-of-his-mate who'd tolerate his unruliness even to the small extent Sylas has.

In the end, Sylas did extend the offer, and Kellan declined. But for all he professed to want to continue serving in this cadre, his disposition has become even more insolent since. Apparently, despite our lord's best efforts, he did take it as an insult.

"We need to speak about the girl," he says in that obnoxiously tart voice of his.

"It appears we do." Sylas motions for the new arrivals to close the door. "Whitt was just advocating that we cart her straight to the arch-lords."

A flicker of surprise crosses Kellan's face, which gratifies me for the second before he opens his mouth again. "I agree. She's the leverage we wanted—we have to make use of her, not waste our time coddling the creature."

I like my stance less now that he's joined me there. If he thinks that's a good idea, maybe it isn't one after all.

August glares at me as if I've betrayed him somehow, his shoulders coming up. He has already taken up doting on the mite, and my youngest half-brother has about as much rein on *his* temper as a jockey who's toppled off a runaway horse.

"As soon as we approach the arch-lords, Aerik will know we're the ones who stole her," he says. "They'll probably find some way to take credit for it—the arch-lords might even hand her back to them so they can throw her back into that cage and keep brewing their tonic. Then all we are to them is thieves."

Oh, we're much more than that. I don't think it'll help the situation to go over our extensive list of crimes in the arch-lords' eyes, though.

Kellan rounds on him. "What do you suggest we do

then? Put her up in our keep as if it's some fancy hotel while we all cater to her whims?"

A furious light flares in August's eyes. "Getting enough food into her to bring her back from the verge of starvation and taking her first bath in who knows how many years aren't *whims*," he growls. "If you suggest we put her in a cage like they did, I—"

Sylas stands with a rasp of the chair legs against the floor that shuts August up. Even Kellan draws up short. The newest member of our cadre might like to bitch at all of us, but there are lines he doesn't cross too, no matter how closely he might toe them.

"There's no point in arguing about it—from either perspective," Sylas says in his laying-down-the-law tone. "It makes no sense that a random human girl could have this kind of power. We don't understand how she came to be that way or how else she might be connected to the wildness. Are there others like her? Is there a way to replicate the effect she has without needing her at all?"

Kellan lifts his nose haughtily. "Is that your main concern: finding a way to return the feeble thing to her 'home'?"

Sylas manages to keep his glower restrained, but there's no mistaking it for what it is. "Are you so caught up in your scorn for humans that you can fail to see she's hardly a permanent solution to our problems, for the same reasons you scorn her? What are we supposed to do years from now when she succumbs to old age and we're still here with the moon and its inevitable waxing?"

The absinthe is still bubbling through my veins headily enough that I barely catch my laugh at how taken aback

Kellan looks. His mouth closes into a sour line, so I ask the necessary question.

"What are you proposing we do with her in the meantime, exactly?"

Sylas spreads his hands. "We have four weeks until the next full moon when we could demonstrate her usefulness to the arch-lords. Until then, we treat her well enough that she'll trust us, we find out what we can from her, we observe her, and at the same time we evaluate how to balance the fallout of Aerik's potential anger—and how we might avoid it entirely. It should be simple enough. From what I've observed already, I don't imagine she's going to ask for much."

"We could speed all that along with the right wine and a charm or two," Kellan says. "Magic her into telling the truth or at least into total compliance."

"No. I don't think she's purposefully hiding anything from us—she's even more bewildered by all this than we are. And she's hardly a threat. We simply need to find the right questions to get at the answers we need. Controlling her with magic might make her *less* inclined to open up if it reminds her of her treatment at Aerik's hands. She's already recoiled at the idea of being presented with intoxicating food." Our lord folds his arms over his chest. "We'll treat her as we should any respected guest."

The other man's lips curl back. "You can hardly expect me to pamper—"

"I *expect* you to steer clear of her if you can't control yourself enough to avoid terrorizing her, kin-of-my-mate," Sylas says sharply. "We want to open her up, not tear her down. But you can leave that to the rest of us."

Kellan looks as if he's bit back a grimace, but he says nothing more, just ducks his head in acknowledgment. Then he marches out with an audible huff.

August turns to our lord. "How do you think Aerik found her to begin with?"

Sylas rubs his jaw. "From what she was able to tell me about her capture—and from that scar on her shoulder— it sounds as though Aerik and his cadre roamed into the human world while caught up in the wildness and came across her. When they attacked her, the taste of her blood must have woken them from their madness. Which gave them enough wherewithal to decide to bring her back with them so they could make more use of her."

"And torment her at the same time." August's eyes flash again. "We *can't* let her fall back into their hands."

"I agree with you completely on that. You don't need to worry about it."

"They'll be sniffing around for her," I can't help noting. "It's quite the prize to lose."

Sylas gives me a grim smile. "And we'll deal with that eventuality when it comes for us. Now…" He taps the notebook lying on his desk. "I'd like to return to my reading, if you don't mind."

His reasoning makes sense, but I'm not sure I like the vehemence with which he's expressed it. I saw how carefully he handled the girl last night, how quickly he attended to her needs this morning. Whatever flaws our glorious leader has, one of them is definitely an over-inflated sense of honor, especially when it comes to the vulnerable. We wouldn't be putting up with Kellan's impudence otherwise.

It won't do any of us any good if he softened to the poor thing as much as August has—or more.

Sylas will hardly appreciate my saying that to his face, though, so I motion to August, putting on an innocent tone. "Come on, Auggie. I believe I might smell something burning. Did you leave the stove on?"

My little brother's eyes widen. I don't smell anything of the sort, so he couldn't have either, but simply saying it sends him hustling out of the room and down the hall. My lips quirk with mild amusement. He can pay me back for the trick with a tussle later.

I shut the study door firmly on the way out. As I head toward the staircase myself, my gaze roves to the bathroom door behind which our "guest" is still washing. My ears prick.

No sounds of water moving against a body reach me. Has she finished already? I'd have thought she would need at least an hour to scrub all the accumulated grime from her skin.

Or is she up to something else entirely?

I stalk down the hall and grip the handle with the ease of centuries' practice in stealth. The latch and the hinges don't make the slightest sound as I ease the door open a sliver.

She isn't in the bath, but she's by it. Sitting on an overturned wooden box—the one for tossing used towels into—her elbow leaning over the lip of the tub. With her back to me, there's no chance of her seeing me. What is she *doing*?

Her hand dips into the tub with a faint sloshing of the water and lifts out the sponge I left for her. She brings it to her calf to rub the pale skin there, her leg canting to the side. The sight of her foot, of the unnatural slant to the bones there, triggers my understanding.

She was too weak and too lame to scramble into the tub on her own, or at least she thought it was too much of a risk to try and possibly slip, bang her head, and drown herself. Apparently she was also too embarrassed to say as much to August when he showed her to the room or to call for help if she realized it later.

Kellan was wrong about that much. This one is hardly demanding pampering.

Without the nightgown or the blanket from last night, her emaciation is even more evident. Beneath the fall of her dark, tangled hair, her shoulder blades jut like a hatchling's featherless wings. The segments of her spine form a picket fence down the center of her back; the angles of her hips are nearly as sharp as the nub of her chin.

And yet there's a delicate grace to her movements that I find myself appreciating, as if she were one of those intricately sculpted twig puppets one of the court craftswomen used to construct for the shows that entertained me in my childhood.

No, more alive than that. A gamboling fawn, perhaps.

The thought slips through my head, and I yank myself back from the door, shutting it as silently as I opened it. I shake those images from my head. August will be out there hunting deer on Sylas's request for our luncheon. We *snack* on fawns.

The last thing I need is to find myself admiring one.

I stride away before anyone can notice I've lingered

here. Even after I throw back another gulp of absinthe, my hands curl into fists.

I wish we had found nothing more than a recipe in Aerik's fortress. Or a rare toadstool. Or a vat of nauseating chemicals.

Anything other than a human girl with grass-bright eyes and a frailness she tries to hide.

7

Talia

The knock comes just as I'm squirming into the blouse left for me on the bathroom floor. I spin around, my feet skidding on the wet tiles. Even with my hand on the edge of the tub for support, I nearly fall.

The blouse's thin fabric drifts to my thighs. The clothes are a little too big on me, the waist of the jeans threatening to slip over my hips, but I've become so skinny I'm not sure what size *would* fit.

"Yes?" I say, managing to push my voice above its now-standard whisper.

Sylas's commanding baritone carries through the door. "If you're finished with your bath, I'd like to speak with you."

Oh. I look at the floor, blotchy with dirty puddles I didn't feel right trying to sop up with the fluffy white towel, and run my fingers into my hair, which is damp but still full of knots I couldn't untangle. Not that the latter should matter. The man-who's-not-a-man on the other side of that door has seen me much worse off. At least now I'm reasonably clean, with a light floral scent from the soap clinging to my skin.

I take a sniff of my arm, weirdly giddy at the proof that I'm no longer a stink-fest, and brace myself in case he's angry about the puddles. "You can come in." Like he really needs my permission.

Sylas strides into the room and stops a few feet from me, eyeing the floor with a puzzled expression.

"I'm sorry," I say quickly, clutching the side of the tub. "I tried not to make a mess, but..."

His gaze snaps to me—to my face and then to my arm taut as it balances me. His mouth tightens.

"You couldn't get into the water. I should have realized. My apologies. The next time—we have a sort of sauna in the lower chambers, with a small in-ground pool you could use instead. It has steps."

He expects me to be here long enough that I'll take multiple baths. It's hard to know what to make of that when I have no idea how often faeries generally bathe.

I glance around. Better not to make myself any more of a nuisance than I already have while I am here, while he's being kind to me. "If there's a mop, I could clean it up—"

He shakes his head before I can finish. "I'll see that it's taken care of. I have something for you that should make getting just about anywhere *other* than into the bath easier for you."

He steps closer, holding out his hands, and that's when I register the object he's brought me. It looks like a snapped off branch, nearly as thick as my wrist, blunt at the narrower end and spreading into a shallow crescent at the thicker end. The crescent is polished smooth, but the rest of the surface is covered in bark.

Sylas turns the branch-staff-thing so the blunt end touches the floor and stands it next to me, studying it. Then understanding clicks in my head.

"It's a crutch?" I say.

He nods. "Not quite tall enough, I think. I had to estimate from memory." His fingers close around the top of the crutch, a few soft syllables slip from his mouth, and before my eyes, the branch *grows*. Just a couple of inches, so it's the perfect height to fit under my armpit.

More magic. How much can he do with it? Suddenly I'm remembering the houses I saw from the bedroom window that looked like twisted-off tree stumps. Did the fae *grow* those homes rather than build them?

Sylas is waiting for me to try out his gift. I'm pretty curious too. I tuck it under my arm, ease some of my weight onto it, and take a few tentative steps away from the tub.

The crutch's base stays steady on the floor, and my damaged foot doesn't ache at all when I don't need to fully press down on it. I wouldn't want to get too used to this thing, since who knows how long I'll be able to keep it, but for now it'll at least allow me to walk around the keep without needing to cling to the furniture or my new captors.

I'm already that much closer to making my escape, and I have the man who brought me here to thank.

And I should actually do that. I give him a cautious smile, not sure how much gratitude he'll need to be satisfied. "Thank you. I really appreciate it."

Sylas offers a restrained smile, so I guess that was enough. A trace of humor gleams in his dark eye. "It benefits us as well, not needing to act as your crutch ourselves."

I wet my lips, hesitating over my next question. "So, it's okay, then? If I wander around this place a bit?"

"Nothing within the keep should pose a danger. Any rooms we'd prefer to keep private will be locked. All I ask is that you stay inside. Aerik and his cadre, perhaps his whole pack, will be on the hunt for you. We can't risk anyone seeing you."

Because then he and *his* cadre would lose me. But it's hard to resent that when he's just granted me so much more freedom than I've had in years.

I drag in a breath and find I have the courage to push a little harder. "You need something from me—like they did. Something to do with my blood?"

I can see Sylas withdraw behind that tattooed, square-jawed face with its vicious scar. The hint of warmth that was there an instant ago vanishes. He called himself a lord, and it shows in both the sternness of his gaze and the lifting of his posture.

"Don't trouble yourself about that," he says. "All you need to know is that we won't treat you the way they did. Would you like to begin your explorations now?"

Part of me would, but a larger part wilts with

exhaustion at the thought of tackling more of the winding hallways. I need to figure out where the main door is and what else this place holds, but right now, I'm ready to crash. The exertion of moving around even this much must be getting to me after all that time in the cage.

"I think—I think I'd just like to rest for a little while," I say.

"Of course. Let me see you to your bedroom."

The room I woke up in is around the corner from the privy where the hall splits, two doors down to the left— important details to remember. Sylas lets me walk in unaccompanied.

I stop on the threshold, taking in the brighter sun flooding through the window and the warmth it brings, the sweet smells of wildflowers and hay drifting in on the breeze, and the spread that's been laid out for me on the table next to the bed: a wooden comb, a hand mirror framed in silver, and a goblet that, I determine as I meander closer, is full of water. A large pitcher sits on the floor next to the table in case I want to refill that or, I guess, the ebony bowl for a quick wash.

This is mine. I mean, it's not, and it's technically a prison cell besides, but I can't smother the tickle of possessiveness, giddy as my enjoyment of the soap smell on my skin, that runs through my chest. I lean my crutch against the wall and flop onto the bed, my lips curling into a smile as I surrender to the coziness of the covers.

It's dark, so horribly dark. Hands grasp at me. A knee jabs my back. A snicker reverberates through my ears. The cold bite of a knife slices into my skin—

And I wake up, gasping and shuddering, sitting bolt upright in my new bed.

It isn't dark at all. The sunlight no longer slants through the window, but an indirect glow fills the room. Nothing's restraining me; nothing's cutting me. Still, it takes several breaths before my pulse stops rattling in my chest at its panicked pace. Sweat has glued my blouse to my back.

I barely remember the dream, only that I was back there, back in the cage, and the bars seemed to be closing in on me as if to crush me completely...

I'm not there anymore. Maybe I'm not totally sure of this new place or what I'm going to face here, but at least I'm not *there*.

Outside my window, a pinkish tint is streaking through the clouds. It must be evening. My stomach gurgles, reminding me that after my first real breakfast in ages, I've gone and slept through lunch. Have I missed dinner too?

I grope for the crutch Sylas made for me—more for his convenience or mine, it's hard to say—and swing myself onto my feet. The muscles in my legs only wobble a little on my way to the door. As I grasp the knob, a quiver of panic shoots through me. Will it even open?

But it does, turning easily in my grasp. I tug the door open, and the smell of roasting meat carries from the staircase to greet me. Oh, yes, I'd like some of that.

It takes me twice as long as a normal person to lurch

down the stairs, but I do it all on my own, so I'll count that as a win. Someone—August, I assume—is humming a buoyant melody in the kitchen, utensils clinking against the cookware. The dining room is empty. I'm even a little early for the meal.

No time like the present to get in some of that exploring, then. Ignoring the tension that twists around my gut with each limping step I take, I head farther down the hall. Sylas said I could feel free to wander. I'm not breaking any of his rules.

I'm just figuring out where I *would* go about breaking them when I'm ready to.

With the dimming of the natural light that appears to seep down through slits at the edges of the ceiling, orbs mounted along the walls have lit up with a flame-like flicker. The amber glow leads the way to a branching of the hall in two directions, just like upstairs. To my right, I find a grand entrance room, with even more orbs beaming along the walls and across the vaulted ceiling. A red-and-gold rug spills across the floor to the broad wooden door striped with reinforcements of gleaming brown metal.

Bronze, I think. Like my cage. Faeries are supposed to be repelled by iron, aren't they? I guess that must be true, and they use whatever other metals they have available instead.

I shuffle along the rug, wincing inwardly at each muffled tap of my crutch. The hall is quiet; no one's around. There's no one here to see me grip the handle on that door and tug.

It doesn't budge—not when I heave it up and down, not when I haul it toward me or shove at it. The door is locked in some way I can't see the mechanism to, which means I can't *un*lock it.

Of course Sylas wouldn't leave it up to me and my accepting of his orders. He gave me those orders, and he also made sure I can't leave whether I want to or not.

I swivel around to make the trek back toward dinner. I've only taken one step in that direction when a lean figure skulks out of the hall, stopping at the edge of the entrance room.

Kellan's silvery eyes glitter as they settle on me, and every inch of my skin prickles in alarm. "What do you think you're doing all the way over here, little mousey?" he asks.

"Sylas—Sylas said I could explore the keep," I stammer. "I was just taking a look around."

"Were you now? Such a coincidence you immediately looked at the front door."

I cling to my crutch, a tremor racing through my legs, but I manage to raise my chin. "It *was* just a coincidence. I don't want to go out there and get caught by the monsters who had me before."

There's enough truth to the statement that it comes out with more confidence than I'd even hoped for, but Kellan doesn't look convinced. He stalks toward me, baring his teeth in a grin that's nowhere near friendly.

"We aren't stupid, pipsqueak—me least of all. And let me disappoint you now. There's magic binding that door and the one at the back, more power than a dung-body like you could ever contend with. You're stuck with us."

He looms over me, still grinning, and I can't stop myself from cringing backward in a cower. His grin stretches. His eyes spark. For a second, I think he's going to say or do something worse. Then he flattens his mouth and whirls with a snap of his flowing vest.

"August went to call you for supper. You'd better come quickly. Who knows how much time you have before we make a supper out of *you*."

8

Talia

The next morning's breakfast is an even quieter affair than the first one, mainly because Whitt doesn't make any appearance at all. With Kellan eyeing me ominously from across the table, I gulp down a small portion of juicy bacon and hash browns with an unusual licorice-like flavor as quickly as I can and then excuse myself.

On my way back to the stairs, my eye catches on a movement beside me. A small mirror hangs on the wall in a gleaming frame, the wood so polished it could almost pass for brass. My face stares back at me, my eyes too big in my pale, sunken face, my hair a dark bird's nest around it. I look like a wraith from one of those horror movies my friend Marjorie started cajoling us all into watching when we were ten.

Does Marjorie still love freaky thrillers? What is she even doing now? She must have graduated high school, maybe college too. She could have a job, her own apartment. She could be married for all I know.

All those possibilities feel as distant from my reality as if they're a movie in themselves. As if I've been stuck in suspended animation, the rest of the world moving on without me while I drifted unknowing beyond time itself.

Maybe that's not totally inaccurate either, but I hate looking like the prison escapee I technically am. If I could wash every trace of the last eight years away with the gurgle of bathwater down a drain, I would. Leaning on my crutch, I tug at a particularly stubborn clump of knots with my other hand.

August comes out of the dining room and catches me at it. "Having trouble with those?"

"I don't know if they're ever going to come out," I admit. The comb one of the fae men left on my bedside table is the first one I've seen in years, and it wasn't up to the job. Maybe I'd have to shear my head to the scalp and start over. The thought of looking even more like an invalid makes me cringe.

It shouldn't matter, but it does. I'm already vulnerable enough without adding to that impression. And it'd be yet another thing my former captors stole from me, if far from the worst.

The awareness of the much more wrenching losses I've suffered rolls through me, suffocating me like my dream yesterday. For a moment, my mind blanks out under the weight of it. When I get a hold of myself again, my skin has gone clammy and my hand is clutching the crutch so tightly my knuckles ache.

August is watching me with a deer-in-the-headlights

expression that sits oddly on his broad face, his muscles tensed and his golden eyes alight but his stance uncertain. "Do you want me to try to help you with your hair?" he asks after a moment's hesitation. "We all have different areas of magic we take to most naturally, and one of mine is all things bodily. I could check out your foot too."

All things bodily. That's why he was the one Sylas called on to knock me out when they dragged me from my cage. I still don't know how much I should be grateful for that —how much it was a rescue versus being thrown from the frying pan into a fire I haven't yet uncovered the full extent of.

But he's been the kindest to me out of all four of my new captors, and I'm never going to get the answers I need if I hide away in my bedroom until that fire is licking at my bedposts. I suck in a deeper breath, willing away the jitters, and nod. "Okay. Thank you."

His usual warm enthusiasm comes back into his face and his voice. "Thank me when we see how much I can actually do for you. Come on—the parlor has good light."

"The parlor" turns out to be an alcove off the kitchen where a few well-padded armchairs—less ornate than most of the furniture I've encountered in the keep—squat in a semi-circle around a matching footstool and a coffee table of pale wood. Big windows look out over a garden of unfamiliar plants in neat rows and a cluster of trees bearing vibrant globes of fruit.

Beyond the orchard, more fields stretch out toward thick forest. In the distance on the left-hand side, spires of peach-colored stone jut high above the tree-tops, dotted with patches of clinging lime-green shrubs. It looks like the kind of awe-inspiring landscape I'd have printed off for my travel-planning scrapbook.

The thought of those long-lost dreams squeezes my throat. I wrench my gaze away.

A door leads out to the garden, simpler and less imposing than the big one in the entrance room. Seeing it, an itch runs through my arms. It doesn't seem likely that Sylas would have protected the front door so carefully but neglected this back one—Kellan even said there was a back one that was magically sealed—but at least I know for sure there's more than one way out.

August motions for me to sit on the footstool and hunkers down on the edge of the chair behind me so he can examine my hair. His fingertips graze my shoulders, warm and gentle.

"Let's see... I should be able to convince at least some of these knots to unwind themselves."

He says a word in that melodious tone all the fae seem to use when casting their magic, and a tickle of energy passes over my scalp. His fingers keep moving through the strands of my hair with only the faintest of tugs. A wisp of heat from his breath grazes my neck. By the time he asks me to turn so he can work on the waves that frame my face, my pose has mostly relaxed. I can't say I feel *safe*, but I'm reasonably sure I'm not in imminent danger while he's next to me.

When August has worked over both sides, he leans back to consider his handiwork. "The ones higher up weren't so bad, but near the bottom there were a lot of strands twisted pretty tight. I couldn't get them all free without breaking some. I could remove those completely?"

I have the abrupt, ridiculous thought that the lower span of my hair is one of the few things I have left from my time in the real world, before faeries and cages. But maybe I'd feel better having it closer to the chin-length bob from when I was twelve and had no idea any of this existed?

"All right," I say. "Just as long as it doesn't end up with big chunks missing or something." Before the words have even finished tumbling out, my face flushes. I'm not really in a position to be making demands.

August just chuckles. "I may not be a trained barber, but I can manage to do a better job than that."

He goes into the kitchen and comes back with what appears to be a large carving knife. My back stiffens automatically. August halts a few feet away, holding the knife with the tip pointing at the floor. "It's an enchanted blade—it'll cut where I need it to in an instant. I promise I'll be careful."

He looks so hopeful that I'll let him finish his work, so eager to reassure me, that I manage to nod. If he wanted to stab me, he could have done it the moment we walked in here, no need for some complicated subterfuge about fixing my hair.

And he's telling the truth. He lifts the hair from my back with another brush of his fingers and slices through the strands so swiftly that I feel nothing but the patter of what remains hitting my shoulder blades. When I glance back, he's got about four inches of tattered tangles in his hand. At least for the few moments before he murmurs another magical word, and they burst into flames. I flinch, but the fire is already gone, my hair only a sprinkling of ashes that August tosses away.

"It's better not to have your hair lying around—it can be used for enchantments and things," he says, as if reminding me of something I should already know, and offers me an easy smile. On him, the gesture doesn't seem to be hiding ulterior motives like so many of the other grins that've been aimed at me since I got here. "Swivel all the way around, and I'll tackle that mis-healed foot of yours."

He'd better not be planning on using the carving knife on *that* part of my body.

I do as he asked, and he picks up my warped foot by the heel to rest it on his knee. It's bare where it protrudes from the leg of my jeans—the fae men didn't bother to give me socks or shoes. A subtle discouragement from attempting to make a run for it or simple oversight since they knew they weren't letting me outside anyway?

August slips his thumb over the lump of misshapen bone, one side of his mouth slanting downward. His light touch doesn't wake up the usual ache. Then he lifts his gaze, his golden eyes darkened with regret so tangible it sends an unexpected flutter through my chest.

"The injury happened quite a while ago?" he asks.

"About eight years," I say, my voice falling back into its previous whisper. "As well as I've been able to keep track."

"Feet are difficult as it is—a lot of little bones that have to fit together just right. I'm not sure I have the skill that I could have set them properly even a week afterward. Now that the pieces have had so much time to fuse together and settle into their new form... It's easier to mend something than to break it apart once it's combined into something new—that would be like trying to magic a cake back into flour and eggs. I'm afraid I'd hurt you worse."

"That's okay." I hadn't really believed he'd fix *that*, I realize. Would Sylas even want him to? The faerie lord gave me the crutch rather than asking August to check the bones. Maybe he could tell from a glance it was too complicated a task, or maybe he doesn't want me recovering *quite* that much.

But I don't think August would have offered up the possibility if he hadn't planned to help if he could. As far as I can tell, he's more disappointed than I am.

"Why are you being so nice to me?" I blurt out, and then snap my mouth shut, my cheeks flaring hotter than before.

August blinks at me. "Why wouldn't I be?"

I grope for the right words. "I just mean—no one else here was offering to fix my hair or my foot… or anything." Even Sylas was brisk and business-like about the crutch. Whitt has barely bothered to pay attention to me at all, and I could do without the attention Kellan has directed my way.

August sets down my foot. "I wasn't needed for anything else, and you shouldn't have to go around uncomfortable if I can change that easily enough. It's bad enough what Aerik and his cadre put you through."

That doesn't explain why he's been so much friendlier than the others, but I guess it's a reasonable explanation. Before I can decide whether to prod further, he reaches out and gives one of my newly trimmed locks a playful but still gentle tug. Tipped toward me like that, his knees nearly touch mine—his unsettlingly handsome face is less than an arm's length away.

My pulse flutters again, this time with a quiver of heat that's not embarrassment.

"We could do something else with your hair," he offers. "Cut more off, change the color—whatever you like. Take you farther away from everything you've had to endure."

I kind of like that idea, and it's a welcome distraction from the new sensations spreading through my body. Mom always said I could dye my hair when I got older. Well, I'm older now, aren't I?

I tamp down on the hysterical giggle that bubbles up my throat at that justification and manage to say, "Another color—I think that would be good."

He gestures to the windows. "Whatever you like. I've got plenty of materials to bolster my magic."

Any color I want? Thinking of my captor with the sunflower-yellow hair and the purple tint in Sylas's, I have to assume even the natural range for fae coloring isn't as restricted as it is for humans.

A memory pops into my head so suddenly it jerks at my heart. A few months before I was taken, I saw a singer whose name I can't remember anymore in a music video, her hair neon pink, and became desperately determined to emulate that look. It seemed like the height of coolness.

I've got no one here to impress with my style and probably using my preteen sensibility for guidance isn't the best idea ever, but it would be a tribute to my old life. The one I was meant to have. And I definitely wouldn't look like a horror movie wraith like that.

"Can you make it pink?" I ask.

August grins. "Absolutely. Wait right there."

He gets up and bounds out into the garden, but not so swiftly that I miss the indecipherable whisper as he opens the door. Yeah, it's got a locking spell on it too. Damn it.

As he crosses the garden to the fruit trees, I can't help watching his muscular stride, taking in the blatant strength of that brawny body and the eager energy with which he carries it. It's a combination that's more appealing than I want to admit.

He isn't just a man. He untangles hair with a word and conjures flames from his hands. He can turn into a wolf— one of those huge, vicious wolves like the one that left the ring of scars on my shoulder.

August has just passed out of sight amid the trees when Whitt strolls into the kitchen, dressed in an indigo housecoat of what looks like satin with gold embroidery along the cuffs and hems. If he's surprised to find me there, he doesn't show it.

"Hmm," he says. "I came to get some breakfast, but it looks like August has been busy. Are you lunch?"

I wince, but the remark is too flippant for me to take it seriously, the total opposite of Kellan last night when he threatened to have me for supper. Whitt's eyes glint as he watches my reaction, and I'm gripped by the urge to play something other than the trembling captive just this once.

"At this point, I don't think I've got enough meat on my bones to make much of a meal," I say.

Surprise flashes across Whitt's face. My pulse hiccups

with the fear that I've made a mistake, but then he barks a laugh.

"We'll see how you turn out after a few weeks of August's cooking, then," he says in the same offhand tone, grabbing a couple of pastries and a heap of bacon out of a basket at the back of the counter and dropping them onto a plate. He saunters out without another word.

The tension from the brief encounter releases from my limbs with a tremor, but at least he's not around to see how much it took out of me to produce that single retort.

August hustles back inside with a couple of glittering fruits that look like rubies in the shape of pears and a handful of bell-like magenta flowers that bob in his hand even when he comes to a stop, as if they're drifting in their own innate breeze. "It'll just take a moment," he promises me.

He dumps his entire haul into a bowl and mashes it together with the energetic pounding of a pestle. He adds a little water from the kitchen faucet, mashes some more, and brings the gloopy mess over to me. "Ready?"

My heart has started thumping as if this was a perilous mission rather than a makeover, and it seems abruptly absurd that this linebacker of a man is going to deliver a dye job, but I've come this far. "Ready," I agree, willing my voice not to shake.

He has to sit even closer to me to work the gloop into my hair, his fingers massaging my scalp and spreading the concoction down through the strands, which still fall to about an inch past my shoulders. When he speaks one of those hushed, melodic words to enhance the dye's effects, his breath washes over my neck again. The fluttering heat returns to my chest, traveling lower in my belly in a way I'm not sure I like.

There's no chance he's feeling anything like that about *me*. I'm a pitiful prisoner he's trying to make himself feel better about keeping locked away.

I don't want to enjoy the tender press of his fingers. I don't want to like him at all.

Whatever his reasons, he *is* being nice to me—extraordinarily nice. Maybe there's a way I can take advantage of that so I can get away from here and all these unwanted feelings ASAP.

I didn't want Whitt looking at me like I was pathetic, but I suspect August is more likely to cooperate if I play up the pitifulness with him. I'm nervous enough about broaching this subject that my voice comes out wavery without any need to feign it.

"August… can I ask you something?"

He kneads more of the dye into a patch of hair at the back of my skull and then eases it out through the rest of the strands there. "Of course. What is it?"

My hands ball in my lap. "I know the reason this Aerik guy kept me and the reason you all wanted me too has something to do with my blood. What's so—what's so special about it? I just want to understand why all this has happened to me."

My words break toward the end. Suddenly I'm choked up, through no act, just honest emotion.

What could possibly have been worth all the other blood spilled, the screams that echo in my memory, the years crouched in that filthy cage? Or maybe to faeries it doesn't need to be all that big a deal to justify that kind of violence.

August's hands have gone still. He pauses for a moment, and then he says, in a more subdued tone than usual, "We don't really understand it either. We only know what it does."

"And what's *that*?"

He inhales slowly. "I think I heard Sylas tell you that we can transform into wolves?"

I nod, suppressing the cringe accompanying the images that rise up in my head. "He did."

"Well, it used to be, a long time ago when I wasn't even of age yet, that the shift was always under our control. It felt right to let our wolves out under the full moon, but we didn't *have* to, and we were just as much ourselves if we did. Then that started to change. We would shift even if we didn't want to. And when we did, on those full-moon nights, our wolves would go wild."

"Wild?"

"Savage." August grimaces. "Nothing in us but the urge to fight and destroy. Like some kind of curse, but we have no idea what might be responsible or how. And the wildness has taken over us for longer and more violently as the years passed. These days, the full moon makes us more like monsters than wolves."

Another memory flits through my mind: hulking, furred shapes lunging out of the shadows. Monsters, indeed.

"That's awful," I say, restraining a shudder.

"It is. But for most of the Seelie, the ones with a decent amount of favor among our peers, it hasn't been so bad for the last several years. Aerik started selling a tonic that if drunk would either prevent the wildness or halt it if it'd already taken over, clear the folk's heads. And as far as we can tell, the key ingredient in that tonic was the blood they were stealing from you."

"Oh." The word falling from my lips is utterly inadequate, but I don't know what else to say. "Has anything else ever helped stop the curse?"

He shakes his head. "Nothing we've ever found or heard of."

A chill spreads through my chest, eating up any heat that remained from August's closeness. I'm the key to taming a savage sickness that has taken over the fae—the only cure they have. How could they ever consider letting me go?

And even if I manage to make an escape, what lengths will they go to in order to get me back?

9

Talia

On my way down the hall that evening, my reflection catches my eye again. I can't help stopping and goggling as I have several times already at the magic August did with my hair.

And it really is magic in every sense of the word. No human dye job could ever have worked like this. Somehow the pink hue sank into my dark brown in a way that lets the natural variation come through without diminishing the vibrancy of the new color. It's a deep, rich pink just a few shades shy of purple, and if I didn't know that humans don't grow hair like this, I'd believe it sprouted out of my head that way.

I still look gaunt, my skin sallow, but the vivid waves elevate those flaws from sickly to something luminous, almost as otherworldly as the fae men who brought me here. That's pretty magical in itself. It makes me feel just a tiny bit more powerful than I did before, but a tiny bit matters a lot when you started with nothing.

As I head to my room upstairs, the sound of lilting music reaches my ears. Curious, I clomp along with my crutch to follow it—down the hall in the opposite direction, to where a narrow arched window overlooks the fields to the south.

Beyond the fields and the low, rolling hills beyond them in this direction, the sun has sunk below the distant forest, leaving only a ruddy glow in the dusky sky that's a close match to my new hair. A brighter illumination lights the field at the outskirts of the cluster of stump-like houses. Amber orbs float like immense fireflies around rugs spread out on the grass amid platters of food and goblets of what from the general vibe must be wine.

Several men and women lounge on cushions scattered across the rugs. Others sway beneath the orbs in time with the tune played on a misshapen guitar by an elegant man with fingers that look a joint longer than they ought to be. Laughter rises up as loud as the music.

One couple is kissing, pressed up against a nearby tree. Another two sprawl between cushions at the edge of the festivities, the woman straddling the man in an embrace so intimate my face heats as I avert my gaze.

These must be members of the larger pack—the faeries who live in those houses. The flickering light falls on one familiar face: Whitt, the rumpled strands of his sun-kissed hair catching the glow as if they contain their own internal sun, his hand raised in a toast. He says something with a grin, and another wave of laughter carries through the gathering.

He's entirely lit up with a radiant energy I don't remember seeing when I've encountered him in the keep. It's impossible not to notice how striking these fae men are in general, but watching Whitt right now, I forget how to breathe.

That's how faeries trick mortals in the tales about them, isn't it? Dazzle them with beauty and wonders so they don't realize just how much the fae are stealing from them at the same time.

Still, I can't tear my eyes away.

A creak of the floor makes me startle. I jerk around as fast as my warped foot allows, my body tensing defensively even though I don't see how I could have been doing anything wrong.

That turns out to be the right reaction anyway. Kellan stands in the shadows of the hall, his lips curled into a smile so cruel you'd think someone cut it into his face with a blade. My fingers tighten around the stem of my crutch.

"Enjoying Whitt's revels from afar, maggot meat?" he says. "That's as close as you'll ever get to them."

I swallow hard. What does he want? "I'm fine staying in here," I say in that pathetic whisper. I can't seem to propel my voice louder around him, not with his silvery eyes fixed on me like blades in themselves.

"Such a docile little lamb." He takes a step closer, and my spine goes even more rigid. "Or perhaps a clown, with that ridiculous cataclysm the whelp has made on your head."

As much as I'm fighting not to react, my cheeks burn. All I want is to get away from him, but he's standing between me and my bedroom. Between me and the entire rest of the keep, really. He has me cornered here at the end of the hall, and with that growing awareness, my breath comes short with panic rather than awe.

He prowls even closer. I think the glint in his eyes might be a sort of pleasure alongside the maliciousness. He licks his lips, making no effort to hide the motion of his tongue, and I'm sure of it then. He wants exactly what he's getting: me, trapped and terrified, at his mercy. He's simply enjoying testing how much he can scare me.

Because he wouldn't *actually* hurt me, not while Sylas has said they're going to keep me safe here. Right?

Under Kellan's cold stare, I can't summon much faith in that pledge.

My heart is thudding, and I just barely hold my body back from trembling. Will he let me get out of this stand-off if I try? I *have* to try—the panic as he closes in is already dizzying me.

I fumble for words, lurching forward with my crutch as I do. "I'll get out of your way. I was just going to bed."

I limp past him as quickly as I can, sticking close to the wall. Kellan watches me go, folding his arms over his chest, his gaze pickling over my skin.

"That's right. Run, little dung-body. Enjoy your lavish bed while you can. You won't have it much longer."

I stumble into my bedroom and slump against the closed door. My limbs aren't just trembling but shaking now, so hard I might vomit. When I close my eyes, images flash behind my eyelids: the bronze bars of my cage, the haughty faces sneering down at me, the gleam of the blade that dug into my wrist.

I'm not there anymore. I'm not there. I remind myself

of that over and over in my head, but my body isn't convinced.

My body knows that all I've done is traded up for a prettier cage and jailors with nicer manners. Well, most of them.

I let myself sink to the floor and summon different images in my mind. The Egyptian pyramids, rising ancient and sublime out of the desert under a scorching sun. The dawn glow filtering green through the thick bamboo stands in a forest near Kyoto. Picture after stunning picture from my collection. There's still a chance I'll make it to those places someday.

Gradually, the tremors fade away. I'm still wobbly as I shuffle over to the bed, but I make it there without falling.

The full moon must be weeks away. I have time before any of these wolfish fae *need* my blood. I've already found out so much more than I knew before.

I've just got to hope that they don't change their minds about how much freedom they're allowing me—or about keeping me to themselves to begin with—before I discover everything I need to.

The bedcovers settle around me, cocooning me in feathery softness. As I tug them closer, the lavender scent in my pillow tickles into my nose. My breath evens out, and sleep pulls me under.

The next thing I'm aware of is a cold, hard surface beneath me. I'm slumped against it, unable to move. Too *weak* to move. Like I've refused to eat or drink for days and even thinking about lifting my arm is exhausting, let alone doing it. I can't find the energy to so much as stretch my fingers.

Then someone is grasping my jaw with bruising force, wrenching my mouth open. Sharp eyes glint beneath spikes of blueish-white hair.

A cloying, viscous liquid flows over my tongue. I sputter and gag, but I'm too weak to push at the hand, too weak to spit the stuff out. My survival instincts kick in against my will, and I swallow, swallow, swallow until my head spins with the magicked wine and my lips are sticky with fruit pulp.

It courses down my throat and into not just my stomach but my lungs—I'm drowning. Gasping, gurgling. Muscles wasted and slack. Helpless, so helpless—

Suddenly I'm sprawled on grass in a forest clearing. The stars whirl overhead. My little brother calls my name, his voice wavering through the twilight. I blink, and I see him silhouetted in the distance, Mom and Dad on either side of him, coming this way.

No, no, they can't. The monsters are coming.

But my body won't move, no sound will travel up my throat. When I called out to them before, I thought I was fighting, struggling to survive, but all I did was give everything up.

Just one word. One cry of warning. A cold sweat breaks out across my skin, my lips part a fraction of an inch—

Claws slash from the darkness, carving screams in their wake. Not again, not—

A hand grasps my arm, and I yelp, thrashing. Thrashing... against the soft sheet tangled around my legs.

I wheeze, my lungs constricted with panic, my pulse thundering in my ears. The air tastes like lavender and wildflowers. Moonlight streams through the gap in the curtains—in my bedroom, or the room that's my bedroom for now, at least.

And the hand still gripping my arm, carefully but firmly, belongs to the massive man sitting beside me on the bed, his milky scarred eye even more eerie in the dimness.

"You were having a nightmare," Sylas says, his voice slow and measured, as if talking to a young child. "You were crying out. There's no easy way to wake from one like that."

No, I didn't wake easy at all. As my eyes adjust to the faint moonlight, I make out a fresh scratch on his unscarred cheek where my fingernail must have caught him when I lashed out.

He heard me in distress and came to shake me out of it, and I *attacked* him. My heart stutters all over again. What consequences am I going to face for that mistake?

My voice wobbles as it spills out. "I'm sorry. I didn't mean—I didn't realize—"

"The dream followed you out," he says, calmly enough that the alarm clanging through me starts to dull. "They do that sometimes. Are you all right now?"

A laugh catches in my throat. How can I possibly be *all right*, even now that I'm awake? But I know what he means.

"Yes," I say. My body is catching up with reality, the panic falling away. "Thank you. It was… awful."

I expect him to get up and leave. Did I wake him up with the noises I was making—oh, crap, did I wake *all* of them up?

But Sylas doesn't appear to be in any hurry to get back to his own bed, if he was even already in it when the nightmare hit me and not burning the midnight oil on whatever it is he does when he's not kidnapping human girls and making crutches for them. How much do fae even need to sleep?

He sets down my arm but stays where he's sitting, close enough that my knee tingles with the proximity of his hip even though it isn't quite touching me. His dark eye studies my face. "What did you dream about?"

A shiver runs through me, just remembering. The memory of my family sends an ache through my chest so sharp I know I can't talk about that. But the rest...

"When the other fae—Aerik and whoever—had me," I say. "There was a point when I gave up. I didn't think I'd ever get away from them, and I just wanted to die. So I refused to eat or drink anything... But it didn't work. When I got weak enough, they forced things down my throat. I couldn't stop them. I couldn't do *anything*. Not even die. It was... the worst I ever felt."

Sylas nods. "I can see how that would be."

I swipe my hand across my mouth. A prickling sensation has formed behind my eyes, but I don't want to cry in front of him. He's seen me in a bad enough state without adding to it.

"I decided that if I had to live, I'd better make sure I was strong enough to do something with that life, even if it wasn't much. I couldn't stand staying completely helpless like that. So I kept eating, and when I could move I did, just to work my muscles a little. Just... just in case." My shoulders tense. "I dreamed it happened all over again—the weakness, the way they force-fed me. That's all."

"They never should have treated you that way," Sylas says firmly. "Some of my fae kin may be pitiless, but I promise you it's far from all of us." He pauses. "Aerik and his men—the wolves that attacked you in your world— were they the first wolves you'd seen roaming? Had you ever seen *them* before that night?"

Does he think they might have planned the attack? I knit my brow, thinking back across the seemingly endless stretch of captivity. My sense of my life before has gone vague and dreamlike, as if *it* was only a happy illusion conjured in my sleep, but I know I'd remember seeing *wolves* wandering around town. It was a pretty small town, but hardly some tiny settlement in the wilderness.

I shake my head. "No. Nothing like that. The biggest animals I remember seeing even when we'd go for hikes are raccoons and one time a porcupine."

"Do you recall ever noticing a raven nearby? Or perhaps a wild rat?"

"There were crows sometimes, but I don't think ravens. They're bigger, right? And we had a wild mouse get into the house a few years before... but definitely no rats." I glance up at Sylas. "Why specifically those?"

He gives me one of his restrained smiles. "I can't help wondering if there was some fae influence in how you came to be as you are. We Seelie have the wolf in our nature, but there are also the Unseelie of the winter lands, who become ravens, and the rats of the Murk... who are better not dealt with at all if one can help it." He moves to get up. "I shouldn't be troubling you with these matters when you need your sleep."

"It's all right." I rub my arms, willing away the last flickers of uneasiness from my nightmare. "Thank you for coming in. I'm glad I didn't have to spend any more time in that dream."

"No doubt you will find yourself there again. Nightmares like to inflict our worst memories on us. If I can, I'll make sure you don't stay in any of them too long."

He turns toward the door, and I wonder abruptly how he speaks with so much confidence on the subject. What kinds of nightmares has *he* had?

I don't think he'll answer that, but him coming to me, helping me, was an opening. One I have to grasp hold of however I can, just like I grasped the bars of my cage to build up the strength in my arms.

"Are you usually awake at night?" I venture. I need to know when my new captors sleep if I'm ever going to escape.

I'd hoped the question would sound innocent enough, but Sylas's expression turns even more opaque than before. "Don't you worry yourself about me, little scrap."

He says the nickname kindly enough, but the rest like a command, not a mere suggestion. Before I can respond, he's already striding out of the room, closing the door behind him.

I sit there in the dark for several minutes, too wound up to even consider trying to sleep. My body slowly relaxes, but another question grips me, one I can answer for myself.

I slip off the bed and limp across the room, leaving my crutch so the tapping won't give my movement away. My balance teeters, and a muted throbbing wakes up in my warped foot by the time I reach the door, but traveling around the keep over the last couple of days has steadied my legs enough that I at least don't fall.

I curl my fingers around the polished wooden knob and twist it ever so gingerly.

It only moves a smidgeon before it catches. I can't turn it any farther, and when I give it the gentlest of tugs, I can tell the door won't budge.

The faerie lord wouldn't let me stay trapped in a nightmare, but that hasn't stopped him from locking me in my room at night.

My mouth has gone dry. I focus on the knob, remembering that moment in my cage when I released the lock. The syllables I practiced so many times before they worked tickle across my tongue with no thought at all. I cling to the fear winding through me and murmur the word with every bit of emotion I can muster. "*Fee-doom-ace-own.*"

The knob doesn't budge. I repeat the magic word again, and again, and then stop, afraid if I keep it up someone will hear me.

Who knows how many different kinds of locking magic there are? Sylas hasn't treated me like my former captors did in any other way, so why would I assume he'd use the same spell to hold me in?

It'll be open during the day. I'll still have chances. But as I shuffle back to the bed, my heart has sunk with an all-too-familiar sense of hopelessness. I close my hands into fists against it.

I made it out of that cage, and I'll make it out of here too. I just have to keep believing that.

10

Talia

When I peek into the kitchen halfway through one afternoon, August is already in a flurry of motion throwing together some kind of epic dinner. Catching sight of me, he beams without slowing down his preparations. "My favorite new assistant! Come in. I've got something for you to stir."

Over the past few days, I've found myself gravitating here more and more often, as if drawn by August's typical clatter like a bee to nectar. The auburn-haired fae man with his human-like ears and his warm smiles has always waved me in eagerly. Nothing appears to make him happier than sharing the secrets of one recipe or another with me—not that I'm likely to use those anytime soon, seeing as most of them involve ingredients I'm pretty sure the grocery store back home won't offer, like cat's milk and hummingbird eggs.

He's the only one of my new captors who makes me feel like I really am a welcome guest and not a prisoner.

Today, I'm soon perched on my usual kitchen stool with a bowl wider than I am propped on my knees and a long wooden spoon clutched in my hand. The dough I'm mixing is a weird combination of sticky and sloshy, but it gives off a sweetly spicy smell that makes my mouth water.

"What's this going to become?" I ask.

"You'll just have to wait and see," August says with a sparkle in his golden eyes. "I promise you'll enjoy it."

"I want to eat it already."

He laughs. "It won't taste half as good before it's baked." He pauses, studying me with sudden concern. "Are you hungry? I can get you a snack."

The thing that appears to make August second-happiest is watching me devour his cooking. Every meal where I manage to consume closer to a full serving—though still nothing like the amount these men-who-aren't-men eat—he perks up a little more. And every day, I have a little more energy of my own.

I'd have thought it'd be in their best interests to keep me weak, but August doesn't seem to think so, and Sylas isn't stopping him. I don't know what to make of that.

"No, keep going with your dinner prep," I say. "I'm not really hungry—this just smells so good."

"And I haven't even added the malvia sugar yet," he says, whatever that is. "I'd make these things more often if they didn't take so long to bake. Easier when I have help, though." He flashes another smile at me and goes back chopping up root vegetables of an odd pale blue color.

"It'll need another five minutes stirring, but if your arm gets tired, I can jump in. Just let me know."

As I continue turning the batter, I glance around the kitchen. It's twice as big as my bedroom, which is pretty big in itself, with three ovens, two islands—one massive and one narrow—and pots and pans of all shapes and sizes dangling from vine-like ceiling fixtures. "It seems like this kitchen is meant to have a whole team working in it."

"Sylas modeled it on the one we had in Hearthshire. We had a full staff there. Back then, I really just noodled around in the kitchen when they didn't need it…"

He trails off with a hesitant note, as if he's not sure he should have said that. That might mean it's important. Sylas said something about Hearthshire, didn't he? I can't remember exactly what.

"Why did you move here?" I venture. I *do* remember the fae lord indicating that it was unusual for August to be doing the cooking—for them not to have staff. I haven't seen anyone in the keep other than him and the three members of his cadre since I arrived here. Whatever work the rest of the pack does, it happens outside these walls.

August sweeps the chopped veggies off the cutting board, his stance uncharacteristically awkward. "Unfortunate circumstances. But we've made the best of things here."

A typically vague answer, the kind I get whenever I ask anything at all prying. I suck my lower lip under my teeth to worry at it. He was willing to open up a bit about my role here, but that involved me directly—and he wasn't keen on talking even about that.

I have to understand how everything works in this

place, where we are and why and all the rest, if I'm going to have a real hope of being anything more than a walking blood dispenser. But it's going to be obvious if I prod too much. I veer back to what seems like a safer subject, hoping I'll get another opening.

"Have you always liked to cook then, even though you wouldn't normally need to?"

August nods, his usual energy coming back into his movements and the gleam in his eyes. "I've mostly trained in fighting, to defend Sylas and the pack if it comes to that. Thankfully there's not much call for combat most days." He shoots me a lopsided grin. "But everyone always needs food, and just about everyone appreciates food that's well made. I like knowing I always have something to contribute."

I glance down at the batter I'm still stirring, struck with an unexpected pang by how much I relate to that sentiment. Isn't that exactly why *I* keep volunteering to pitch in rather than sitting back and simply observing, which I know he'd happily let me do? I want to show I can give something back.

"That makes sense," I say.

"I came by it pretty naturally." August sets a frying pan on one of the stoves. "With all the physical training, I was constantly getting hungry between meals and scrounging around in the kitchen. But even as a kid, I wasn't satisfied with just a piece of bread and cheese, so I hassled the head cook until she taught me some of her tricks. In some ways, it's kind of like warfare, figuring out which elements will come together and cooperate or clash."

I never would have thought of cooking like that. "I'm

glad you did learn. With the food you make, I don't think anyone could *not* get their appetite back quickly."

He laughs. "Then my plan is working. Here, give that a couple more whirls and it should be done."

I put my elbow into the last few stirs, the batter thicker against the spoon now, and try to think of what else I might ask him. Before I land on anything, Sylas strides into the kitchen through the back door.

I'm not sure I'll ever *not* be intimidated by the giant of a man with his mane of purple-brown hair and intense, mismatched eyes. My pulse hiccups and my mouth snaps shut before his gaze has even settled on me.

"August is putting you to work, is he?" he says.

The other man leaps to snatch the bowl from me, giving his lord a hasty but respectful bob of his head. "I just thought—since she likes hanging out in here anyway—"

"It's fine," I say quickly. "I'm happy to help out." It does feel good to be doing something useful. Something that's actually me *doing* it and not just a part of my body being stolen away.

Sylas considers me as if he can see that unspoken thought, but he doesn't remark on it. He gestures me up and toward him in the parlor area. "There's another way you can be of use. Come sit with me."

I can't exactly deny him, even if I'm less sure of his good intentions than August's. I walk over, confident enough with my crutch after a few days of practice that it's more an amble than a lurch now. At another motion from Sylas, I sink into one of the armchairs. He pulls another up closer to me and sets a bag of waxy fabric on the coffee table next to us.

"What am I doing?" I ask, fighting the urge to shrink into myself with his powerful form so close. He might rule here, which means he's the one keeping me captive, but he hasn't hurt me. So far.

He takes a sprig dotted with tiny orange leaves from the bag. "I've gathered some of my medicinal herbs from the garden. I'd like to test and see if you have any reaction to them. Just on your skin, nothing that should affect you too strongly if you do react."

That doesn't sound like a huge imposition. But— "Why?"

"You're obviously not a typical human being," he says evenly. "I'm curious to see how else that might bear out and whether it could allow us to determine what exactly makes you unique."

Why my blood can cure this wild curse the fae are suffering from and no one else's can. If he figures that out, would that mean they might be able to replicate the cure without needing me? I'm all for *that* possibility. And the more helpful I am, the more helpful these men will hopefully become when I'm asking more of my questions.

Obediently, I stretch out my arm, bare beneath the sleeve of my T-shirt. I rest it on the arm of the chair, the skin on the underside somehow even paler than the rest, nearly translucent. Blue veins crisscross the delicate bones. August's incredible meals have started filling me out from my half-starved state, but it hasn't been that long. I'm still thin enough that I want to wince, seeing myself.

Sylas moves methodically, so different from August's enthusiastic vigor. He crushes a few of the orange leaves between his thumb and forefinger and then rubs the paste that forms onto my skin just below my wrist. He waits, observing. "Do you feel anything unusual?"

I shake my head. "Nothing I wouldn't expect to."

After a little longer, he wipes the herb off, studies the faint pink spot it left on my skin, and hums low in his throat. It mustn't be anything all that exciting, because rather than spend any more time on that reaction, he retrieves another sprig from his bag, this one bushy as a squirrel's tail—if squirrels came with lavender fur.

That stuff sends a faint stinging sensation through my skin when Sylas applies it. He has me describe the feeling, wipes it off, examines the slightly darker pink mark, and rubs a cool gel onto it that absorbs the sting. Apparently that wasn't anything unexpected either. He immediately moves on.

We've gone through five herbs, none of them provoking any response that holds Sylas's attention for more than a few seconds, before I gather the courage to find out if my cooperation has earned me any of *his* cooperation in return.

"August said the four of you haven't always lived here."

Sylas pauses and looks from me to his cadre man. August ducks his head and throws himself even more energetically into stuffing the roast he's working on now. "August seems to have a habit of mentioning things he doesn't need to," the fae lord says, his tone mild but low enough that there's a hint of reproach in it anyway.

Is Sylas upset that August told me as much as he did about the curse? I didn't mean to get him into trouble. "I — He didn't say very much," I add quickly. "But you said something when I first got here, about somewhere called Hearthshire… That's where you used to live?"

The lord's mismatched gaze comes back to me, and my skin prickles with the impression that he's again seeing a lot more than I said. Then he chuckles, a deep rolling sound that's only a tad less unnerving than if he growled. "The little scrap listens well. Why do you want to know about Hearthshire?"

I can't exactly tell him that I'm hoping someone will slip up and offer a tidbit that'll aid my eventual escape. But I have other, more innocent reasons I can give that are still true.

"I've been living in your world for years, and I don't know anything about it. I haven't *seen* anything of it except the room my cage was in and this keep. I can't help… being curious."

"We were gone from Hearthshire long before you came to the Mists," Sylas says, returning his attention to his herbs. "Long before you were even born, from the looks of you. It's better for all of us if we look forward instead of back."

I can't really argue with that. "What do you see looking forward?" I ask instead.

A small smile curls the lord's lips. "Better things, if we're wise in how we make our moves. I'll take care of that, one way or another."

He doesn't look me in the eyes as he says it, training

his gaze on my arm and the bright green herb he's rubbing into my skin now. A shiver creeps down my back.

I'm going to be a part of those moves—and it's hard to believe that the way I end up fitting into their plans will be better for *me* in the long run.

11

August

"Just one more tartlet?" I implore, waggling the pastry at Talia. "Otherwise I'll think today's baking wasn't up to snuff."

The human gives me that hesitantly fierce look, as if she knows I'm not being serious but isn't quite confident enough yet to call me on it. At the same time, her lips twitch with a smile, and the blush I adore more every time I see it brings color to her wan cheeks.

Knowing that she's comfortable enough with me by now that she trusts I won't really push the issue—that she can take my urging her to eat her fill in the friendly spirit with which I mean it rather than as a threat—fills my chest with warmth. In just a week, she's come a long way from the skittish, cringing girl who could barely speak above a whisper. I'd like to think I can take at least a little credit for that.

I can definitely take credit for the softness that's

starting to fill out her features and frame, smoothing out the harsh angles of starvation. Since the first morning when she picked at her breakfast like a mouse, she's worked up to what I think must be close to a human-sized meal. After so many years without any humans around, my frame of reference is shaky.

"I'm full, I promise," she says, setting her hand on her still-concave belly, her voice quiet but clear. "You're going to give me a stomach ache."

"All right, all right." I grin at her and pop the pastry into my mouth instead.

"Let's not give her the impression we're trying to fatten her up for the slaughter," Whitt drawls from across the dining table.

I can tell he's teasing, but Talia's obviously not as sure of him. Her shoulders tense with a restrained flinch. Then she shoots me a swift little smile as if to reassure me that she knows that's not my intention, and a swell of affection rushes through my chest.

She's been through so much. When I think of Aerik and his cadre, of the state in which they kept her and the cage we found her in, of the reactions that show just how much they traumatized her, anger hazes my mind. I want to storm right back into their fortress and tear the lot of them apart. I *would* rend them into pieces if giving into that desire wouldn't screw over my own cadre. But if Aerik or his people ever set foot on our territory...

My fingers curl, my claws prickling beneath the tips. I focus on Talia's bright green eyes and the strikingly rich pink I transformed her hair into, and the fury recedes. She's been through so much, and yet she can find the space to care how I might take my older brother's hassling. The hard part is stopping myself from gazing at her for too long.

As Kellan has clearly noticed. He bares his teeth in a sneer where he's sitting next to Whitt. "Yes, let's all become mudlickers and organize our lives around *her*."

My hackles rise again, but Sylas shoots me a sharp look, and I manage to hold my tongue. It's only through our lord's grace that I haven't already ripped the mangy asshole's throat out.

Sylas stands, the meal done, and I get up to collect the plates. He motions to Whitt. "I would see you in my study now."

Whitt dips his head. "I can barely contain my excitement." Despite his sarcasm, he follows our lord out without hesitation.

One of his runners came by the keep this afternoon. News about the Unseelie incursions, maybe? Have they launched another assault?

I clench my teeth, holding in my impatience that Sylas doesn't yet consider me astute enough to add something to the larger strategy discussions. How am I supposed to learn enough to have something to contribute if I'm shut out?

This isn't the time to campaign for more responsibility, though. Sylas is still deciding how we're going to handle Talia and *her* unique contributions to our situation. He's taken in what I've had to say about that. I have to be ready to speak up for her again if I need to.

It doesn't matter how important she is to us—she still deserves better than to be passed around like a bargaining chip. I can't let other concerns distract me and then fail her.

This time I won't let the worst happen.

I carry the dishes to the sink I've already filled with hot water and fermented shearvine juice. Within an hour in that potion, all the bits of food still clinging to the ceramic surfaces will have dissolved. I lope back to the hall, passing through the kitchen doorway just as Kellan swipes his foot toward Talia and knocks her crutch out from under her.

Talia squeaks and tumbles onto her knees. Kellan looms over her, his laugh so vicious she winces, and every thought in my head blanks out beneath a roar of fury.

I hurl myself at the other man, the roar bursting from my throat. My fist slams into the side of his head before he's had a chance to turn fully around.

Kellan staggers backward, catches himself, and springs at me with a snarl. I land a punch on his jaw, but he manages to knee me in the gut. I dodge another blow and leap at him again, conscious of nothing but the thunder of my pulse and the rageful red tinting the edges of my vision.

He *attacked* her, that poor slip of a thing not even half his weight with no means of defending herself, and he is going to pay.

My teeth twinge as they lengthen into fangs; my shoulders start to hunch with the instinct to unleash my wolf. I can fight in either form, but the animal is faster, freer. Kellan slashes at my face with fingertips already sprouting claws—

—and a force larger than either of us rams between us, shoving us apart.

Sylas plants himself there with his arms spread, one hand gripping my shoulder and the other Kellan's. The growl I was about to let out dies in my throat under my lord's scrutiny.

"Get a hold of yourself," he barks, and jerks his head around to level his glare at Kellan too. "Both of you. Are you my cadre, or are you whelps barely off their mother's teat?"

My muscles are still clenched with anger, but the flare of adrenaline is already tapering off. A sickly sense of shame trickles through me. And I was just bemoaning that he doesn't invite me into his higher strategy discussions. Small wonder.

"He hurt Talia," I say, because if I'm going to be shamed, Kellan is owed at least as much. "Kicked her crutch away so she'd fall. I was—"

"Defending her?" Sylas fills in with a dark rumble in his voice. He tips his head toward the stairs. "It doesn't appear she's appreciated your attempt all that much."

I glance past him, and my heart plummets. Talia has scrambled over to the foot of the steps. She's crouched there, a pose not so different from when we found her in Aerik's cage a week ago, her expression as terrified as it looked then. She holds her crutch braced in front of her like a shield. She's *trembling*, her breath coming in shallow gulps.

The shame that gripped me before is nothing compared to what rolls over me at that sight. We rescued her from fae who acted like monsters toward her, I've been doing everything I know how to help her heal—and what could she see me as after that display of violence but a monster just like them, ready to snap the second he's angered?

I would never lash out at you like that, I want to tell her. *You have nothing to fear from me.* But why in the lands should she believe me?

"Talia," Sylas says gently, "you're in no danger. The fighting is over. I'll deal with these two. No one will hurt you."

Her hands squeeze tighter around the crutch, but she nods in acknowledgment, her breath catching and then starting to even out.

Sylas's tone softens even more. "Do you need me to help you upstairs? I think you'd best retire to your room for the night."

She holds still for a few more seconds, getting her trembling under control, and then pushes herself upright with a shaky determination that makes my heart ache twice as much as before. "I—I think I'll be all right," she whispers.

"I'm glad to hear it. I'll see that you're not disturbed."

She bobs her head again and limps away up the steps, her crutch wavering in her anxious grasp. I feel every fall of her feet like an additional jab of guilt.

When she's out of view, our lord lowers his arms and turns back to Kellan. His voice comes out taut with the anger *he* knows how to control. "I told you to leave her be."

"She wasn't hurt," the other man says dismissively. "I was merely reminding her not to get too cozy around here, since this whelp seems to be doing everything he can to spoil her."

Sylas's voice drops even lower. "Just this once, because surely the kin-of-my-mate would never ignore a direct command, I'll assume you forgot that I specifically said we *want* her to be comfortable so that she'll cooperate in every way we need. To make sure the message sticks this time, I'd have you attend to her in some way to make up for it, but I suspect seeing you is the last thing she'd like right now. The upstairs lavatory could use a good scrub, though."

Kellan draws back. "You're not actually—"

"*Someone* needs to take care of it, and I'd rather not risk anyone else from the pack seeing our guest for the time being. Get to it, and don't let me find out you've been terrorizing the little scrap again."

Kellan's mouth tightens into a grimace, his displeasure obvious, but he turns tail and stalks up the stairs without another word.

Sylas rounds on me. "It's bad enough we can't rein in the wildness one night out of a month without you giving yourself over to it when there's no moon to blame. However you may feel about Kellan, he *is* your cadre-fellow. Every disagreement can't turn immediately into a brawl, or we'll make more broken bones than decisions."

"I know." I lower my head. "He's been picking at her so much, and then seeing him menace her physically as well—I had too much anger building up, and it burst out."

"I don't fault you for defending her. Just attempt it with words next time before bringing out the fangs and the claws. Go for a run. Let out that energy and clear your head. And do that again the next time you notice tensions building inside."

"Yes, my lord."

It's less punishment than Kellan faced—barely any punishment at all. As I head to the back door to follow his orders, my shame over disappointing him fades quickly.

What doesn't fade is the image of Talia's frightened face, the way she gripped her crutch as if she thought she might have to fend us off with it. I bow down over the grass beside the garden, the change rippling through me with a rush of exhilaration the way it's meant to be when our wolves come out, but my stomach stays knotted.

How many times has Kellan pulled stunts like that when none of us were close enough to catch him? How long will it be before his hostility turns even more brutal?

I don't think he'd kill Talia knowing what having her alive means to all of us, but I wouldn't put it past him to injure her, possibly even badly, and count on begging forgiveness. It's hard to imagine Sylas actually kicking him out of the cadre over an offense against a human.

But she shouldn't have to live in fear of him... of all of us.

I look toward the orchard, my mind already traveling past it to the fields and forest beyond. Maybe I can find her a real means of protecting herself—just enough to spare her the worst of his malice.

I stretch my wolfish limbs and set off at a trot toward the edge of the Mists.

12

Talia

Taking an afternoon nap is becoming a habit of mine. I've started staying up into the early hours of the morning, watching from my window and listening to the footsteps and door clicks that seep through the walls, forming a picture of the fae men's comings and goings. The nap gives me a chance to catch up on the missed sleep. My body doesn't seem to appreciate it, though. I'm always groggy when I wake up.

I rub my eyes in the warm sunlight and scoot to the edge of the bed where I left my crutch. I've gotten used enough to walking that my bad foot only twinges a bit when I put my weight on it. Since I can't count on always having the crutch when I need it—as Kellan went out of his way to prove a couple of days ago—I'm trying to lean on it as little as possible. I use it for balance more than anything until my foot starts outright aching from the pressure of walking.

I've also been working on moving silently. It's clear that faeries have keen ears—like wolves, I guess. Sylas came barreling down the stairs to intervene the second August collided with Kellan the other day.

Stealth isn't easy with the wooden end of the crutch bracing against the hard floor. I set it down as carefully as I can manage, make sure it's steady before taking a step, and lift it straight up so it doesn't scrape the floor. I'm going to need to rely on it more when I'm ready to get out of here so that my feet themselves don't make too much noise with my uneven gait. No matter how I try, my warped foot catches on the ground a little every time I raise it.

Along the hall and down the stairs, I only slip up with the crutch and tap it on the floorboards once. Not bad. I'm getting there. Considering that I still have no concrete idea how I'm going to get past the locks or find my way out of the fae world afterward, I've got plenty more time to practice.

I expect to find August in the kitchen. As I slip through the doorway, my body tenses just slightly in anticipation. An image flickers through my head: his face twisted with fury, his fist hurtling at Kellan's face, his animalistic roar ringing through the hall.

He was protecting me. I know that. I know it, and my pulse still stutters when I remember how he looked and sounded in that moment.

He's been so sweet to me, but he's no more a man than the others. He has one of those monstrous wolves inside him. I can't ever forget that.

Scary as that might be, it doesn't change the fact that I

find him *less* scary than his companions. The kitchen remains my favorite hangout spot.

There's no sign of his dark auburn hair or well-built body in the room right now, though. I'm about to head back out when a clinking sound reaches my ears. As I glance around, Whitt emerges from the pantry that's just off the cooking area.

His sun-kissed hair is in typical disarray, his stride as jaunty as ever, but his high-collared shirt and trim slacks look more rumpled than I'm used to, as if he's slept in them. Maybe he has. There was another party outside the keep last night, one I could still hear strains of music and laughter from until I finally let myself sleep. He didn't emerge for breakfast *or* lunch today.

When he catches sight of me, he cocks his head. There's a glaze to his eyes as if he's not quite seeing me after all.

"Are you all right?" I find myself asking, even though on the scale of scary Whitt is definitely at the upper end. He's never been mean to me like Kellan, but he hasn't ever been *nice* either.

He makes a humming sound and brandishes a bowl of something he must have grabbed from the pantry. "I will be. Perfect hangover cure."

Something that counteracts the effect of faerie-world intoxication? That could come in handy. A shiver runs through me with the memory of the pulped fruit my former captors shoved into my mouth when they wanted me particularly compliant.

"What is it?"

Whitt ambles over to the parlor and flops into one of the chairs with a leg casually draped over the padded arm. "Much too precious a delicacy for a mite like you," he declares, warmly enough. "You wouldn't know what hit you."

My body balks for a second before I force myself to limp over. I haven't really talked with Whitt before—maybe I should have tried. He might not go out of his way to be friendly, but he seems pretty free with his words. Maybe he'd tell me some of the things the others are keeping secret. Especially while he's hung over.

"I've survived all the faerie food I've eaten so far," I remind him.

He hums again and takes a swig from the bowl, which I can now see holds a syrupy liquid a slightly lighter shade of pink than my hair. He swirls the rest against the sides of the bowl and scrutinizes me with eyes the same bright blue as the ocean under a beaming sun. A perfect match for his hair, not so much for his temperament.

"You want a taste, do you?" he says, a sly glint lighting in those eyes. "I suppose that sort of boldness should be rewarded."

I sink into the chair next to his, and he hands me the dish. It's like an oversized mug in his broad hands; in mine, it's more like a mixing bowl. I raise it to my lips and manage to take a sip without spilling it down my chin.

The syrup coats my tongue, lighting up a giddying warmth everywhere it touches. It's fruity and sweet—so sweet my gums tingle—but rich at the same time. I'm overwhelmed by the flavor in an instant, and at the same time I want to gulp and gulp until I've filled myself to the brim with it.

"Oh, no, you don't, my overeager friend." Whitt snatches the bowl back from me before I can pour more into my mouth. He takes another swig and grins at me, looking a little giddy himself. "I'm sure you never had anything half that delectable back in your own world."

I think of cotton candy at the summer fair, of sugar cookies at Christmas, of crème-filled chocolate eggs left by the supposed Easter Bunny. If all those flavors were somehow combined into one, it would almost reach the wonder of that pink stuff.

Instead of answering, I hold out my hands. "Could I have a *little* more?"

Whitt chuckles and passes the bowl back. I take a bigger swallow than could really be called "a little" before he pulls it out of my grasp. "Watch you don't drown yourself in that, mite."

My head tips back against the cushioned chair, the warmth swelling from my belly all the way to the tips of my fingers and toes. Why get hungover if you could just have this "cure" to begin with?

My thoughts spin around that question and bounce off another consideration of cures. My head feels heavy when I lift it to look at Whitt. "I'm a cure. Not for hangovers. For going wild when it's a full moon."

"Indeed you are." He winks at me and throws back the rest of the syrup. "Wouldn't want to try the hair of the dog approach there. A pity we can't package you up in the pantry so easily."

Hair of the dog. I've heard that expression before—from my parents, way back when?—but I don't remember what it means, if I ever knew. The entire contents of my head have started spinning now, but it's an exhilarating sensation, like whirling around on a merry-go-round.

I cling onto the thread I'd meant to pursue, pulling the words from my mind as if they're unravelling from a spool. "You talked about a tonic—you could keep a tonic in the pantry. Why didn't you just keep using that? Why did you come looking for me?"

"Oh, we didn't know it was you we'd find. We just wanted our own means of making the tonic. Aerik didn't often share with us, you see. We're somewhat out-of-favor with most of our Seelie brethren. And he did enjoy holding that over our heads. No more!"

"Because of me?"

"One way or another." Whitt tosses the empty bowl onto the coffee table and stretches in the chair, more cat-like than wolfish in that moment. A very large cat that could sprout claws just as sharp. "No more living on the fringes of the Mists, human drudges just around the corner. No more half-sized keep for a home. No more dwindling pack. As soon as our lord and master gets on with sorting it all out."

A bit of an edge has crept into his flippant tone, but my attention has stuck on something else. The fringes of the Mists? Humans just around the corner? Are we *close* to the regular world here, then?

I want to ask that, but when I open my mouth, all that tumbles out is a breathless laugh. My mind isn't just whirling but soaring now—I'm suddenly sure that if I reached up I could brush my fingers over the ceiling. The colors of the chairs with their leafy patterns are so vibrant they make me want to cry for awe. Am I even still sitting in one or am I floating?

"You *did* like that syrup, didn't you?" Whitt says with a laugh of his own. "Feed you on this every day, and you'd be happy enough."

In some distant part of my brain, it occurs to me that this isn't normal. It isn't right. No regular food or drink would give me this giddy, soaring sensation. It might not be the cacophony of sounds and color that the pulpy mash put me through, but this—Whitt's hangover cure—it's plenty intoxicating in itself.

I can't quite bring myself to care, though. I reach upward, in the grips of the notion that if I just angle my arms right, I can flap them and fly off the chair like a bird.

Whitt leans toward me, his bright blue eyes sparkling, the same pleased glow in his face that I saw when I watched him at his party the other night. "What are you trying to do, little birdie?"

"I don't know," I say, and giggle so hard my ribs vibrate with the sound. "Is this what you have all those parties for? To float like this?"

"Something like that. Don't fly too far now."

"No. That wouldn't be good. I might hit my head on the ceiling." I giggle even harder. My gaze latches on his face, smiling and so bright. "You're beautiful. Are all faeries beautiful?"

His glow diminishes at that comment, as if the act of pointing out his breathtaking looks drains some of the power from them. His mouth tightens. Is he mad at me? I didn't mean to make him mad.

I was supposed to be asking him about something—about the Mists. About fringes. They moved here from a long way away. Here is close to humans.

Is it close to home? What is home, even? I've lived in Fae Central for almost as many years as I had where I was meant to be.

For some reason, that realization provokes another laugh. My head lolls in the other direction.

Whitt tsks, his good humor seeming to return. "Never did meet a mortal who could handle their—"

"*Whitt*," a voice growls, cutting through the glittery vibe of the moment with a tone so dark it might as well throw a shadow over us.

I crane my neck around and squint to focus. Sylas strides into the pantry, glowering at Whitt and then moving to my side. He looms over me, a mountain of a man. I clap my hand over my mouth, since he's obviously not happy about something, but a giggle leaks past my palm anyway.

"What have you done to her?" he says. "I told you she didn't want anything inebriating."

"She changed her mind," Whitt replies. His voice has gone strange, with a tone I don't think I've ever heard before. Flat and brittle, as if it might snap if he speaks just a little more forcefully. "She practically begged me for a taste, I assure you."

"Did she know what she was asking for?"

Whitt is silent for a few seconds. "It didn't hurt her any. She's loving it. It wasn't any of the harsher stuff."

"That's not your call to make."

Sylas descends on me and scoops me up in his arms. "I'm fine," I tell him, unable to stop myself from grinning. "It was *de*licious. Now I can fly!"

"I think we'd better fly you up to bed so you can sleep this high off safely, little scrap." He tucks me against his broad chest and gives Whitt one last glance. "Stay here. I've got more to say about this."

Being carried in his arms feels even closer to soaring. The heat of his chest encircles me, and the flex of those solid muscles against my body sends a deeper tingling through me.

He's looking after me like he always does. My fiercely stalwart protector. I want to lean into him, drink in the rich earthy smell that wafts off of him and lick that smoky tang off his neck. Mmm.

I shift against Sylas, and he adjusts me so his corded neck is just out of reach. Spoilsport. Instead, I watch the ripples in the wood grain on the ceiling flow by. "I'm not tired. I don't need to sleep."

"Then you can just rest until you do need to. I'll bring your dinner up."

"Not hungry either. That syrup filled me right up."

"I can see it did." His tone is dry. I don't think he's angry at me. A jolt of panic shoots through me at the thought that he could have been angry, even though I've just decided that's not the case. Everything is backwards and upside down.

But my body is still light as air. My thoughts bubble around in my brain like fizz in champagne.

"I was trying to be friendly," I tell Sylas.

"Of course you were."

We're in my room—I don't remember the door opening, but here's the bed and the window with the sun beaming outside. Sylas shuts it. No flying that way. Not a good idea anyway. I snicker to myself.

Sylas sits me down on the edge of the bed and steps back. The loss of contact sends a pang through me. "Are you going? I didn't mean—if I made a mistake—"

He chuckles. "If you did, it's a mistake most of us make at least once."

"Not you."

"Even me. Let's not get into the time I got myself fully drunk on duskapple wine when I was a whelp even smaller than you are. I grew a whole new orchard of emeraldfruit trees before one of my tutors caught me."

I blink at him in disbelief. "You were *never* smaller than me."

That declaration provokes an outright laugh. "It *was* a very long time ago. And to answer your question, I'm not going quite yet. I came looking for you because I made something for you. I'll show you now, but we can go over it again tomorrow if the instructions don't stick. All right?"

"You made me a present?" I peer at him, aware that my smile has turned goofy. "You're very generous for a kidnapper."

Sylas's mouth twitches in the other direction, some of his humor fading. He holds up a strange wooden contraption only a little bigger than his hand, like thin branches curved together to form a sort of cage—although you couldn't keep anything in it, the "bars" are too far apart.

I tip my head, taking it in. "What's that for?"

"Your foot. The crutch isn't an ideal solution. You attach this brace around your calf, and it'll offset some of the pressure so you can walk with less pain using just your two legs." He pauses. "Not something anyone could steal or kick away."

Like Kellan. In my current state, that terrifying moment feels centuries ago. Still, the idea of walking steadily without the crutch appeals to me even in my daze.

I swing my feet against the side of the bed. "Show me how to put it on?"

Sylas slides the device over my ankle, talking me through each step as he centers my foot on thin, padded slats across the bottom and tightens bark-like strips around my thin calf. They grip my skin but hardly weigh on it.

I stand up and take a few experimental steps. My body sways, but I think that's from the giddy dizziness. With the extra support, my warped foot holds me up just as well as the good one.

I spin around and stagger. Sylas catches my arm to keep me from falling. Still watching out for me, making sure I don't get hurt. I want to hug him, but his expression sobers me enough that I don't try.

"It'll take some time for the muscles in your leg to adapt," he says. "And your foot may still hurt, especially if you're on it for a long time. But the brace will help."

"Thank you." I peer down at the contraption and then up at him. The question spills unguarded from my lips. "Why are you helping me like this when you don't really want me going anywhere?"

Sylas's face darkens. "We may have use of you, but that's no reason to torture you. Make what you can of what you're given." He gives me a careful nudge toward the bed and leaves without another word.

Abruptly, even through my joyful lightness, I find myself wondering whether he even likes me.

13

Sylas

On my way to my study after a twilight run, I pause outside the girl's bedroom. With my ears pricked, I can make out the soft rise and fall of her breath even through the door, rhythmic but not slow enough to indicate she's sleeping.

She's often still awake when I come by and cast the magic that locks this door. I can imagine it must be difficult to sleep when she can clearly sense her situation here remains precarious. There's no way I can reassure her of her fate when I'm not sure of it yet myself.

Why should I even want to reassure her? The security of my pack and our chance to redeem ourselves in the arch-lords' eyes come before concern for any human. If the image of her vivid green eyes, turned more vibrant in contrast with the striking hue August added to her hair, lingers in the back of my mind even when she's not in front of me, I can blame that easily enough on my long dry spell. She might be a scrap of a thing, but there's a loveliness to her delicate form that I can't deny.

Taking lovers from among our dwindled pack poses too much risk of adding tensions where there are enough already. My cadre has stolen off beyond the Mists from time to time to sate their lustful hungers with mortals, but I've held myself back from indulging in even that brief satisfaction. I thought it would be a distraction. Now it seems the lack of indulgence may become a distraction in itself, too much pent-up hunger.

Better I don't even enjoy *looking* at Talia. Any desire I develop for her will only interfere with my decision-making. I'll have to find my own chance to go on the prowl.

The thought sends an unwelcome pang through me, as if I owe any faithfulness to one long gone from this world. I shake off the sensation and murmur the spell word over the door knob.

I called a meeting before I went for my run. August arrives at my study at five minutes before the hour, typically over-eager. Kellan stalks in exactly on time, his way of keeping to the letter of the law while making it clear he won't give me a shred more respect than he has to. Whitt ambles in a few minutes late with an air of nonchalance as if he hasn't realized, smelling faintly of absinthe.

I can tell his carelessness is feigned. His shoulders give him away, stiffening just slightly as he crosses the threshold, as if bracing for a scolding. In the hazy afterimages that filter through my dead eye, a ghost of his form bows its head beseechingly—so unlike the man that I know that it's not a reflection of any past dealings we've had.

Perhaps it's an exaggerated echo of his apology yesterday when I laid into him for sharing his edible entertainment with the girl. Perhaps my eye sees some future in which he'll have more to apologize for.

That's a disturbing thought if there ever was one. Criticism tends to roll off Whitt like water off a duck. What could he possibly do that even he would feel he needed to kowtow for forgiveness?

There's no way of knowing what the fleeting impression means. It's gone before I can study it, as always. I focus on what I can see in the here and now with my unmarred eye.

"You've all had some time to interact with the girl," I say, sweeping my gaze over my cadre. "Some of you in more… acceptable ways than others. I feel it's time we go over what we've learned and see what picture we can piece together from it."

Whitt props himself against the side of one of my armchairs. "Well, as we saw yesterday, she responds to cavaral syrup like any regular human would. I haven't observed anything differently from afar either."

August glares at the other man before turning to me. "I haven't seen any signs that there's anything otherworldly about her either. Other than the effect of her blood under the full moon, I'd say she's fully human."

"Perhaps we should test her blood under other circumstances and see what comes of that," Kellan suggests with a narrow, predatory smile. "There are plenty of other body parts she could spare that we could sample as well."

August's muscles bunch as if to spring, but I remind him of his obligations with the clearing of my throat. That doesn't mean I'm going to let Kellan's remark go unchecked, though.

The trouble is, he isn't entirely wrong.

"We will not be mangling the poor thing's body in any way beyond how Aerik has already harmed her," I say with the full force of a lord's command. "If we need to sample her blood, we'll do it as painlessly as possible."

August's head jerks toward me. "You can't really mean we're going to—"

I hold up my hand to halt him. "She's a mystery—a mystery that must be investigated. If her blood can affect us in other ways, and we present her to the arch-lords without determining that, we could undermine our position or even cause some catastrophe down the line. As I said, we won't hurt her."

He stirs restlessly but manages not to argue. "You tested those herbs on her skin—did you see anything from that?"

I shake my head. "I haven't observed anything that would suggest she has other innate powers. If I hadn't experienced the effect of her blood myself, nothing would indicate to me that she's anything other than a perfectly ordinary human girl."

Well, "ordinary" isn't quite the word for her. To have withstood the abuse Aerik's cadre subjected her to for all those years and still have fought like she did when I first plucked her from their cage—to be making her tentative steps toward exploring this place rather than staying huddled in her room in a quivering ball—there's an extraordinary resilience to her soul. It hints at so much more to be discovered. Perhaps *that* is why her face lingers in my mind.

She certainly can't be considered a mere cowering victim.

"I think you haven't pushed her hard enough," Kellan tosses out. "Dabbing her with herbs in between feasts. And this one, coddling her in the kitchen like she's a pet puppy." He jabs his thumb toward August. "There's no reason for an 'ordinary' dung-body to have the power to affect us like that. Either she isn't all human, or she's had some sort of magic worked on her."

"If she has, she doesn't know about it," I say. "You can't push knowledge out of a being if it's not there to begin with."

"You can push it from her dust-destined body. Terrify her and see what comes out when she's provoked enough. Aerik and his lot left her to languish, but who knows if they ever really came down on her." Kellan's eyes flash. "You complained that I wasn't following your orders, but all I want to do is test her to find out what you claim to want to know. Or do you not really want answers after all, my *lord?*"

He puts such a disdainful sneer on the title that my lips itch to draw back in a snarl. Instead, I take a step toward him, my chin high and shoulders flexed, reminding him that I'm more powerful than him in more than just name. "Your 'test' resulted in nothing more than putting her into a state of panic. Or did you make some useful observation you haven't bothered to share?"

Kellan tenses, but he holds his ground and my gaze. Oh, he is getting bolder with his defiance. "You haven't given me the opportunity to pursue my approach further. It seems you value this dung-body over your own pack— over your cadre. Most would see that as an absolute failure of rule."

I do snarl then, my voice coming out in a growl. "If you're unhappy with my leadership, I've already made it clear that you may find yourself another lord at any time, kin-of-my-mate."

"I'd be happy to show you the door if you've been having trouble finding it," Whitt pipes up, ever cavalier.

"Threatening rather than facing up to your failures. How impressive of you," Kellan snaps back at me.

"It wasn't a threat. It was a statement of fact. Here is another one—one you should heed. I rule this keep and this pack, and I will not be insulted to my face or have my orders disregarded without consequence. The bond between us can be broken, Kellan, and if *you* break it, you'll have no one to blame but yourself for the result."

We stare each other down for a few seconds. A glimmer dances in Kellan's eyes that's so wild I'd almost think he's caught in the full moon's light. With a twist of my gut, I brace myself for the worst, but to my relief, he lowers his gaze. He dips his head just enough to indicate he's recognizing my authority.

Recognizing it only by a thread, though. I don't like how close he's coming to forcing my hand. I swore I'd do right by him, that I'd give him the best life I was capable of offering, but if his behavior outright threatens the stability of the cadre, I can't give him a pass.

Does he think I will? Or is he simply testing just how close he can get to that line so he can stay right on the other side of it?

In that moment, I'm not sure which would be worse.

"You *are* soft on the girl," he says, still keeping his head bowed. "The crutch, and now this brace for her foot?"

"I explained my reasoning before," I reply. "The more comfortable she feels, the more she'll cooperate. If you hadn't interfered, I might have asked for a sample of her blood to test already and had her willingly offer it, no torment necessary. *You're* letting your enjoyment of the torment cloud your judgment."

He says nothing more, but his denial radiates from his stance. He probably thinks blood gained through torment will serve us better.

And he might not be entirely wrong. Did I need to share that brief story of my childhood follies with the girl? Does it niggle at me more than it should when I see her off-balance?

Surely she's earned at least that much respect when we're asking so much from her, though.

I can't see anything more to be gained from this discussion. I motion toward the door. "It sounds as though we've covered all our observations and made our stances clear. Let us continue to observe, and I will take additional steps as I see necessary. If you wish to test the girl in some way, you pass it by me before taking action. Are we understood?"

My cadre gives me a round of murmurs of agreement. Kellan hurries out, muttering something inaudible under his breath. As August moves to follow him, I hold him back.

"You returned from roaming late these last two nights. It's not like you. Have you found some new venture to occupy your time?"

My eyes are keen, and August is too much of a novice at the art of deception to completely suppress the flicker of guilt that crosses his expression. Whatever it is he's been up to, he thinks I won't approve.

"I've just been restless," he says. "I took some long runs to work out that extra energy, like you suggested."

I hadn't expected him to take runs so long he hadn't returned when I finally took to my bed. Is there more to it than that, or is his guilt simply at the memory of how he lost control of his temper toward Kellan—and the fact that he needs to put that much effort into avoiding doing so again?

It would be much easier to fulfill my role if being lord came with the power of telepathy as well. But I've known August since he was a literal whelp, and I trust he wouldn't do anything he believed could harm the pack. Whatever he might feel guilty about, it's of a personal nature. I can be benevolent enough not to pry... for now.

"If anything should come up that you believe I should know, don't hesitate to come to me," I say.

He nods and lopes out—perhaps to take another of those runs.

Whitt heaves himself away from the chair with a

chuckle under his breath. When I aim a sharp look at him, he gives me one of his wry smiles.

"For such a little mite, she's certainly opening the fault lines wide, isn't she?"

Then he saunters into the hall, leaving me stewing over how much truth there might be to that statement.

14

Talia

The knock comes just as I'm pulling my blouse over my head. Thankfully the rest of me is already dressed, other than I haven't fit the wooden brace around my leg yet. I tug the hem of the shirt down to the waist of my jeans and sit up straight at the edge of the bed. "Yes?"

"May I come in?"

Even if I didn't recognize August's mellow voice, I'd have guessed it was him simply from the fact that he asked first. It's not as if this is really *my* room.

"Of course," I say, and find I don't know what to do with myself.

August has never visited me in my bedroom before. He walks in with unusual hesitance, as if I might yell at him to get out despite what I said. As scary as he was when he attacked Kellan, he's never been anything but cheerful and considerate with me. That's probably why seeing his handsome face sends a flush over my skin like it does so often these days.

He might be kind to me, but he follows Sylas's orders. He's helping keep me prisoner. How can I have a crush on him? Apparently I'm still twelve somewhere in my head. Delayed development due to emotional isolation. That's totally a thing, right?

Labeling it as some kind of delusion doesn't make the effect go away, though. I just have to make sure I don't start *acting* like a swoony preteen. If I will the tickling heat away from my face, can I make it leave?

It was bad enough that I started throwing compliments at Whitt and snuggling into Sylas when I was drunk on that syrup. What would I have done if I'd run into August in that state?

"Are you already serving breakfast?" I ask. The typical kitchen smells haven't come trailing after him this morning. My head is still a bit muggy from my late night monitoring the sounds of the keep—I woke up earlier than I'd have liked, in the grips of a nightmare not quite loud enough to bring Sylas to my door.

"Oh, no, I'll be getting right on that as soon as I've talked to you." August smiles and shuts the door behind him, glancing back at it as if worried someone will notice.

A chill runs down my back. I can't forget that I barely know him. That he's fae, not human. That there's no way for me to be sure he'll be consistent in his kindness even when he's following his own conscience.

I curl my fingers into the bed covers, ready to shove myself onto my feet if I need to. But August doesn't make any aggressive moves. He walks closer, his smile slanting in a way that looks more sad than anything, and reaches into the satchel slung over his shoulder. He... winces? And then pulls out a small leather pouch closed off with a drawstring.

He tosses the pouch onto the bed next to me as if he can't get it out of his hand quickly enough. Even though it lands a couple of feet from me, I flinch.

"Sorry," August says quickly. "It's hard for me to handle that, even contained in the leather. It was hard getting it at all." He laughs a little sheepishly, running his hand through his dark auburn hair.

The pouch lies there on the duvet motionless. I eye it to make sure it isn't going to sprout little fangs or spew out spiders or some other horrible thing, and then I glance back at August. "Why? What's in it?"

"Salt." His mouth twists again as if even the word bothers him. "I had to go to the human world to get it. It and iron are the only two materials toxic to fae."

I was right about the metals then, but I don't know what to make of this gift. I pick up the pouch and tug it open with careful fingers.

It does indeed hold a teaspoon or two of chunky salt crystals, the mineral scent mingling with the musk of the leather when I lean close. My brow furrows. This doesn't make any sense.

"Why are you giving this to me?"

August ducks his head, a shadow darkening his golden eyes. "I don't trust Kellan. He's already pushing the boundaries, and he's made it clear he likes harassing you. There isn't enough salt in there to really hurt him, but if he comes after you, if you think he might hurt *you*, toss that in his face while you call for help, and it should get him to back off long enough for one of us to get to you and stop him."

It takes a moment for the full import of what he's said to sink in. He's giving me something that I could use against him and his colleagues. He's putting my security over his loyalty to his cadre and his lord—only in a small way, but more than it would ever have occurred to me to hope for.

I'm abruptly ashamed of my nervousness at his behavior. He was acting shifty on my *behalf*, not against me.

He raises his head to meet my eyes again, and I can't tune out the flutter that passes through my chest. He's earned that affection, fair and square.

"Thank you," I say. "It really means a lot. I guess…" I have to keep the pouch somewhere the others won't notice, but where I can easily grab it. I tuck it into the hip pocket of my jeans, making sure it's out of sight but with the cord right where a hasty finger could snag on it.

August clears his throat. "I also wanted to apologize. For the other day, with Kellan. I don't regret stepping in, of course, but I shouldn't have leapt straight into a fight. I was so angry, seeing him treat you like that—but then I scared you even more. That's the last thing I would have wanted to do."

He sounds so torn up about it that I immediately believe him. Without thinking, I scoot forward so I can reach for his hand. A flicker of surprise crosses his face, but he squeezes my fingers, and the longing to have him wrap his arms right around me, to envelop me in his protective intent, floods every other thought from my mind.

It takes me a second to find my words again. "It's okay. I know you were only trying to help." I'm not sure I was really scared of him in that moment or just tangled up in the memories of the wolves I faced before, the violence of that past encounter echoed in the fight in front of me.

August grips my fingers a little tighter and then lets them go. "Still. I won't let it happen again."

The pouch forms a soft pressure against my hip. He got it from the human world—from the world where I belong. The one I have to get back to.

After he's made a gesture like that, it feels like a betrayal to ask the question rising in my throat. But I have to know. "Whitt mentioned that the keep is on the fringes of the Mists. Did you have to go very far to get to the human world?"

"It wasn't any trouble getting there," August says. "The harder part was finding a bit of salt in a situation where I could grab it without having to come in too close contact. But that didn't take too long either." He beams down at me, his stance relaxed now that he's gone through with his minor mutiny and received my gratitude. "Things are hard enough for *you* without having to worry about that jackass tormenting you."

If I can get out of here, what Kellan wants to do with me won't matter anyway. I run my tongue along the backs of my teeth, searching for a way I can ask exactly which direction the human world is in and whether there's any special procedure to getting out of the Mists that won't tip him off to my hopes.

Maybe if I come at it in a roundabout sort of way…

"Whitt made it sound like it's a bad thing, living on the fringes," I say. "Like things haven't been so great for you since you moved."

August's eyebrows rise. "Look who's got the big mouth now. Yeah, we've had some troubles."

"But what's so bad about the fringes? I mean, if it lets you get to the human world quickly whenever you need something there…"

"As you've probably noticed, a lot of fae don't have the highest opinion of humans, so being close to them isn't seen as a good thing. What everyone wants is to be close to the Heart of the Mists. It's the source of our magic, and the closer you are to it, the more of that power you absorb. Living out here, after a while we can't work our magic quite as well."

The Heart of the Mists. There's a reverence in the way he says it that sends a tingle over my skin, as if the name itself holds a kind of power. I make a show of glancing around. "Where is the Heart compared to here?"

August waves his hand to the south. "We always build our fortresses so the main door faces it. In theory, that makes it easier for the power to reach us."

So, that means the farthest fringes—and the human world beyond them—must be to the north. I smile at him, grateful and relieved despite the guilt nibbling at my gut underneath. "You must miss being closer to it."

"I do, but—it couldn't be helped. Sylas is doing his best to make things right. Kellan is always grouching about it, as if he wasn't even more involved in—"

August snaps his mouth shut before the rest of that

sentence tumbles out. He makes an apologetic grimace. "You don't need to worry about that either. And, you know, I'm not the only one looking out for you. Sylas doesn't want you harmed either."

The faerie lord has done a lot more for me than any prisoner should really accept. I look down at the brace leaning against the end of the bed. My chest constricts with a sudden wave of emotion.

"Maybe he doesn't, but none of you would let me leave if I wanted to, would you."

I say it as a statement, not a question, and August obviously can't deny it. His expression clouds, his hands stirring restlessly at his sides as he searches for a response.

He doesn't confirm my comment, but at least he doesn't completely change the subject. "I guess you have family back there that Aerik stole you from."

Splashes of red on green flicker through my mind. My heart is suddenly thudding. I grip the edge of the bed and swallow hard. Stole me from them—that's one way of putting it.

"Yes." My voice comes out quietly, an uneasy tension coiling through my ribs. Who *will* I be running back to when I get my chance to escape?

Mom and Dad and Jamie are long gone. There was my aunt and uncle and the baby they had on the way—God, that kid will be eight years old by now—but they lived the next state over, if they're even still in the same town. I never knew their exact address. We only saw them a few times a year. My grandparents on Dad's side lived on the west coast, and only visited over the Christmas holidays. I'm not sure what city they live in. I don't even know their first names. And Mom's parents were all the way over in Greece. I only met them twice.

Of course, I'm coming at this all wrong. I'm twenty now, not twelve. Twenty-year-olds don't need family to take them in. They're supposed to get jobs and their own places to live, like adults do.

Thinking about all that makes my pulse thump even harder. I drag in a breath, and August steps close enough to grasp my shoulder tentatively before drawing his hand back just as quickly. "I'm sorry. I didn't mean to upset you now either."

"No, it's just—It's a lot to wrap my head around." I touch my pocket. "I really do appreciate the protection. And you just talking with me. That makes everything easier."

His smile returns, so pleased my heart aches at the sight. "Do you want to come help me whip up some breakfast? You're my best assistant."

I manage to laugh. "I'm not sure how high praise that is when it seems like I'm your *only* assistant." My insides still feel all tangled up. I inhale again, right to the bottom of my lungs. "I'll be down soon. I need a minute or two, if that's all right?"

"Of course, absolutely." He bobs his head to me and lopes out of the room with typical exuberance.

I find myself gazing toward the window—toward all that open space I still haven't gotten to experience, even though I'm so much more "free" than I was in my cage. What's going to be waiting for me in the world Aerik's cadre ripped me from more than eight years ago? What am I going to do once I get there—how am I going to *explain* any of what I've been through? If I say I was kidnapped by faeries, everyone will think I'm insane.

It doesn't matter. That's the world where I belong—the world where men-who-aren't-men won't be fighting over how to use my blood. I'll be able to figure things out one way or another. I just have to get there.

And now I know which direction to run in.

I strap the brace around my calf the way Sylas showed me, take a few testing steps to make sure it's secure, and then head out. I don't feel quite as steady as I did with the crutch, but the independence of not needing to hang on to an entire other object makes up for it.

Walking slowly, I feel no more than a slight pressure around my muscles, and the wooden strips across the base produce only a faint scuffing sound. I'll have to practice until I can eliminate that altogether.

As I come up on the bend in the hall, my balance wobbles. I catch myself with a hand against the wall—and an urgent voice filters through the door just behind me.

"Our forces managed to push them back, but there were a lot of Seelie losses. They're getting cleverer with their tactics."

My body goes rigid. I don't recognize that voice. It doesn't belong to any of the four men who've appeared to be the keep's sole inhabitants. I thought Sylas wanted to prevent anyone else from seeing me and possibly tipping off my former captors.

But maybe he's making arrangements for whatever he's going to do with me next, and that means setting aside a little of that caution.

What forces were pushing back who? It sounds like

some kind of battle. I stay in place, my ears straining to make out the response.

Whitt's dry voice answers, terse in a way I've never heard before. "Has there been any recognition of our pack's contributions?"

"No mention of us so far. It's been pretty chaotic. I'm not sure how well they're keeping track of who's joined the patrols anymore."

Whitt lets out a sharp sigh. "Hang in there as well as you can. We're all worse off if those Unseelie bastards gain more ground. Is there anything I could send you back with that might give you an advantage, from what you've observed?"

"No, nothing so far."

"Well, if anything comes up, reach out to me at once and I'll see it done. Our lord will be glad for any chance of winning some glory in the conflict. You're dismissed."

Dismissed—the stranger is about to leave the room? My nerves jump, and I lurch farther away so clumsily my foot brace scrapes against the floorboards.

If I had proper use of both my feet, this would be where I'd make a dash around the corner to the stairs. But I don't, and I can only imagine the racket the wooden slats would make if I attempted a sprint—if I even manage to run rather than fall flat on my face after a few steps. I scramble forward as quickly as I can while keeping my balance, but I've barely moved when the door flies open.

Whitt storms out. He grabs my arm, yanking me around to face him. His ocean-blue eyes remind me more of a tsunami now, his fingers grasping painfully tight.

"What are you doing skulking outside my study?"

My mouth opens and closes. I can't seem to work any sound from my throat. "I—I—"

"Don't give me that wide-eyed act. I know you were out here listening."

He tugs me toward him, his grip pressing into my muscles exactly where Aerik's man used to clamp down as he readied to cut my wrist. The breath shudders out of me.

"Well?" Whitt demands, but I've lost my words completely. He glowers down at me. "If you're going to sneak around here like a crook, maybe it's time Sylas locked you up in that bedroom permanently."

A sharper surge of panic blares through me. To be shut off from the rest of the keep—to lose so much of the little freedom I've regained— What other punishments will they inflict on me? Maybe they'll think I don't deserve any better than a cage after all.

I gulp for air, trying to recover my voice, but my chest has constricted too tightly. A flood of cold washes through my body. My heart batters against my sternum. I'm suffocating like in that dream.

Help, I want to say. *Help, I'm drowning.* But I can't force my vocal cords to form the words—and I'm not sure Whitt would care anyway.

15

Whitt

The dust-destined girl twitches in my grasp like a rabbit in a snare. As shudders wrack her body, her wide eyes stare at me, so hazed with terror I'm not sure she's even seeing me. Her breath wheezes in her throat.

My fingers tighten around her arm, holding her from collapsing now. Is she having an attack of some physical ailment? Or are these dramatics just a way to get herself out of trouble now that I've discovered her lurking outside the room that holds my most closely guarded secrets?

It doesn't really matter which it is. If Sylas finds us like this, it's me he'll lay into for frightening her, even though *she's* the one who violated my privacy in my own blasted home. As if I'm not even owed one *room* to conduct my work as I see fit—meddling with my affairs—wretched female looking to gain any advantage—

I tamp down on my fury as well as I can. Heart take me, I don't have the patience for dealing with this, but I'd better find it before our glorious leader rains down twice as much on me.

And I'll work on finding it somewhere he isn't likely to stumble on us, thank you very much.

I tug the girl to the next door down: my bedroom. Better she see that space, as much of a mess as it no doubt is—I honestly don't know; I have better things to do than pay attention to the state of my bedcovers—than my office. Most important items in the office are tucked away or unintelligible to her human understanding, and Ralyn is long gone through the secret passage that allows direct transit between the room and outside, but I'd rather not take any chances. I hadn't expected to find this mite lurking nearby in the first place.

My bedchamber turns out to be in an even worse state than I would have predicted. Discarded shirts and slacks litter the floor, and the blankets slump over the side of the bed in a rumpled waterfall of fabric. One of my pillows has made it all the way to the other end of the room, and sitting on that pillow is a crumb-scattered plate I really should get around to taking back to the kitchen at some point. A couple of goblets rest nearby, one of them tipped on its side in a thin, sticky puddle of evaporated wine.

Perhaps it's been a tad too long since my periodic, manic tidy sessions.

At least the space doesn't outright smell, other than a fair tang of fermented fruit that some might consider almost pleasant. Not that my unintended guest appears to be in any state to draw judgments. She's still gasping, one hand pressed to her chest over her heart, the arm in my grasp shaking. Her heart is racing loud enough that I can hear its beat without even leaning close.

She really is terrified. If this is an act, it's a better one than I've seen any evidence she's capable of. I'd started to think she was made of stronger stuff than this. A couple of snappy remarks were enough to send her into a total meltdown…?

My mind trips back over the words I said, and understanding hits me. I threatened to have her locked in her room—shut away in one small space where she can't speak to anyone, can't even pretend she's an actual guest here. That bedroom Sylas gave her is leagues above the hospitality Aerik offered, but perhaps the suggestion of being caged at all was too much. And I did grasp hold of her rather brusquely on top of that.

It wasn't a huge offense, but there aren't many fae who'd come out of years of torment with their minds unscarred, let alone mortals.

My stomach twists, torn between shame over making myself an Aerik-like figure and irritation that I have to deal with this problem at all. If Sylas had just shipped the girl off to the arch-lords and let them decide what to do with her in the first place—

But she is here—he wants her here—so I must play with the hand I'm holding.

"Hey." I pitch my voice as low and soothing as I can manage, bending down so I'm on her level. What would Sylas say to calm her down? Or August—he's gotten awfully chummy with the mite. Let's see if I can channel my inner over-eager whelp.

"It's all right," I go on. "Nothing awful is going to

happen to you right this minute. You startled me. We can talk about it—you can explain."

Talia sinks down until she's sitting on the floor. Tremors keep running through her body, but at least the wheezing is tapering off. It occurs to me that having her wrist still in a death-grip probably isn't helping the situation. I release her arm, hesitate, and give her an awkward pat on the back. "There, there. You've got nothing immediate to worry about. Everything in here is fine."

The statements ring hollow in my ears, but the girl's shoulders come down a little. To outright lie diminishes a fae's connection to the Heart of the Mists, so I avoid it as much as possible, but I do have quite a lot of practice at speaking around the truth in convincing ways.

She blinks at me, her eyes really focusing on me for the first time since the panic hit her. Another shudder shakes her scrawny frame. She braces her hands against the floor and drags in a deep breath.

"I—I'm sorry," she says. "I just—I couldn't help it—I couldn't *breathe*—"

I stay crouched across from her and cock my head. "But you can now. All's well that ends well?"

A shocked laugh tumbles out of her, so she must be nearly recovered. She rubs her hand over her pale face and into that shock of deep pink hair. It's the sort of vibrant hue you'd typically only see on the purest-blooded of fae. On a human, as natural as August has made it look, it's incongruous.

And yet I can't stop the memory rising up of that face lit with laughter the other day in the parlor, how lovely it became in the giddy glow of the cavaral syrup. Maybe if I gave her some more of that, she'd calm down faster, and I could enjoy that recklessly gleeful side of her again...

I clamp down on that thought and shove it away before it can even fully slip through my consciousness. She's not here for me to *enjoy* her in any way. I shouldn't even want to.

When the girl looks up at me, it's with an expression as if she still thinks I might toss her into a locked room and throw away the key—or perhaps even hit her. I wince inwardly. Did I really come across that vicious?

"I was listening," she admits, her shoulders hunching. "I heard a voice I didn't recognize, and I was confused, so I was trying to figure out what was going on. I only caught a little of the conversation."

I don't think Ralyn and I mentioned anything particularly sensitive. Nevertheless— "None of us here will take kindly to eavesdropping—not even Sylas would be pleased about it."

She nods. "Are you—are you going to tell him? Honestly, it's the first time. There's just so much about this place I still don't understand..."

The muddled little mite. I have to admit that if *I* were in a similar situation, I'd be listening at every door I could. She is resourceful and determined, even if her traumatized emotions sometimes get the better of her.

In some ways her bewilderment is Sylas's fault, for keeping her here while still holding her at a distance. How could she know what to make of us? So far we've barely decided what to make of her.

Thank the lands that soon enough she won't be our problem anymore.

"We can keep this first transgression between ourselves," I say, forming as firm an expression as I could manage. I'm not so practiced at that—usually I leave the authoritarian posturing to our lord. "But only this once. If you want to know something, you *ask*, and if we don't deign to answer, you weren't meant to know it. If I catch you spying again, I can't give it a pass as a mistake. Clear?"

She nods again, more vigorously this time, her stance slumping with relief. "Completely clear." Then she pauses. "Can I ask—who *were* you talking to?"

I almost guffaw at the balls on this smidge of a girl. I definitely will need to keep a closer eye on her while she's in our midst. "I can tell you that it was an expected visitor —by Sylas as well as myself—and while he'd mean you no harm anyway, I'm ensuring he never encounters you. That's all you're going to get. Now come along. You've got most of the keep to scamper around in still—you don't need the use of my rooms on top of that."

As I direct her to the door, her gaze darts around the bedroom, really taking it in for the first time. She's wise enough not to remark on the overall state of disarray. Good girl.

She scurries dutifully off toward the stairs. I pull my gaze away before I'm inclined to admire the slim curves that her body is shaping into or the deftness with which she's adapted to that brace on her foot. No doubt she's off to canoodle some more with August in the kitchen. There are several words I could say about his decisions in that regard, but it's not my place when it hasn't caused any real trouble *yet*, so I can manage to keep them to myself for now.

The encounter has left an uncomfortable edginess in my nerves, though. I'm in no mood to saunter downstairs and make small-talk around the table, which is all we *can* make with our "guest" looking on. I hadn't really wanted to be up this early to begin with, but duty called, and now I'm too awake for the bed to have any appeal.

Instead, I prowl back into my study, push aside the sliding bookcase, and speak the word to open the hatch only Sylas and I can access. I step into the narrow chamber on the other side, secure the shelves and hatch in place, and head down the tight spiral of steps.

At the base, another word magically unseals the door. I duck out, stretch my lips, and let my wolf spring forth.

The joy of how naturally my beast emerges from my skin at times like this only makes the memories of the wrenching transitions under the full moon more horrible in contrast. I set off at a trot, soaking in the warm breeze tickling through my fur and the banquet of scents my wolfish nose picks up even more easily than when I'm a man. I make a full circuit of our territory every day. It can't hurt to take it in earlier than usual this once.

A few of the faded pack members are already up and about. As I travel past their cluster of houses, they tip their heads respectfully to me. I eye the buildings, going over my mental tally of who remains and who I've sent to join the arch-lords' border patrols. Can we spare anyone else?

We need to keep some good fighters among us, of course. A pack that becomes too weak begins to look like prey to those with a hunger for conquest, and I happen to know through my contacts that there are at least a couple of lords who've eyed our domain. Not because they want this fringe-land, but because Sylas has a reputation for being a powerful leader if no longer the official prestige, and it'd elevate anyone's status to say they cowed him.

The fact is, we can't send a large enough force to the arch-lords for them to be all that impressed anyway. They're as likely to see our meager contribution as a sign of how far we've fallen rather than how dedicated we are to their cause. No, our best bet will be if Ralyn or one of the others abroad susses out a strategy none of the others have picked up on. Wits can win the day as easily as strength if we use them right.

Or Sylas could present the gift of the girl, and then we wouldn't *need* to prove ourselves so much in other ways.

I pass into the forest, where the shadows drape the ground with patches of cool and the scent of pine fills my nose. I test it periodically for any taint of an intruder. About halfway through the stretch of woodland, I catch another wolfish whiff, but it's a familiar one—one of our sentries.

One of ours, and loping toward me. I veer off course to meet her and pull myself back into my regular form so we can speak.

As the sentry comes into view between the trees, she does the same. It's Astrid, gray-haired and wiry in both forms, her face just beginning the transition from wrinkled to wizened. She's getting to the point where I'd have pulled her off sentry duty so she can spend more time resting her old bones if I didn't know she'd sooner slash my face off than accept.

Astrid has fought in more skirmishes than I have, and she intends to fight alongside us until those bones give out completely. She wouldn't still be here otherwise.

"Is there trouble?" I ask.

She lets out a short huff. "Not yet, but I can smell the start of it. One of the Copperweld cadre was sniffing around the borders, wanting to know if we've had any human girls come wandering onto our territory. I told him no, but he looked as if he'd have made his own investigations if I hadn't showed my teeth."

Copperweld—that's Aerik's domain. My back tenses. "Good that you did," I say. "A lost servant is no excuse for them to intrude on our territory. If a human does ramble this way, let the keep know first."

She bobs her head in acknowledgment and slips back into the shadows, leaving me twice as uneasy as before.

Aerik's cadre is making inquiries all the way out here already. Do they specifically suspect us, or are we simply an easy target, one they had less concern about offending with their attempted imposition?

Either way, it amounts to the same thing: the mite is now bringing yet more trouble down on all our heads.

16

Talia

After another of August's extravagant dinners, Sylas catches my elbow on my way out of the dining room.

"Come with me?" he says with the inflection of a question but the air of a command.

As he leads me down the hall, my pulse kicks up a notch. Did Whitt mention my eavesdropping to the fae lord after all—is he going to rebuke me in some way he doesn't want his cadre to see?

Sylas doesn't show any sign of anger or disappointment, striding along in his usual powerful, assured way. I can tell he's keeping his speed in check so that I don't fall too far behind. The brace on my foot taps against the floor as I hustle along, not wanting to seem like I can't keep up.

When he heads down the steps to the keep's basement,

a deeper prickling races beneath my skin. I haven't been down there except for a few baths in the small sauna room with its hot-tub-like pool. The thicker shadows and the cooler air that seeps through the wood make me uneasy, and when I pushed myself to explore a little farther once, I found the few other rooms along the hall were locked.

Not tonight. Sylas opens a door farther down from the sauna and motions me in. Two steps inside, I stop in my tracks, staring.

It's not that the contents of the room are so alien. No, what's startling is how familiar they are: a flat-screen TV, a shelving unit of DVDs, a device I don't fully recognize but can identify as some kind of game system. The shelves at the other side of the room are stuffed with paperback and hardcover books in regular human-style bindings. Sure, the wooden shelves and the unit holding the TV look as if they've grown right out of the walls rather than being constructed by regular means, and the long, curving sofa that stretches through the middle of the room is upholstered with what looks like woven willow leaves, but still. I haven't seen this much evidence that the world I remember really does exist since I was torn from it.

Tears I can't suppress spring to my eyes. I inhale slowly, trying to steady myself, and propel myself toward the sofa. "This is—why do you have all this stuff?"

One corner of Sylas's mouth turns up with apparent amusement. "We fae enjoy a variety of entertainment. If we can bring humans themselves over, why not their amusements as well?"

"I just—I wouldn't have thought—" I'm not sure I

have the words to explain how bizarre it is imagining the imposing faerie lord chilling out in front of the latest Hollywood flick. If I found them, I'm afraid they'd end up coming out in a way that offends him.

"It's mostly August who plays the games," Sylas says, ambling past the TV. "Helps him work out some of his aggressive impulses. We have to replace the controllers rather more frequently than I'd prefer."

It's not difficult to imagine the exuberant fae man perched on the sofa with controller in hand, whooping in triumph as he kicks digitized ass in a fighting game or sports simulation. My own mouth twitches into a smile.

"What part of this collection is yours?"

Sylas motions to the DVDs. "Mostly the movies. A… past associate of mine introduced me to human cinema."

I step closer, peering at the spines. Some of the titles I don't recognize—movies that must have been from well before my time or that came out after I was stolen away—but others jump out at me. *Mean Girls. Zoolander. 17 Again. Legally Blonde.* They stir up memories of surfing through Netflix on sleepover nights.

I glance at Sylas, unable to stop my eyebrows from rising. "You like the comedies, huh?"

Is there a hint of embarrassment in his smile now? He laughs with a casual shrug. "I have enough drama and combat in my life here. It's fascinating how humans can make an entire story where nothing happens that really matters, and everyone ends up with what they deserve, happy or not."

Maybe *I* should be insulted by that assessment of my species' efforts, but I find it too funny that he likes watching this stuff at all. The comment spills out unthinking. "You'll have to catch me up on some of the good recent ones."

Sylas gives me a measured look as if trying to decide whether I'm serious. I can't really tell whether I am myself —it's impossible to picture sitting next to this regal giant of a man while he laughs at some slapstick joke and tosses back a handful of popcorn. Does he sit through the comedies with nothing more than one of those restrained smiles? Or maybe he does loosen up now and then... though that doesn't mean he'd want me seeing him like that.

In the end, he chooses not to address my remark at all. "Any time you'd like to relax in here, just let me, August, or Whitt know and we'll open the room for you. I thought you might need more to keep you occupied beyond acting as kitchen servant."

"I really don't mind helping with the cooking," I say quickly, in case he's gotten the idea that August pressured me into that job somehow. The faint pressure of the pouch of salt in my pocket makes me feel extra defensive of the younger man. Then I pause. "Why do you keep this room locked at all?"

Sylas's lips twitch again, but this time it looks like he held back a grimace. "Kellan has some strong opinions about anything to do with humans, as you've undoubtedly observed. He wouldn't go out of his way to damage what we've collected here, but if he happened to wander in when he's in the wrong sort of mood—it's easier to simply ensure that set of circumstances never occurs."

Then I'll be safe from that brute in here too. I'm liking

this setup more and more. For however long I'm still staying in the keep, at least.

That last thought brings a gloom over me. I sink onto the sofa and pick up a video game magazine someone—August?—left tucked into the crease by the arm. My gaze skims over the computer-generated warrior on the cover, the bold headlines—and snags on the date of the issue beneath the title.

For a second, I just stare at it, my body rigid. Sylas looms closer, frowning. "Is something the matter?"

"How long ago is this magazine from?" I ask, my voice sounding distant to my ears.

"A moon or two ago," Sylas says, which I guess means a month. "You look as if something about it disturbs you."

"No—I mean, sort of—" An awkward laugh spills out of me. "I just didn't realize how long it's been. I was trying to keep track of the years while I was locked up in that cage. I thought I had. I thought it'd been only eight. But it's actually been nine."

I'm twenty-one, not twenty. Three hundred and sixty-five more days than I counted have passed since I lost my home.

It shouldn't be a big deal. What's one more year in the grand scheme of things? But the knowledge hits me like a punch to the gut.

Where did I miss it? How warped had my sense of time become while Aerik held me prisoner that I didn't catch on that it'd been far too long?

Sylas sits carefully on the sofa a couple of feet away from me. "I'm impressed that you managed to keep track even if not totally accurately," he says. "How did you determine the passing of the years?"

I twist a strand of my hair around my finger, pulling tight as if the sting in my scalp will offset the horror of those memories. "There was a night pretty early after they took me when I heard all this howling, loud enough that it reached all the way to the room with my cage. The next day the men said something about how they were glad they only had to bother with "it" once a year. And then it was ages, I almost forgot, until it happened again. I figured if it's something you all do once a year, then it was a way I could keep track."

"That was important to you."

I shrug, my head drooping. It seems like such a minor victory now that it's almost silly. "It was one small way I could hold on to *something* I understood. Knowing how long it'd been, how old I was… I was afraid I'd forget, so I marked myself as well as I could."

I hesitate and then ease down the waist of my jeans to where the thin scars mark the skin over my hipbone. Eight of them where there should be nine. "I must have been so exhausted on one of those nights I slept right through the howls. What is that racket all about, anyway?"

"The Wild Hunt," Sylas says. "You judged right—we take it up once a year. It's a sort of holiday, a celebration… The arch-lords race through the human world on horseback and the rest of the Seelie follow in our wolf forms. For some, it's the only time they venture among humans at all—a chance to snatch up new servants or whatever else they might want that they can't find here."

Servants they maybe treat only slightly better than Aerik and his cadre did me? Or that they treat *worse*, because those servants have no special blood to grant them a tiny respite? I shudder.

Sylas looks away. When his gaze returns to me, it's as solemn as I've ever seen it. His voice comes out even lower than usual, deep and grave.

"Our kind doesn't generally *hate* humans. Kellan is not the norm, and neither is Aerik. Many mortals live among us for a long time, mingle with our families, find some sort of place in our domains that they're satisfied with. August's mother was fully human, you know."

I'm startled by that revelation only for an instant. Suddenly all the kindnesses the other man has shown me makes a lot more sense.

"But mostly you—the fae—bring us here to be servants and things like that?"

He tips his head in acknowledgment. "I can't say the norm is to see humans as equals either. In most cases, your people are simply a means to an end."

"Like animals. Something you can own."

"Yes. Which isn't hate or hostility. It's just…" He sighs as if he's not sure how to finish that sentence. "But I have seen plenty of suffering too, and I don't wish to perpetuate that."

"You've given me a lot," I have to acknowledge. "You got me away from Aerik."

"But I'm also keeping you here, when no doubt the realms of the fae are the last place you'd prefer to linger."

He pauses and then turns to face me more fully.

"Talia, I don't expect you to like what I'm doing or to approve of it. If there was a way that I could ensure security for my people without your presence, I'd escort you back to your home this second. But my entire pack depends on me, now more than ever, and this 'curse' affects all my Seelie brethren as well. With so much on the line, I can't let you go without more answers. But I promise I will give you whatever comforts I can to ensure you're *not* suffering, and that any decisions I make, they're not made lightly."

Something about that statement brings a lump into my throat. I hate that I'm still a prisoner, and I'm frightened of what's to come when he makes those decisions… but right now, at least, I'm not frightened of him. How could I tell him that my life should matter more to him than his own and that of all the people counting on him?

It does mean something that what happens to me matters to him at all, even if not as much as those other things.

"All right," I say, a rasp creeping into my voice.

He studies me. "In light of that, there's one request I'd make of you that I know you may recoil from. If we're to find another cure that works so that we can release you without losing that boon, I need to understand everything I can about your blood. I'd like to take a sample from you to test."

I flinch automatically, a jolt of panic racing through me—a rush of images: elbows and knees pinning me down, blue-white hair and daffodil-yellow, a glinting blade, the slice into my wrist. My lungs start to constrict like they did when Whitt made his threat the other day, but Sylas has spoken so calmly and gently that the sensation doesn't turn completely suffocating.

Closing my eyes, I travel away in my head to a bamboo forests and sublime mountains. After a few gulps of breath, my thoughts stop spinning.

He asked, rather than just taking. He's *not* like my former captors. And if he can figure out some alternate cure by studying my blood, then both our problems will be solved.

"Okay," I whisper.

Sylas's smile comes back, though the edges of it look pained. "You're made of strong stuff, little scrap. I thought I might put a movie on now—perhaps there's something in my collection you're familiar with?—and that would help take your mind off the procedure."

Is that why we're really here? I can't argue against his strategy. My gaze has already shot to the stack of movie cases, starving for something from home. "That sounds good."

As I get up to consider my options, a sharper awareness cuts through the muddle of my momentary panic. Sylas has opened up a lot. I should use this chance while he's feeling particularly generous to find out more that *I* need to too.

"You have a lot," I say as casually as I can manage. "I guess when you're close to the human world here, it's pretty easy to go back and forth?"

"It certainly wouldn't be much trouble if there's anything missing that you'd particularly like to see."

That's not quite what I'm trying to get at. I worry my lip under my teeth, pretending to be absorbed by the movie selection. "I wouldn't want you to have to waste your magic or whatever just getting me a movie."

The fae lord hums dismissively. "The boundaries aren't so solid as to need an enchantment to breach them. On the fringes, one can slip from one world to the next without even meaning to if one isn't careful."

Then I could slip through too, all on my own. Relief settles in my chest alongside a twinge of guilt at manipulating the conversation to my own ends. Of course, I doubt he'd have admitted that fact if he thought there was any chance at all that I could escape the keep to make use of the information.

"I think this one will do it," I say, pulling out a superhero parody Mom and Dad took me and Jamie to see in the theater not that long before Aerik ripped me away from my life.

Sylas pops the disc into the player, and I find myself frozen on the sofa, caught in a surge of more conflicting emotions than I can pick apart. The act of watching the movie is familiar and *right* but so distant from what I've been living through for almost a decade. I remember jostling with Jamie trying to grab the seat closest to the center of the row and Dad jokingly threatening to banish us to the back of the theater. The echo of salty, buttery popcorn laces my mouth.

It's a bittersweet distraction, but it does stop me from flashing back to my grimy cage. Sylas dabs a clear salve on my wrist to numb the skin, and I keep my eyes fixed on the TV screen as he cuts a small nick into my skin. I don't even check what he's collecting the blood in. It's barely enough time for the movie's characters to crack a few jokes and flub a heroic rescue, and then he's murmuring a spell over my arm that seals the skin, a kindness Aerik never bothered with.

"Thank you," the fae lord says, getting up. "I'll let you watch the rest of the film in peace. The door will lock behind you when you leave."

He brushes his hand over my hair in a gesture just shy of a caress, and that brief contact brings my awareness crashing back to the present with a flutter of my pulse. I watch him go, feeling abruptly tingly and wondering if I wouldn't have rather he stayed and watched with me.

I don't end up finishing the movie. It doesn't take long before the bitterness of the associations overwhelms any sweetness. Even in a superhero fantasy version of reality, there are far too many reminders of all the things I've lost that I might never get back.

When I emerge from the room, the keep is quiet. I creep up the two flights of stairs, practicing the steps that provoke the least noise from my foot brace. Singing voices filter through the walls; Whitt must be hosting another of his revels.

I *am* starting to feel a little more at peace, if not overjoyed with my situation, when I turn the corner and Kellan appears, his icy silver eyes glittering.

My heart stutters. I stumble backwards instinctively— not far enough. Kellan marches right up to me without hesitation and shoves me into the wall. He pins me there, glaring down at me, but with a smirk twisting his lips that shows he's as much delighted as he is angry.

"Going to cry for help, maggot meat?" he snarls under his breath, the light in his eyes almost feverish now. "We can find out how quickly one of my claws will slice out your tongue."

My body trembles. I grasp at the wall, wanting to make sure that when he lets me go—*if* he lets me go—I won't collapse. "Please. I just want to go back to my room."

"Hmm. Think you're so safe in there, do you? I could open that door if I wanted to. Imagine the fun we'd have then."

He bares his teeth and kicks my bad foot—not hard enough to break the brace but enough to send a lance of pain through the sinews. I gasp, and the stairs creak at the far end of the house.

Kellan jerks away from me and stalks off with his chin lifted haughtily.

I slump against the wall, hugging myself as if my heart might explode from my chest if I don't hold it in. No, I can't stay here. What if he comes back?

It's only when I've staggered into my room, gasping to fill my lungs, that I remember the salt. I could have used it, could have forced him to back off.

But would that really have helped anything? I'd have shown my hand, he'd demand that Sylas take it away from me, and I think Sylas would agree, even if he laid into Kellan for harassing me too. I've got to hold onto that gift until I *really* need it, until it's my only chance.

As I shake off my daze, I find myself staring blankly at the doorknob. What Kellan said about being able to unlock it comes back to me. It's magic that holds me in overnight, of course. Why would fae bother with keys when magic is something I can't steal?

But maybe…

I can't test the idea yet. I crawl into bed and tuck the covers around me, the shivers not quite subsided. My foot keeps aching. The ghost of Sylas's affectionate touch lingers on my hair, but the memory of Kellan's assault stays with me much more vividly.

It doesn't matter how kind some of these fae men are. They all want to use me in one way or another, it's only a matter of how painfully. I *have* to get out of here.

Time slips by. I might doze a little in the quiet of the keep. Then there's the faintest of footsteps outside my door. Someone stops to cast their magic.

After they've left, I count to one hundred in my head, and then do it again, and then again, just to be sure. When I'm convinced that whichever of my captors bespelled the lock must be long gone, I peel off the covers and limp across the room to the door, fishing the leather pouch out of the jeans I didn't bother to take off.

I pour the salt into my hand and press it against the fixture just below the knob. I hold it there until the coarse grains have bitten into my palm. Then I brush them back into the pouch and ever-so-carefully twist the knob.

It turns. I inch the door open a fraction of an inch, just enough to be sure, and hastily close it again. My heart thumps, but not with panic this time.

I can get past the locks. I can open the doors and leave the keep. I know which direction it is to the human world, and that if I go far enough, chances are I'll stumble into it.

There's nothing left to stop me but my captors

themselves. I can't go while Whitt is partying with the pack outside—someone's bound to notice me, no matter how drunk or high they get. But he rarely gathers them two nights in a row.

Tomorrow… Tomorrow I could be free.

17

August

The rain rattles against the parlor windows, blurring the landscape beyond them into a watercolor painting. It's a summer downpour, though, not a refreshing shower. With the panes closed, the air inside the keep has gotten uncomfortably humid.

My muscles itch to be active, but my wolf doesn't fancy a run in that muddy chaos. I roll my shoulders and head down the hall instead.

Kellan is prowling back and forth near the stairs, his mouth set in an even sourer scowl than usual. He catches my eye.

"We could be done with days like this if our 'lord' would get his head out of his ass. Much more of this, and I'll think that head's gone as soft as a rotten fruit."

My stance tenses, my jaw clenching. I manage to hold myself back from a growl. I *can* keep my temper, as much as this asshole tests it.

"If that's the way you feel, go ahead and bring it up with him, and we'll see how soft he is about that," I retort instead.

There's a feral air about him that I don't like at all. In the dim hallway, his eyes shimmer like coins through murky water. "You won't fight me over it because you know I'm right. Someone's got to make him see this dawdling is only going to screw us all over."

He's trying to provoke me. I don't need to dignify that statement with any response at all. It's true that it only rains like this on the fringes of the summer realm; in Hearthshire, we never had to deal with more than a pleasantly mild shower. But his solution isn't right at all. He wants to present Talia to the arch-lords like she's a doe cut down on a hunt. And he'd clearly like to take a few bites out of her first.

I turn my back on him and jog down the stairs to the basement, where I find the girl herself, poised stiffly just beyond the staircase. When she looks at me, the anxiety shining in her gaze sparks a rage twice as blazing.

"Did he chase you down here?" I demand.

Talia flinches, and I mentally cuff myself across the head for my tone. I still have to be careful how I let my aggression out around her. A beast is scary to witness no matter who its anger is aimed at.

I will my voice to even out and my balled hands to open. "If he's been hassling you again, you can tell me about it. Sylas will get him in line."

I hope so, anyway. Kellan's talk lately has been creeping too close to mutiny for my comfort. If he doesn't like his lot here, why doesn't he go back to the two-faced family he came from?

Because there's nothing but crumbs left of them, and he thinks he deserves better.

"Nothing's happened today," Talia says, which makes me wonder what's happened other days that I haven't witnessed. She did look as if she was limping more than usual this morning. "Is he gone yet? I just—I thought I'd go to the entertainment room after breakfast, but obviously I couldn't open the door, and when I was going to come looking for you or Sylas, Kellan was hanging around near the top of the steps…"

She doesn't need to explain why she didn't like the looks of that situation. I let out my frustration in a rough breath. "He's still up there, but I can open the room for you. And make sure the coast is clear before you head back upstairs."

"Thank you. But—were you going to use the room?"

So worried about imposing when we're the ones who've essentially imprisoned her in the keep. I offer her a reassuring smile. "Not at all. I was going to work out my urge to punch Kellan's face in a way that won't get me in trouble with Sylas. I've got a… what would you call it? A small gym down here."

Talia brightens much more than I'd have expected at that information. The eagerness in her expression takes her from pretty to stunning so abruptly my breath catches. I glance away for a second to make sure I don't come across as leering.

"For exercising?" she says. "Can I—can I see it?"

I grin back at her. "Sure. Allow me to give you the

tour."

She follows me down the hall in the opposite direction from the sauna. I watch her steps from the corner of my eye, but not just to appreciate her slender form. She's *definitely* favoring her once-broken foot more than she normally is.

My fingers curl into fists. Maybe I won't plant one of those in Kellan's face, but Sylas can't complain about me informing him that the asshole must have been harassing Talia again.

Sylas asked me to keep the gym locked because there's equipment in here he wouldn't want Talia getting her hands on unsupervised—we use the space for combat training as well as pure exercise—but I can't see how she'll get into any trouble with the swords and daggers while I'm here. They're all shut away in the cupboard at the far end of the room anyway.

As we walk in, the lantern orbs in the corners of the ceiling light up with their orange glow. Talia blinks at them, still awed by the magic that's so ordinary to me. How ridiculous is it that she's spent so much of her life in our realm yet gotten to experience so little of what it can offer?

I want to see how her eyes would widen and her lips part in amazement if I took her out to the lunar tree grove to watch the flowers bloom and sing by moonlight. Or to the Shimmering Falls, where the water glitters like crystal and tastes sweet as fresh honey. I want to pull metals from the earth and show her how I can talk them into forming a blade or a bracelet.

But it isn't safe to let her leave the keep—for her or for

us. And maybe that longing is beneath me. Whitt would scoff at me for being so keen to please *anyone*, especially a human girl.

I beckon for Talia to follow me all the way into the room. A thick layer of moss covers most of the floor, providing a firm enough surface for aerobic exercise and sparring with enough cushioning that no one's likely to break any bones if they take a hard fall. I like the rich loamy scent it adds to the air and the feel of it under my feet, dense but springy.

A leather punching bag dangles in one corner, the material mottled with thinning patches. That piece of equipment gets a lot of use. On the opposite wall, branches form bars at varying heights. Next to them rests a stack of metal weights. It's probably a good thing the weapons cabinet is closed, come to think of it, because I'm not sure Talia would have quite as enthusiastic a reaction to the space if she caught a glimpse of all those killing blades and the target dummy that's definitely seen better days.

She walks up to the wall with the bars and grasps one that's well above her head. I'm about to warn her not to strain herself when she hefts herself up, curling her back and legs so she can rest her feet on the bar's underside. Wiry muscles I hadn't realized were quite that strong stand out in her slim arms. She tips her head back to smile at me upside down, her hair streaming like a pink flame, and then flips back around, careful in her landing.

"Good to know I haven't lost the basics from lack of practice," she says. My surprise must show on my face, because a blush colors her cheeks. "When Aerik had me—

I didn't want to let myself get too weak. I'd exercise as well as I could using the bars on the ceiling of the cage. I don't know how useful those muscles are for anything other than dangling off of bars, but…" She shrugs as if embarrassed to have admitted that much.

"Arm and shoulder strength like that can help you with a lot," I say quickly. "I'm impressed. You should have told me sooner you needed a workout space."

Her blush deepens. "It wasn't—I mean, it didn't seem as important— It's been amazing just getting to walk around, so I guess I was more focused on that." She waves toward the rest of the room. "Don't let me stop you from whatever you were going to do. Unless you wanted to use the bars?"

"No, go ahead, that's not where I'd usually start anyway."

As I meander toward the punching bag, I can't help watching her a little longer. Determination sparks in her eyes as she grips the bar again. There's no mistaking the enjoyment she gets out of putting her body to work. It warms me, seeing that. Thinking about how she managed one small act of resistance even while battered and starved in that filthy cage.

The small curves of her breasts rise beneath her shirt with the stretch of her arms, and a headier sort of warmth, one I don't let myself look at too closely, travels down my chest to my groin. I jerk my gaze away and train my attention on the punching bag. Now I've got more than one kind of energy I need to work out of my system.

It only takes a minute or two for me to shed the distraction of her presence and fall into the familiar groove of punches and side-steps. I weave one way and another, sometimes focusing only on the angle of my strikes and the force of the impact, and sometimes picturing Kellan's sour face and letting my fists fly with some of that pent-up aggression.

As I intensify the workout, I tug off my shirt like I typically do so it doesn't end up a sweaty mess. The perspiration that breaks out as I pummel the bag some more cools my skin. I've worked a satisfying burn into my arms and chest when I finally step back and take a breather.

Talia is still standing by the bars, but she's stopped her own exercises. I glance at her, worried that my violent display might have frightened her even when directed at an inanimate object.

When our gazes meet, the emotion in her eyes isn't anything like terror. No, there's a hunger in the dilation of her pupils—one I can taste a moment later in a faint musky tang that carries through the air between us.

She yanks herself around to grasp the bars again, flushing so darkly even her neck has reddened. A matching flush washes through me with a flare of my own desire. My wolf stretches within me, roused by the urge to stalk right over there and pull her into a kiss, dig my fingers into that vibrant hair, taste the sweat that shines on her skin. She's such a tantalizing mix of sweetness and strength…

By sheer force of will, I hold myself back. She might welcome the advance. She finds me attractive—I've sensed it in her bodily reactions as we've worked together in the kitchen, when I came to her with my offering of salt the other night. But no doubt she isn't sure what to do about it or even if it'd be safe for her to try to do something, considering she can't have had much experience in that area before Aerik stole her from her world.

The one small mercy she's had in the midst of so much torment is the result of more disdain: Aerik's pack has always recoiled from the idea of sexual relations with humans. They sneer at those who take on mortals as lovers —and those like me who are the direct result of a coupling like that. It appears the most intimate of violations is the one indignity they didn't subject her to. The problem is, it wouldn't necessarily be all that much safer for her to act on her desires with me.

The human lovers of the fae tend to meet dire ends. I should know.

The chill of that long-ago horror winds through my lust, dampening its heat. As much as my blood stirs at the thought, I can't offer Talia what she wants, what *I* want, especially when she's barely had a chance to explore what that even is.

If she builds enough courage to make her own advances, though… Heart help me, I'm not sure I could resist.

I heave another blow at the punching bag, but my fist glances off the side in my distraction. Is there a way I can make sure the attraction between us never reaches that point? A way that she could release her hunger just as I'm letting loose my aggressions into this sack of leather? A possibility rises up in my mind.

If I have the chance, I have to at least try—for both her sake and mine.

18

Talia

In what I intend to be my last evening in the faerie realm, dinner centers around a large roast bird that looks like an elongated turkey, which August calls a "flame pheasant." I've got to say that his cooking means there'll be a few things I'll miss about this bizarre supernatural world. The pheasant's meat has a rich, smoky flavor that's so delicious I find myself licking the leftover juices off my fork.

For dessert, he serves bronze-skinned apples carved so they appear to be blooming out of rings of crisp pastry, topped with a dollop of cream. Be still my heart. I'd already planned on stuffing myself as full as I could tonight, since I don't know how long I'll need to find my way back to the human world—or how long it'll take me to secure myself another meal once I do—but I'd have gorged myself tonight anyway.

August had a few apples left over in the kitchen after

his carving and baking. As I lean back in my chair, savoring the caramel-sweet aftertaste lingering in my mouth, I consider asking him if I can take one up to my room. I could say I sometimes wake up in the middle of the night hungry, and I know he'd jump at the chance to get more nourishment into me. Then I'd have a little food to bring on my uncertain journey.

But Kellan's gaze pauses on me more than once with its usual cold glint. I've never asked for more food after a meal before. I should have thought of that, established a pattern—now any deviation from my normal routine could rouse suspicions.

I'll be okay. *Someone* in the human world will have to be willing to help me… right?

Will I even come out in the same town I was taken from? There's no reason to assume I will. What if I end up in some country where I can't speak the language? Or hundreds of miles from civilization in the Amazon jungle or the Antarctic tundra? I dreamed of traveling to epic landscapes like those, sure—but with proper preparations and supplies. Stranded with nothing but the clothes on my back and a permanently injured foot, it'd be less an adventure and more a catastrophe.

My pulse thumps faster. I get up, letting the rasp of the chair legs against the floor cover my shaky inhalation. Whatever happens, I'll figure it out. I have to try. If I stay here, I'm pretty much guaranteed to meet an even worse fate, aren't I?

August has already swept around the table to clear the dishes. He meets me in the hall with a playful little bow, so attentive in his enthusiasm that I can't suppress a pinch of guilt at the huge secret I'm keeping from him. Maybe he'll be glad when they wake up and find me gone, though. He's doing what he feels he has to, but he obviously doesn't like that they're keeping me captive.

"Shall we descend to the sauna?" he asks.

Oh, right, this is a bath night. I hesitate, but it isn't as if I can make my escape yet anyway. From what I've gleaned about their schedules, the four fae men won't all retire to their bedrooms until the early hours of the morning. A soak in the hot water might even do me some good. Since Kellan's assault yesterday night, my foot's still aching more than usual.

"Of course." I give him my best everything-is-perfectly-normal smile and walk with him down the stairs to the basement.

My bathing routine requires a bit of an awkward arrangement. After my difficulties with the tub upstairs, Sylas didn't want to risk that I might lose my balance on the slippery floor and injure myself with no one around to hear me call for help. So, while I take my bath in the little in-ground pool, August sits on a chair behind a folding screen he set up, giving me most but not all of my privacy.

Sometimes it's nice having someone to talk to, and I've wobbled on the slick tiles enough times to appreciate the security of the measure too. But when my thoughts take a darker turn, his presence only reminds me of how much I *am* still a prisoner, as much as we might like to pretend otherwise.

Inside the sauna room, August dips his head to me and takes his spot behind the folding screen. I sit on a stool to take off the wooden foot brace and then peel off the rest of my clothes. Steam floats through the small room, condensing on my bare skin. I drag it into my lungs, some of the tension I've been holding in easing in the humidity's embrace.

Gripping the edge of the pool, I limp down the steps. Now that I've gotten used to the brace, I can't ignore how uneven my gait is without it. Sylas has aided my escape without even realizing it. I just hope someone in the human world will be able to look at it and figure out how to construct something similar for when my current one wears out or breaks.

The water closes around me all the way up to my chin, hot enough to melt even more of my uneasiness. It holds a slight salty scent, but not enough that it stings if I rub my eye with a wet hand. I tip my head back, my hair floating around my shoulders like pink seaweed. The currents propelled by the jets beneath the surface of the water tickle across my waist.

For a few minutes, I drift in pure indulgence. Then I grab the soap from its dish near the steps and get to work on the actual washing. The bar gives off a welcoming smell like a summer forest with all the vegetation at its most vibrant, and it lathers quickly between my hands.

I massage the bubbles into my hair down to the roots, dunk my head several times to rinse it out, and then rub every other inch of my skin. I'm never again giving anyone the opening to claim that I stink if I can help it.

I'm business-like about it, my awareness of August's presence never fading, but when my fingers brush over my breasts, a quiver of giddy sensation runs through my chest. Closing my eyes against it doesn't help one bit. The memory rises up of seeing August in the basement gym this morning—of the sculpted muscles flexing beneath his sweat-damp skin, the power with which he wielded them, his rhythmic breaths in time with his movements. The look in his eyes when he caught me watching him, their golden gleam turning molten.

More heat than I can blame on the water courses through me now, leaving me dizzy. I suck in the steamy air.

"Are you all right?" August calls from behind the screen. The genuineness of his concern only puts me more off-balance.

"Yes," I say, and grope for something to steer my wayward mind in a less provocative direction. "I— Sylas told me your mother was human."

There's a momentary silence and then a startled but not offended chuckle. "He did, did he? Did that surprise you?"

I consider. "I don't think I know enough about fae to have any idea whether that's a surprising thing."

"It's not—not really." His chair squeaks, and I picture him leaning back in it. "Pure fae are essentially immortal when it comes to old age, but the trade-off is they struggle to have kids. So ages ago, when one or another got a hankering for an heir, sometimes they'd steal away a pretty lady or handsome gentleman to help with that process. At this point, I doubt there's any of us that haven't got at least a bit of human blood in there somewhere, even if some turn up their noses at the thought."

"But that's not the only way fae have kids," I say. "Sylas and Whitt and Kellan—they didn't have a human parent, did they?" I'm assuming Sylas would have mentioned as much instead of just August's if they had.

"It isn't the only way," August agrees. "Now that there's been so much intermingling, it's not even all that common. The faded fae—which is most of us, with blood that's already quite mixed—don't have as much trouble producing children. And now and then those pure enough to be called true-blooded manage it despite the odds. That's why Sylas is a lord and Whitt and I aren't. Our father had him with his soul-twined mate, both of them true-blooded, so Sylas is as well. Whitt and I came from lesser dalliances."

Hold on a second. "You're all *brothers*?" They do have similar builds, and they're all gorgeous in their own ways, but they have such different coloring the possibility never occurred to me.

August laughs. "He didn't mention that part, then? Yes, we're half-brothers. Well, all of us except Kellan. That's typically how a lord forms his cadre—with his faded siblings and sometimes those of his mate…"

He trails off into a sudden silence, as if realizing he might have said too much. I watch the surface of the water ripple in front of me. "If Kellan's not related to Sylas, why did he include *him*?"

"They are related, in a way," August says evasively. "Why are you asking all this, Talia? You don't have to— I mean, none of us would force you to… end up in a situation like that."

His energetic voice has turned abruptly awkward. A situation like what—like getting pregnant by one of them? Is *that* what he thinks I'm wondering about?

My cheeks burn, but a flutter passes through my belly. Now I *am* thinking about it—about the act that gets women pregnant, anyway. About what it'd be like to have August touch me, take me as a lover. So much for finding an unprovocative subject.

"No," I stammer. "I wasn't—I wasn't thinking that. Not that way."

Perfect. Now that begs the question of how I *was* thinking about it.

Before I can find the words to dig myself out of the hole I've unwittingly tumbled into, August clears his throat. When he speaks, his tone is as gentle as I've ever heard it. "It's all right. What you've felt, what you've wanted. Totally natural impulses for any living creature to have, fae included."

Does he *know* about the kindling of desire I've experienced when he's around? Oh, that's a silly question, isn't it? If I could pick up on some sign of those desires being returned when I've got no experience with those urges at all, how obvious must mine have been to him? Augh. Maybe I should drown myself to avoid any further embarrassment.

"We don't have to talk about it," I mumble.

"I didn't want to put you on the spot. I just—" He draws in an audible breath. "It might be easier for you if you have another way of… addressing those feelings, without me or anyone else involved. And from what I understand, the pool is a rather good place for that."

Despite my mortification, curiosity nips at me. My voice comes out even quieter. "What do you mean?"

"I gather the jets can be, ah, very stimulating to

females, if you place yourself so the water moves between your legs."

If my face was burning before, it's a wonder it doesn't outright incinerate now. At least August sounds equally— and adorably, damn it—self-conscious about the subject. And I can't help wondering how he found out this fact about "females." How many women has he brought down here, fae or otherwise?

I don't actually want the answer to that question.

Possibly the only sensible thing to do would be to climb out of the water and scrub this entire conversation from my mind as thoroughly as I can. But with his words, a tingling has shot through the sensitive parts at the apex of my thighs, and I can't help wavering.

This is my last night among the fae—or at least, if I don't make it, it's my last night with anywhere near this kind of freedom. I don't have anywhere else to go just yet. Why *shouldn't* I take advantage of this moment, do something that's insensible—something that might be very enjoyable if the clamoring of my bodily instincts can be trusted.

August doesn't think there'd be anything wrong with it. He wouldn't have suggested it otherwise.

I move through the water to one of the circular protrusions that shoots a stream of water into the pool. When I'm standing in front of it, the current strikes the top of my belly. I ease closer and hook my elbows over the edge of the pool to pull my body upward.

The jet ripples down my belly and hits the sensitive folds below. A bolt of sensation races through me, so intense a gasp tumbles from my mouth.

And it doesn't stop. The intensity builds, pleasure swelling from that spot down through my hips and up to my chest with every passing second the pressure continues. I've never felt anything this *good* in my life.

I grip the tiles harder, my head slumping forward. I want to hold on tight; I want to let go. I'm not sure which of those impulses even makes sense.

The heady surge of sensation seems to reach its peak. It continues radiating through me with the lick of the current against my sex, gripping me with a demand I don't know how to fulfill. I need *more*. There's something just beyond my reach. My whole body quakes with the longing, but I have no idea how to get there.

The need is desperate enough to cut through my embarrassment. My voice comes out hoarse. "August, I— I don't know— It's not enough—"

He manages to piece together that frantic jumble well enough to figure out what I'm asking. "You could add your hand?" he suggests, low and rough, as if he's as affected as I am.

I shift my weight so one elbow can hold me up and dip the other arm beneath the water. My fingertips glide over the spot just above my folds, and my body lights up as if I've struck a match inside me. Oh, yes, that's it.

I press against my hand, my breath spilling over the tiles, my hips straining to reach that higher peak I haven't yet discovered but can sense lies so, so close. The pleasure blazes through me faster.

Closing my eyes, I find myself imagining August is standing in the warmth of the water beside me, that it's *his* hand stroking over me. His fingers exploring this tender part of me.

The thrill of that idea sweeps me to even greater heights. My breath shudders. I rub myself with a little jerk, the current still gushing against me, and it's like a firework erupts from within. It bursts through my body, shocking a cry from my throat and quivering across every nerve.

In the aftermath, I sag against the pool wall. The bliss fades, but echoes of it still ripple through me. I feel wrung out with delight, all that urgency released—and yet a pang rises up inside me with the desire to do it all over again.

Did the release make the feelings August was trying to help me work through better or worse? I can't tell. But, oh, I don't think I can say I regret it either way.

"Talia?" August says tentatively, bringing my attention out of my body. How long have I been floating there, reveling in the moment?

I lift my head and drop my feet to rest them on the pool floor. "I'm fine. I'm… good."

That simple statement must convey a lot more than just the words, because August's response comes out so heated it sends a tingle straight to my core. "I'm glad to hear that."

He must have heard a lot. I made at least a few sounds during that… interlude, or whatever I should call it.

A fresh flush creeps across my cheeks, but it's not quite as intense as before. Apparently I've burned through some of my capacity for mortification.

I glide through the water to the steps and clamber out. While I towel myself off and dress, August stays behind the screen, but every particle of my body is aware of him there. Everywhere fabric grazes my skin, new tingles race through me.

He was on the other side of the room, he couldn't even see me, but somehow it feels as if he really was right there with me, boosting me to pinnacles of pleasure I'd never imagined.

When I'm dressed and strapped into my foot brace, I tug at the hem of my shirt, anxious about looking him in the face after all that. "I'm done."

August steps out, his eyes smoldering the moment they meet mine. For a second, I can't breathe.

He walks over to me like he's stalking his prey. I brace myself automatically, but I find I'm not actually scared of him. Even if I should be.

He stops a couple of feet away, his muscles flexing with restrained power. If anything, his gaze has only gotten more intense. I'm caught in his golden stare. It doesn't feel like such a bad place to be. A flicker of my earlier giddiness returns, coursing through me from head to toe.

August licks his lips, and my gaze follows the movement. "I thought giving you an outlet would make resisting easier," he says in that same low, strained tone. "It turns out I was wrong. You have no idea how badly I want a taste of you—just *one*."

As if the words are a magnet tuned to me, my body sways toward him unbidden. His control snaps with a groan. He cups my face and captures my mouth, the scorching press of his lips setting off a rush of sensation even more intoxicating than anything I summoned alone.

It can't be more than a few seconds of that dizzying paradise before he wrenches himself away, his hands dropping to his sides. I just barely restrain myself from snatching after him to yank him back.

"Just one," he says again, as if trying to convince himself. He inhales deeply and seems to get a grip on himself. "Maybe I should let you go on upstairs by yourself."

Yes. This can't be anything more than it just was. But I don't want him to think he's violated me in some way, especially when this might be the last chance I have to clarify that.

"Thank you," I say, as emphatically as I can, holding his gaze with a fervent smile so he knows I mean for everything.

As I slip out of the room and head to the stairs, it occurs to me that the list of things I'll miss about this place has just gotten longer.

19

Talia

I sit with my back against the wall next to the bedroom door so I can hear the comings and goings in the hall as clearly as possible. In the afternoon, I napped as long as I could to make sure I wouldn't inadvertently fall asleep now, but I still have to jerk myself into alertness a couple of times when my eyelids start to droop.

When footsteps pause outside, I hold my breath. There's a murmur so faint I can't make out the word, and then whoever that was moves on. The door must be locked now—until I put my salt trick to use.

I was right that Whitt wouldn't be hosting another party tonight, but I'm guessing he's the one who takes the longest coming up to the bedrooms. I'm shuffling my feet against each other to keep me awake when the final set of footsteps finally reaches my ears, rounding the corner to the rooms where the fae men sleep.

Of course, going to bed doesn't necessarily mean dozing off just yet. I wait longer, anticipation buzzing through my nerves, my pulse already hiccupping.

I'll only get one chance. One chance, with no idea what really awaits me once I leave the keep. What if Aerik or someone from his cadre is prowling around out there? What if I stumble out of the Mists into a human war zone?

I press my hands against the floor to steady myself. Whatever happens, happens. All I can do is take it one step at a time. I *can* do this.

When the keep has been silent for long enough that my skin starts to itch with impatience, I wait a few minutes more. Then I ease onto my feet. The fae might have good hearing, but surely a few small sounds won't be enough to wake them.

The salt crystals hiss into my hand. I push them against the knob like before, and a quiver of energy darts through me. A few of the crystals crumble into a dust so fine I can't see it after it falls from my hand.

I snatch the rest back against my palm. When I peek at the salt, it looks like I've lost almost half of the meager amount I started with. Counteracting the magic must damage the crystals in the process.

What if this isn't enough to get me through the outer door too?

I drag in a shaky breath and fight off the suffocating sensation rising through my chest. I won't know until I try.

After dropping the remaining salt into the leather pouch for safe keeping, I edge the door open so slowly the hinges don't make the slightest squeak. I close it behind me, knowing that the appearance of me still being inside could buy me vital minutes or even hours if one of my captors walks by, and head for the staircase with carefully even steps. My fingers squeeze the pouch tight.

As I make my slow, measured way down the hall, the foot brace only rasps faintly against the floorboards a couple of times. Both moments make my heart lurch, but its thudding is the only answering sound I hear. No one stirs in the other rooms.

The stairs are trickier to handle silently. I grip the bannister and lower my warped foot first, making sure it's stable, and then set my sturdier foot down beside it. I probably look like a toddler taking her first steps, but about a century later, I'm finally on the main floor.

I'd thought I'd slip out through the back door, which I've studied plenty of times from the kitchen and which is closer to both the stairs and my eventual destination. But when I try the kitchen door, I find that's locked too—maybe to ensure I don't go scavenging for butcher knives in the middle of the night?

I hesitate outside it, clutching the pouch of salt, and then push away. I can't risk using up what power the crystals still contain getting into the kitchen and then not making it outside from there. The front door it is.

The evening's bath might have soothed the pain in my foot a little, but by the time I reach the expansive entrance room, an ache has already formed right where the bones are set wrong. Maybe I should have brought the crutch for extra support, but I can't risk going back for it now.

I'm not letting myself think about how much farther I

might need to walk, or how much more my foot might hurt by the end of all this. I won't think about anything except getting past that door.

Once I'm away from the keep, at least I can vary my gait a little without worrying so much about keeping quiet. If I get to the forest past the fields to the north where I'll have some shelter, I might even find a branch I can use in place of the crutch.

I creep across the thick rug through the darkness. As I reach the broad door, I pour the last of the salt out of the pouch. I press it against the handle, willing it to work.

The crystals fragment against my skin, powder drifting from my grasp and wisping away. When I tug on the handle, it gives. My spirits leap, a smile stretching my mouth. I pull harder, my eyes fixed on the crack where the fresh night air will flood in over me—

A body hurtles at me, crashing into my side and slamming me to the floor. My head smacks the boards at the edge of the rug. Pain splinters through my skull, and a yelp of surprise and agony bursts from my lips for an instant before a heavy hand slaps against my mouth. Sour breath spills over my face.

"Thank you, little dung-body," Kellan snarls under his breath, barely visible above me other than the manic silvery sheen in his eyes. "Thank you for proving me right. We'll see how much you like the results, won't we?" He grins, a faint glint catching on teeth partly curved into fangs.

The hard weight of his body crouched on top of me sends me spiraling back to the times when my former captors would pin me down as brutally as they could manage. My lungs seize, panic hazing my vision. My limbs start to flail, but Kellan rams his elbow into my ribs, leaving me gasping. He wrenches both my arms off to the side under his free hand. The knobs of his knees dig into my thighs.

Claws prickle against my wrists and over my cheek where he's clamped down on my mouth. He digs them in deeper, enough that a cool trickle of blood seeps over my skin. His eyes flash brighter. His mouth opens wide, fangs growing, jaw extending—and a pounding of feet from down the hall jerks his attention away.

His grip prevents me from turning my head to see, but there's no mistaking Sylas's voice. "Get off her, Kellan. *Now.*"

"This piece of maggot-meat was about to walk right out that door, Sylas," Kellan says. "*That's* what she thinks of all the effort you've put into your hospitality." He raises his hand from my mouth and curls his fingers. "Let's make sure she doesn't have anything like a chance again. I think I'll start by scratching out those eyes and then snap off both her feet for good measure."

A wordless wail tears from my throat. I whip my head to the side, squeezing my eyes shut, feeling his muscles shift and the air brush my face as he swings his clawed hand—

With a lurch, his weight falls off me. There's a growl and a snapping of jaws, bodies thudding against the floor.

My eyes pop open to see two huge wolves now wrestling each other on the floor just a few feet away—the one now on top dark furred with one eye scarred through, the one attempting to heave him off paler and leaner.

I shove myself backward, but there isn't very far to go. My shoulder hits the wall. I flinch, the panic tightening around my lungs, the lack of air dizzying me.

The Sylas-wolf lunges for the Kellan-wolf's neck, but Kellan twists away at the last second and slashes his lord's muzzle. They roll, Kellan getting the upper hand only for a moment. A second later, Sylas hurls him back against the floor. Blood flecks the paler wolf's fur. Like the blood— like the blood—

I clutch myself, longing for an image of a peaceful landscape to retreat into, unable to tear my attention away from the chaos before me.

But it's almost done. This time, Sylas manages to jam his paw against the underside of Kellan's chin. His claws rake bloody lines down to the other wolf's throat. With a ripple of his body, he's a man again, holding the struggling wolf down with his still-clawed hand like a vise around Kellan's neck, a feral glimmer in his unmarred eye. A jagged cut slices across his temple, bisecting one of his tattoos.

"*Yield*," he demands, half growl, half bellow. "Yield, and you can leave with your life. By the Heart, Kellan, don't force my hand. You know Isleen would never have wanted this."

Kellan glares up at him, his teeth still bared, holding his wolf form. His muscles tense. He has to be able to see he's beaten, doesn't he?

Maybe he does. Maybe he just doesn't care.

His wolf appears to go limp as if in submission. Sylas starts to release his choke-hold—and Kellan flings his body to the side. Not slashing out at the larger man. No, he whips his head around, his fangs and claws aimed at *me*.

One paw scrapes across my ankle, smashing the thin slats of the brace into splinters and carving through my flesh. Agony spikes up my leg. I heave sideways on my shaking limbs, not fast enough to outpace those gaping wolfish jaws descending on me.

But I don't have to outpace them. Sylas springs, grabbing Kellan's throat and slashing through the jugular with one powerful stroke.

Blood gushes down the beast's chest. Kellan slumps onto the floor inches from my feet. His life flees him with a grotesque gurgle and a twitch of his furry limbs.

In another shudder, he's shifted back into the man with the sallow orange hair and silvery eyes. Those silvery eyes don't gleam at all now. They just stare dully at me, unblinking, while a scarlet puddle spreads across the floor beneath his head.

I push myself farther away, along the wall toward the door, a tremor wrenching through me. He's dead. Completely and utterly dead. My stomach lists queasily.

I've never watched anyone die before.

He died—because Sylas killed him. The fae lord kneels over the other man, his chest heaving. His claws retract into his bloody hands. He can't seem to tear his eyes away from his former comrade, his face stiffening in a mask of horror.

He slit his cadre member's throat for *me*. To save me from being mangled by those fangs and claws.

As my stomach lurches again, a draft of cool air licks over my arm. My gaze slides from Sylas to the front door, which is standing ajar. Darkness and the rustle of the breeze over the fields beckon from beyond it.

I could still make a run for it. I'm bleeding and my brace is broken, my pulse is thundering and my breath still coming short, and maybe Sylas would give chase—but I have some kind of chance. For all I know, I might stumble out of the Mists into the human world just a few feet from this building.

Staring at the sliver of freedom, my body recoils.

I could dash out there into darkness and uncertainty, into a realm where every other being I meet might happily throw me back in a cage, chop me up, or worse—and if I'm lucky, scramble beyond it to a world I don't know how to even start belonging to. Or I could stay here, with the only people who've shown me any kindness in nine long years. With the man who just killed one of his own rather than see me blinded and hobbled.

How can I really say I'll be safer out there than Sylas has just proven I am within these walls? Whatever his reasons for detaining me, he won't allow this prison to destroy me, no matter how much *he* has to sacrifice.

And it was a sacrifice. When I look at him again, his anguish is still plain on his face. I'm not sure how much he actually *liked* Kellan, but he definitely didn't like killing him. To the very last, he tried to avoid that ending.

But when push came to shove, he chose me.

My head swims, exhaustion and emotion welling up inside me. Then a determined impulse pierces the rest, driving me onward.

I half-limp, half crawl around Kellan's limp body to come up beside Sylas. His head has drooped as he reaches to shut his comrade's eyes. I hesitate and then extend a shaky hand to touch his shoulder. My voice comes out in a raw whisper. "I'm sorry."

The fae lord's gaze jerks to me. He blinks at me, looking momentarily, unnervingly dazed. A furrow creases his brow. He opens his mouth, and I have the sense that he's summoning his voice from deep down inside.

"*You* have nothing to be sorry for."

"I'm sorry you had to—I'm sorry it ended up like this."

His mouth twists, not a smile but maybe a shadow of one. "It was a long time coming. The worst you did was speed it up a little."

He hefts himself to his feet, and for the first time I notice the other men in the room. August and Whitt come up to join their lord. They must have been here all along—they'd have heard my cry and the scuffle at the same time Sylas did. They hung back while he decided what justice to deal out, as I guess he would have wanted.

Sylas considers the partly open door and the leather pouch that fell from my hand next to it. "I don't suppose you'd enlighten me as to how exactly you removed the magical seal from the lock?"

I suck my lower lip under my teeth. That's not just my secret but August's too.

The sight of the pouch must tip the younger man off, though, and he's loyal enough to own up. "It must have been—I didn't think—I was only trying to give her a way to fend off Kellan after he kept harassing her—"

Sylas turns his impenetrable stare on August. "Just spit it out. What did you do?"

August winces. "Salt. I gave her salt. Only a little."

Whitt lets out a hoarse guffaw. Sylas's lips pull back with a hint of a snarl, but his voice stays even. "We'll deal with that blunder later. For now, we'd best prepare our cadre-fellow for his final send-off."

20

Talia

They perform the funeral indoors in the same room where Kellan met his end. From snippets of overheard conversations I'm not totally included in, I gather that isn't typical, but Sylas thinks it's best not to reveal Kellan's death to the rest of the pack just yet because of the questions it would provoke.

Thin morning sunlight streams from narrow skylights in the vaulted ceiling. Sylas and his remaining cadre stand around Kellan's body, wrapped now in a thick gray shroud in the middle of the space. The leafy fronds of a fern-like plant circle the corpse, their cut stems giving off a pungent herbal odor. The blood that spilled by the door—his and mine—has been wiped from the floorboards.

No one asked me to witness this ceremony. I could have stayed in my bedroom or tucked myself away in the parlor as if it wasn't happening. But I can't shake the gnawing awareness that Kellan died at least in small part because of me. My presence pushed him over whatever edge he'd been teetering on into territory Sylas couldn't accept; my escape attempt brought those tensions all the way to the surface.

I might have thought of him as a monster; I might not be the slightest bit sad that he's gone, but I won't pretend away his death or my role in it. The others should know I'm not that much of a coward. Sylas should know how much I really do recognize his grief.

I stayed here rather than running, and I still think that was the best choice I could have made, but I don't want the fae lord to regret it. I'm still not sure exactly what last night's events are going to mean for me going forward. For now, I'm here, watching from the far side of the entrance room, present but not participating.

Sylas, standing by the head of the corpse, lets his powerful baritone carry through the air. "As lord and cadre-fellows to Kellan of Oakmeet once Thistlegrove, we honor the last of his time in this world and convey him to his end. He has stood with us in combat and never shied away from a threat."

"He was generous with his advice whether it was wanted or not," Whitt contributes, earning him a sharp look from the fae lord.

The tense set of August's jaw suggests he's having trouble coming up with anything at all positive to say for his colleague. "He was firm in his convictions," he says finally, his mouth slanting closer to a frown.

It's a good thing I'm not expected to speak. I'm not sure a compliment like *He had a way with insults* or *He really knew how to terrify a girl* would go over well in this context.

Sylas lifts a sparkling goblet. "As kin to my mate, I recognize him as family and send him off as family. May the summer sun embrace him with all its warmth."

My gaze flies to his face. Kin to his *mate*?

August said Kellan wasn't related to Sylas like he and Whitt are—that he had another reason for joining the cadre—but if Sylas has a mate, where is she? Why hasn't anyone mentioned her?

Why does something drop out of the pit of my stomach at the thought? It isn't as if he ever—or I ever wanted— Maybe he's set off some of the same feelings August has in me, but I wouldn't have expected them to lead anywhere. I don't think I'd even hope for it to.

Would I?

Sylas drizzles a shimmering liquid from the goblet over the shroud. The fabric lights up for a few seconds before swallowing the glow.

Whitt and August bend down and move several of the fronds so they cover Kellan's body from his feet to his shoulders. Then they step away. Whitt backs up to the front door, where he leans against the doorframe, pulling a flask from his pocket. August drifts backward until he comes to a stop beside me.

Sylas begins to walk in a slow circuit around the body, rhythmic words falling from his lips in a language I don't recognize. It sounds like magic, like an incantation. A shiver prickles down my back.

"Is this what it's always like?" I murmur to August. "Or do cadre members get special funerals?"

"I believe the ceremony is essentially the same as this, other than we'd usually conduct any funeral outside," August replies in a matching low tone. "Sylas would know better than I do. Most of it is the lord's responsibility. This is actually the first funeral I've participated in as cadre, and I only watched one before that when I hadn't yet received my place."

I can't help glancing up at him, startled. I've gathered that the fae men are much older than they look, and with all the aggression I've already witnessed among faerie kind, it's hard to imagine he's experienced so little death in his life so far.

August must be able to guess my thoughts. He grimaces. "Did you assume we kill each other left and right? I haven't been a very good model of fae decorum."

"No, I just— Two deaths doesn't seem like very many in general." In my mere twelve years in the human world, I'd already been to one funeral—for my great-grandmother who passed on when I was seven.

"I told you we can essentially live forever. So taking a life—the life of a fellow fae—through violence is a much more serious matter than it is for humans. You're likely stealing not just decades but centuries. Most fights end just before a killing blow. The victor requests a yield, and the loser offers it up, usually with specific consequences attached."

"Sylas asked Kellan to yield," I say, remembering last night's skirmish with unsettling clarity.

August nods. "It's the only honorable way. If Kellan had given his yield last night, Sylas probably would have banished him from this domain. Most would take banishment over death. He could have ended up gathering stragglers into a lordless pack of his own or found another lord willing to take him in for his services."

But Kellan hated me so much that he was willing to die just to take one last stab at wounding me. My throat closes up. No wonder Sylas looked so agonized afterward. For all I know, Kellan is the first person—the first fae—he's *ever* had to kill.

And he did it for me. A human, a girl he's barely known two weeks—an interloper who'd been in the process of *betraying* him.

How can I make sure he never regrets an act as colossal as that?

August touches my shoulder, just briefly. That fleeting contact is enough to stir a rush of heat into my skin despite the dread creeping through my chest. My mind jolts back to yesterday's other unexpected event—to the pool and August's voice encouraging me to find my pleasure, to the blaze of his kiss afterward.

He didn't want to do anything more than that—he wasn't going to let himself. Maybe that's why he pulled his hand back so quickly just now. I think I hear a hint of a rasp in his voice when he speaks next, but maybe it's sympathy rather than desire.

"You can't blame yourself for what happened. Kellan knew what he was doing. He knew he was acting against Sylas's orders. He made that choice."

But you could also say I forced the issue to a head.

"I hope Sylas didn't get too angry with you about the salt," I venture. And how does August feel about my use of that salt?

If he saw my escape attempt as a betrayal of his trust, he doesn't show it. "It was nothing I wasn't prepared to face when I got it for you." He pauses. "I can see why you'd have wanted to leave, but... I'm glad you changed your mind."

"I am too," I say quietly. At least, I think I am.

I hug myself, and the brush of my arms against my torso wakes up other memories, other feelings that shouldn't have any place at a funeral. I'm too aware of August's presence beside me. Not knowing what to do about the shift in our relationship only makes me more uneasy.

I squash the emotions down, but it's possible they're what spurs the other question that's been tickling through my mind, though I'm too uncertain to phrase it quite as a question. "Sylas said Kellan was the kin of his mate."

August hesitates. "Yes," he says. "Half-brother. He was originally part of her cadre as Whitt and I am to Sylas, but after the trouble that brought us here, without her, Sylas offered to take him on. He thought it was only right."

The weird twinge that ran through me earlier returns. "His mate was banished—she was sent somewhere they can't be together?"

"Ah, no. It's not my place to get into it. Sylas will tell you if he decides to. I'll just say that hers would have been my first funeral as cadre if we'd had her body to conduct it."

That's horrible, but what's even more horrible is that some part of me is *relieved* she isn't still out there somewhere.

My gaze returns to Sylas, who is still chanting,

kneeling beside the shrouded body. Does it make things better that Kellan wasn't a man he necessarily would have chosen for his cadre if it hadn't been for awful circumstances, or worse, because he's killed not just a member of his cadre but the half-brother of a woman I assume he loved and already lost?

Just thinking about it makes my stomach ache.

Sylas says a few final words and extends his hands over the body. A light bursts through the fabric, a golden aura so bright I gasp. As it contracts, the fronds, the fabric, and the corpse beneath shrink too, until there's nothing left of Kellan at all—nothing but a pool of cloth and a gleaming gem nestled in its folds.

Sylas picks up the gem, which fits perfectly in the hollow of his palm. When the sunlight catches on it, it beams as if it's a miniature sun in itself. I have trouble associating Kellan's soul with anything that beautiful, but I guess that's what all fae are made of, deep down at their core.

No wonder they would sneer at humans whose bodies turn into dirt and dust.

"What will he do with the jewel?" I ask August.

"Kellan will have given him instructions about where he'd want his essence laid to rest. I'd guess probably in his family's original domain, Thistlegrove. It isn't theirs anymore, but lords are obliged to honor those kinds of requests—when Sylas has an opportunity to journey that way." August exhales as if shedding a great weight. "Well, it's done now." He turns to me, his gaze traveling over my body to the ankle he bandaged just hours ago. "How's your leg?"

The slash of Kellan's claws dug too deeply into my flesh for August's magic to fully seal it. It took the wrapped fabric packed with some of Sylas's medicinal herbs to stop the bleeding completely. "It's still a little sore," I say. "But a lot better since you worked your magic on it."

"I should make sure the gauze doesn't need changing."

He crouches down beside me, his fingers gliding over the wrapped fabric as he examines it. Heat courses up over my skin, and I think a gleam of desire passes through his golden eyes, but he doesn't look up at me or make any further move.

What happened between us that once, he obviously doesn't mean it to happen again. It *was* only a kiss, even if it feels like much more than that.

Sylas marches over to where we're standing, his attention fixed on August. Something in his stride and the intensity in his expression sends an uneasy ripple of recognition through me, though I can't say why. "Does her wound require more attention?" he asks.

"Not yet, from what I can tell," August says. "The binding of the flesh I managed appears to be holding."

"Good. Let's proceed with care." Sylas steps closer, his gaze rising to meet mine, and just for an instant, something flashes through his unscarred eye. A flicker of heat in the darkness that solidifies my sense of recognition.

The way he stalked over just now reminded me of how August approached me yesterday by the pool: predatory and possessive. That flicker wasn't far off from the searing look the younger man gave me before he kissed me.

It's gone now, though, only grim weariness left. Maybe

I imagined it, or maybe it was merely concern because of my injury. I am still an object of value here, even if Sylas sees me as a person in my own right who's worthy of protection, more than just a means to an end.

"I'll construct another brace for you," he says. "Assuming you found the first one suitable?"

"Yes," I say, my gut knotting at the much less pleasant memory of how that first one was broken. "It helped a lot. But you don't have to go to any trouble—I still have the crutch—"

He waves off my concerns before I've even finished expressing them. "It's a small thing to offset the fate you nearly met last night."

We haven't talked about what led to that horrifying moment—about my attempt to escape—other than Sylas replacing the magical lock on the front door and confirming I had no more salt to break the spells. He hasn't pushed the subject, and I'll admit I've been nervous about bringing it up myself. What if he's angry with me underneath all his authoritative poise?

I do want to make one thing clear. "Have you had any luck with testing that sample of blood you took from me? If you need more to try other things—anything I can do to help you figure out how it works…" And how that effect might be replicated, so I'm no longer such a precious commodity as well as a person…

"I'll let you know if anything comes of it or if I require more from you," Sylas says, in a tone that indicates he hasn't discovered anything all that useful yet.

Disappointment winds through my ribs, but I raise my chin against it. I might want the fae lord's protection, but I don't think it'll help my situation if I take on too much of the role of a victim.

Sylas taps my jaw with the lightest of caresses, and I'd swear another flicker of heat unfurls in his one dark eye. "You should get yourself some rest, little scrap. I don't imagine you had much last night. August, I need to speak with you."

The younger man hurries to follow his lord down the hall, shooting me a quick, reassuring smile over his shoulder. I swallow hard. He'd better not be getting into even more trouble over how *he* protected me.

Whitt sweeps across the room a moment later. He pauses by me, observing me watching his two comrades. His teasing voice comes out with more edge than usual. "Plotting which of us to off next, mite?"

I wince and hug myself tighter. "I didn't—Even with Kellan, I never wanted—"

A glint dances in Whitt's blue eyes, coolly amused and maybe a little unsteady. Not really how I'd expect a man to look minutes after putting a close colleague to rest. I remember the flask I saw him retrieving. Is he even sober?

He isn't even a *man*. None of them are. I have to keep remembering that, no matter what else happens.

"We like you more than we liked him," he says with a chuckle. "That isn't saying much, so I wouldn't let it go to your head."

As he saunters off, my stomach sinks. What if I made the wrong choice, staying here?

If I did, I don't think there's any taking it back now.

Talia

When night falls, I'm wide awake. I must have dozed too much during the day between restless tossing and turning in my bed.

I sit by my bedroom window for a while, watching the fields and the forest beyond sink into almost total darkness. The moon is nothing but a thin sliver. Just past the halfway point before it's full again.

Whitt's last snarky remark echoes through my head. I flop down on the mattress, hoping that my body will take the hint and relax, but my heart keeps thumping a little too fast. My thoughts flit through my mind like nervous birds in an undersized cage.

Kellan is gone, but he was never the real threat. The real threat is the power of my blood and what using that power could mean for Sylas and his pack.

Maybe it won't be so bad if I stay here. If I made it back to the human world, I'd be starting over from scratch anyway—no friends, no close family, no full education, no money. All the dreams I had will be even more out of reach than when I was twelve. My life there could be pretty awful.

The keep has plenty of space for me to roam around in; I've been able to keep myself entertained. I get to gorge myself on three fantastic meals every day. The atmosphere could be outright peaceful without Kellan's harassment. We might even get to the point where Sylas feels comfortable letting me go with them outside during the night when it's less likely anyone will spot me.

I'd take that living situation over not living at all any day. He could collect a little of my blood once a month as he needs it, as gently as he did that once…

But as soon as the cadre starts distributing that "cure" beyond the keep, Aerik will catch on, won't he? He'll know they must be the ones who broke into his fortress and ran off with me. If he can prove it, will he be able to reclaim me? I don't know how faerie laws work.

And it's not just about having the cure. Sylas wants to regain the status he lost, to return his pack to a better home closer to the Heart of the Mists. Can he do that while keeping me, or will he have to turn me over to these arch-lords and let them treat me however they like?

I trust him not to let anyone abuse me while I'm under his roof, but can I be sure he wouldn't hand me over to someone he knows might be cruel where he doesn't have to witness it?

The memory of the way he looked at me this morning, the momentary heat in his gaze, swims up through those uneasy questions. Fae men *can* find me desirable. August made that much clear, even if he didn't want to follow through on his interest. I've felt Sylas's body against mine before—I know how thrilling his powerful presence can be. Thinking about him now, a tingle forms between my legs where the jet and my own fingers stroked the sensitive folds to so much satisfaction yesterday.

What if I gave him a little more incentive to keep me around? Showed him I'm willing to not just cooperate with his tests and rules but to become his lover as well? Obviously he'd never become as devoted to me as he must have been to his former mate, but every bit of affection I can encourage in him is one more reason for him to hold on to me rather than send me away.

As I turn the possibility over in my mind, more tendrils of warmth unfurl low in my belly. My understanding of the actual act of sex comes mostly from the awkward health classes in middle school and a book my parents gave me after a hasty version of "The Talk." I know which parts come together and all that. It's hard to imagine sharing my body like that with… well, anyone, let alone Sylas with his massive frame.

But everything about my time here tells me he'd be careful with me. He wouldn't want to hurt me.

I might even enjoy it.

Once the idea has taken hold, I can't shake it. I roll one way and the other on the bed and finally sit up.

Only a glimmer of starlight shines through the window. The room is so dark I can barely make out the door.

It's probably locked. I wouldn't be able to go to his bedroom anyway. I'll just walk over there and show myself that, and maybe then I'll be able to set aside these thoughts until at least tomorrow.

I pad across the floor on my bare feet, my nightgown teasing across my lower thighs. The trek sends my mind tumbling back to last night, to gripping the knob like I am now and to all the stress and pain that came after.

My throat squeezes shut. I close my eyes, just holding onto the door.

Tonight can't be like that. Kellan is gone—as gone as any living thing can be. And I don't have any more salt. I'm going to twist the knob, and nothing will—

It turns in my grasp, smooth and silent. I'm so startled I let go, and the latch clicks back into place. Staring at the knob, I swivel it again, and it releases just like before.

They didn't lock me in tonight. Is that Sylas's way of repaying the trust I showed him by staying—giving me free run of the keep even while they're sleeping? I can't imagine he overlooked that security measure by accident this soon after I broke past it once.

Now that I know I *can* go through with my plan, I'm suddenly a whole lot less sure of it. I ease the door open, and then I stand there peering into the hall for several heartbeats, not quite able to convince my feet to move. The thoughts that brought me to this point rise up again. More heat pools between my legs.

The unlocked door is a gift. It could almost be an invitation. I think I'm more likely to regret ignoring it than accepting it.

I slip into the hall and make my slow, limping way toward the other end where my captors have their bedrooms. I noted them in my explorations before—at least, the ones that opened at my curious nudge. Whitt's was locked to me until he pulled me into it in the middle of my panic attack the other day; Kellan's I never saw at all, not that I'd want to.

Sylas and August never bothered to secure theirs, I guess thinking there was nothing in there they needed to hide. It was easy to tell which was which even with my quick peeks. Sylas's had larger, grander furniture in vibrant rosewood, everything neatly in its place, while August had clothes hanging from the bed posts, and the air held a whiff of fresh baking that must have carried with him from the kitchen.

Sylas's room remains unlocked. The soft rumble of his sleeping breath travels through the darkness. With the curtains drawn over his window and only faint light seeping from the hall behind me into the room, I can only make out the vaguest shape of his bed and his large form beneath the covers. The distinctive scent that reaches my nose, like rich earth and woodsmoke, tells me I'm in the right place.

My pulse starts to race. Where do I go from here? Can I really just walk right up to him and…?

It seems I can. My feet carry me to the massive bed—it's got to be at least half again the size mine is, and mine's already the biggest bed I've ever slept in. This one is high, too. I rest my hands on the edge of the mattress, my eyes adapting as much as they can to the darkness, watching Sylas's sleeping body sprawled down the middle of that expanse.

Maybe I could just curl up next to him and see what he'd like to do with me when he wakes up? My coming here should be a pretty clear proposition. I have the feeling I'll make a fool of myself if I try to express my intentions in words.

I turn to heft myself onto the bed ass-first, roll to lie on my back—

A muscular arm shoves me down into the mattress with much more force than I was prepared for. A squeak slips from my throat. Sylas stares down at me, braced over my body with his arm clamped across my chest, so close the fall of his wavy hair grazes my cheek.

My lungs have only just started to clench in panic at being pinned when his expression shifts from defensive to confused. As his brow furrows, he sets his hand beside me and pushes himself higher, still peering at me. I can't shake the sense that his ghostly scarred eye sees just as much as the dark whole one.

"Talia?" he says, his baritone thickened by the sleep I've woken him from but his gaze now fully alert. "What are you doing?"

His entire body is still hovering over me, its heat teasing through my nightgown and over my skin. His knees feel almost scorching where they've settled on either side of my thighs. I can see enough in the darkness to tell he isn't wearing anything from the waist up. His shoulders and chest are all sculpted muscle, even more impressive than when hidden under his shirts, the stark black lines of his tattoos swirling and twining across his brown skin.

A weird shivery tingle races down through my belly. I can't tell whether I'm more terrified or turned on. Every nerve is quivering with the knowledge that this man is dangerous, and I'm definitely not half as scared as I should be.

"I—I thought—" I manage to force my voice out of its timid whisper. "I thought you might like some… company."

Even with my awkward phrasing, the insinuation clearly isn't lost on him. He blinks, the furrow in his brow deepening, but the heat I saw before sparks in his unscarred eye before he tamps down on it.

"And why did you decide to offer that company *now*, like this?"

I open my mouth and close it again. It'll hardly work to win his affection by telling him that's what I'm attempting to do. Even thinking of putting it into words makes me feel duplicitous, as if I was doing something slimy.

I don't know what to do other than ignore the question entirely. Tentatively, I raise my hand to touch the side of his chest. His skin is surprisingly smooth over all that hard-packed muscle, and it seems to flare with heat the second I touch it. "You don't like me?"

The way he closes his eyes with a strained grimace suggests *that* isn't the problem. When he looks at me again, it's like a flame is dancing in the dark iris. He keeps his voice steady, but there's a roughness to it that wasn't there before.

"I like you just fine, little scrap. But I don't think this is about liking. Your fate doesn't depend on you submitting yourself to my whims—is that understood? I'll do as right as I can by you regardless of whether you warm my bed, and I always intended to do so."

I guess my motivations weren't so difficult to figure out. I wet my lips, and Sylas's gaze tracks the motion. His attention, the closeness of his body, and his obvious attraction are making me dizzy in a way that's nearly as intoxicating as Whitt's drugged syrup.

"We could still… do something…"

I must sound so naïve. He lets out a sound that's halfway between a chuckle and a groan and pushes off me, settling onto the bed a couple of feet away. "Go on back to your room, Talia. If this is what you really want, for your own sake and not out of fear, you can come back another time when you're sure of that."

I swallow hard against a swell of emotion. The fact that he's sending me off for my own good, even when he's not at all disinterested, extinguishes any fear I still had in me, leaving only the embers of my desire. A desire I'm clearly not going to see fulfilled tonight, thanks to the way I went about it.

But lying there next to his warmth, his smell twined around me and every inch of the stately room speaking of his authority here, I have trouble convincing myself to limp back to my lonely, spartan room. The conviction sweeps through me with so much certainty it takes my breath away: as long as I'm near him, no one can really hurt me.

"Could I stay here?" I venture. "I won't bother you." The bed has more than enough room for both of us. We could lie at opposite ends and barely brush fingertips with our arms outstretched.

Sylas offers another ragged chuckle and runs his hand

through his hair. "Are you attempting to test my self-control? I told you—"

From somewhere inside me, I find the bravery to interrupt. "I really mean just to sleep. I—It feels safer in here than in my room." Although that's an awfully selfish reason to impose on his privacy, isn't it? A flush burns across my cheeks. "It's okay. I'll—"

I move to push myself off the bed, and Sylas catches my wrist. When I glance back at him, there's something so haunted in his gaze it squeezes my heart.

Whatever emotion that was, he masters it a moment later. He drops my arm and shifts farther across the bed, leaving more room for me. "Fine. Only to sleep. Just keep your hands to yourself."

The hint of a growl in his voice sends another of those giddy shivers through me. I lay my head down. "Thank you."

When I drift off, it's with a vision of his hands moving over me like the currents in the pool's water.

22

Sylas

$\mathcal{I}$ wake up painfully hard. The scrap of a girl isn't even close enough to touch, tucked under the sheet at the far end of the bed with her head nestled in my other pillow, but the memory of her lithe body beneath me has been floating through my head all night. That and her scent: woodsy and sweet but not syrupy, like maple sap that hasn't been simmered to tameness.

I want to drink it off her skin. I want to watch those delicately green eyes dilate with pleasure.

I'm going to explode right here in the bed if I don't rein in thoughts like that.

She's so deeply asleep that she doesn't stir as I get up. I pause by the door to my en-suite lavatory, taking in the softness of her face in sleep, the contrast of the pale skin with the deep pink hair falling around it.

She must have meant it when she said she felt safe in

here. With me. She sounded as if she meant it, but the words were so jarring I couldn't fully accept them.

A bittersweet pang echoes through my chest, but it does nothing to diminish the erection tenting the fabric of my drawers. If I *am* going to be safe for her in every possible way, I'd better take care of that.

I lock the lavatory door, because I'm not sure I could control my hunger if she wandered in while I'm in the middle of satisfying these urges, and turn on the water in the shower alcove. It thrums through the pipes and rushes over me in a hot stream. I comb it through my hair and let it cascade over my body, and then I bring my hand to my throbbing cock.

I'm keyed up enough that just that first touch sends a bolt of pleasure through my loins. Bracing my other arm against the wall, I bow my head to the shower spray still raining over me and grip myself firmly.

As I build up a rhythm, stroking from head to base, I can't help picturing Talia kneeling before me. Her pink hair slicked back from her face. Her perfect Cupid's bow lips wrapping around my erection. Her tongue slicking a heady line along the underside of my cock while she gazes up at me in a haze of desire.

Would she cringe if she knew I was thinking of her that way? I can't believe she understood just what she was offering last night, hesitant and stuttering. That mouth has never taken a cock into it; no part of her has been so penetrated.

But she wasn't *un*willing. Regardless of how well she understands carnal acts, there was no mistaking the tang of arousal she gave off while I loomed over her.

I want to do right by her, to make up for the horrors she's been subjected to under Aerik's roof and now mine. But Heart help me, I want to take her too, so badly the memory of her gasp when I first caught her last night sends me careening right over the edge, balls clenching, semen spurting against the wall.

I haven't come this hard in ages.

Afterward, I don't feel quite as unburdened as I was hoping. My cock softens, but a knot of lustful tension remains coiled behind my groin. My chest still tightens at the thought of walking back into my chamber and seeing her in my bed.

Well, there's one way to douse most of my lingering desire. I switch the tap to cold and let an icy torrent pour over me until even my bones are chilled.

The frigid deluge leaves me fully alert and focused. I dry myself briskly, pull on fresh drawers and my dressing gown, and start toward the door.

I'm still a few strides away when my ears pick up a sound that stops me in my tracks. It's the slightest intake of breath but with a husky note that shoots straight to my groin.

As I stand there motionless, the sounds that follow draw a picture that quickens the blood in my veins all over again. A rustle of fabric. A whisper of hair against a pillow. A murmur of a groan, muffled as if against a bitten lip.

The fire inside that I tried so hard to expel and then extinguish flares up all over again. My wolf rears its head, urging me on with its animal appetites.

I walk to the door and push it open. When my gaze falls on Talia, she's lying still beneath the sheet, her head tipped to the side, her expression innocent. But the faint daylight that spills around the edges of my curtain reveals a deep blush in her ivory cheeks.

My dead eye conjures a ghostly image that swims over her face for a moment: those same features turned wanton with a carnal hunger. A thicker tang of arousal scents the air. As I breathe it in, I lose my grip on the vast majority of my good intentions.

I prowl over to my side of the bed, holding her gaze. The words roll scorching over my tongue. "And what have you been up to, my little human?"

Her eyes widen. Her own tongue flicks across her lips, and by all that is dust, I'm hard again. "I—Nothing," she stammers. "I just woke up."

I sit down and reach across the mattress to slide my hand under the sheet. My fingers curl around her arm. Tugging by the elbow, I raise it to bring her fingers level with my nose.

Her cheeks flame hotter when she realizes what I'm after, and her arm twitches as if to yank away. I've already gotten the whiff I expected, the musk of the slickness that must be seeping from her sex. I raise my eyebrows at her as if to say, *Care to try again?*

I wouldn't have thought her face could turn any more red, but it's nearly as bright as her hair now. "I was only— I woke up, and I felt so… wanting, and I thought maybe if I took care of it myself— I didn't know how quickly you'd be back."

She was taking the same tack I did. Not quite so inexperienced in these pleasures as I assumed, it seems. I wonder if it would have worked any better for her than it has for me. It's taking every shred of control I have left not to lick those fingertips and then bury my face between her legs to see how much more of that exquisite nectar I can draw out of her.

"And where did you learn how to do that?" I ask teasingly, not really expecting much of an answer.

Talia wets her lips again. "August showed me."

With a skip of my heart, my vision goes red. Every instinct in my body clangs with the need to claim and defend what is *mine*. My lips are already curling back from my teeth, fangs emerging, before I catch hold of myself enough to register the anxiety flickering across the girl's face.

I manage not to outright snarl, but the question comes out plenty harsh as it is. "He did *what*?"

She flinches, and seeing that, I suppress a little of my burst of temper under the shame of scaring her.

"It—it was in the pool," she says, her voice falling into the whisper that was all she could manage when we first found her. "He just told me how I could use the jets and my hand… He didn't even watch or anything—he was behind the folding screen the whole time."

That doesn't explain why he was making suggestions like that in the first place. That impertinent whelp—I'll cuff him across the head so hard his ears ring for a week.

I inhale slowly, settling my inner animal as well as I can for the girl's benefit, not August's. My voice comes out still fierce but not quite as curt. "Is that all?" Did she come here last night planning to act out what he's already shown her? My gums itch to set my fangs free.

She lowers her eyes. "He kissed me. Only once, and

only very quickly. He made it sound like he didn't think he should have done even that."

Another snarl rises in my throat. He *shouldn't* have done it. And he never bothered to mention his partial seduction of our convalescent guest to me? In that moment, the transgression angers me more than his secret gift of salt.

And I'm man enough to admit that some part of that anger is because I now have to ask this question: "Was it him you were thinking of when you touched yourself?"

Her gaze darts back up to meet mine. Her face, paler after my display of ire, flushes all over again. Her answer slips out so soft it's barely a murmur. "No. I was thinking about you."

The rest of my fury crumbles away under a wave of triumph, more than I'd have expected to feel over one tiny human girl. No, not a girl, not really. She's a woman coming into her own, bit by careful bit now that she has the room to find herself—and this woman wants me, with every beat of her racing pulse.

She still carries so many wounds, old and more recent. There's still so much she hasn't yet experienced. The passion I'm capable of might scare her as much as my anger did. But I can make her mine as much as anyone should while she's in this state.

I let go of her arm, unable to tear my gaze from her bright green eyes. "Show me."

She blinks. "What?"

I tip my head toward her body, desire roughening my tone. "Show me how you would pleasure yourself."

Her lips part, and for a second I think she'll refuse in

embarrassment. Then, ever so slowly, she tucks her hand back under the sheet. From the corner of my eye, I track its movement down her torso, but my gaze stays fixed on her face. She stares right back at me, clearly still nervous, but with a gleam of excitement as well.

I can mark the exact moment she finds the perfect spot between her legs. Her eyelashes quiver, and she sucks in her breath with a little hitch. Her head pushes farther into the pillow instinctively.

My renewed erection strains against my drawers, but this is for her, not for me. This is to give her a taste of the reality of whatever she's imagining, of what she pictured happening last night.

All the same, I intend to relish every moment.

I bend over and brush my lips to her soft cheek. The essence of her, that wild sap-sweet smell, floods my nose, enflaming my hunger. I kiss a gentle path from her cheek to the crook of her jaw, with the slightest nibble of the tender skin there.

Talia arches farther back with a gasp that's almost a whimper. I tease my mouth down the side of her neck, tasting her with a swipe of my tongue. Her breath breaks into shaky little pants that make me want to unleash my desire and devour her like a beast.

No. She is mine, and I'll treat her like the precious being she is.

As I continue to attend to her neck, I glide my hand over the silky fabric of her nightgown to cup her breast. My fingers trace a lazy circle around the small mound. She trembles at my touch, her hips shifting needily beneath the sheet. More of her delectable musk laces the air.

When I skate my thumb over her nipple, I earn my first full moan. She turns her head toward me, seeking me out. No force in the lands could stop me from claiming her lips.

I kiss her deeply, reveling in the tart sweetness of her mouth, in the invigorating sounds that course from her mouth into mine as my thumb urges her nipple into a stiffened peak. Skies above, there's so much I want to teach her about the pleasures her body is capable of.

I drop my mouth to her collarbone, slicking my tongue across the delicate ridge and grazing my fingers over her chest to her untended breast. Her hips are rolling now as if grappling with the hand between her thighs.

"Take yourself all the way," I say against her skin. "Find your pinnacle, Talia."

Her groan sends a violent throbbing through my rigid cock. "I—I can't seem to get there."

Oh, my lovely innocent. I nibble my way along the edge of her scarred shoulder, back up her neck, until I reach her earlobe. "Are you aching to be filled? Dip those eager fingers right into your slit."

A gasp that's almost startled leaves her lips, but I can tell from the motion of her arm that she's following my command. Her eyes roll up, a strangled sound following them. "*Oh*."

"That's right. Give yourself over to it."

I'm not sure I've ever seen a vision quite as erotic as this nearly untouched woman chasing her release. The flush in her cheeks is only delight now, no embarrassment, and her irises flare so brilliantly they put emeralds to shame. I ease down her body to draw one of those pert nipples into my mouth through her nightgown. A cry shudders out of her.

"I still can't— Would you help me?"

Her voice is so fraught with need there's no way I could deny her request, even if I wanted to. I trail my hand down her arm to where her own hand is pressed tight to her pussy, the heel of it by her clit and two of her fingers curled inside her channel. Watching her expression, I apply a hint of pressure over her clit, and then a little more, my thumb stroking over the inside of her thigh where the slickness of her arousal has spread.

That small assistance is all it takes to carry her over. Talia closes her eyes and opens her mouth. With a choked cry, her head jerks back against the pillow. Her whole body quakes against mine with the force of her orgasm.

As her shudders subside, her hand goes slack beneath mine. I raise my arm to collect her against me, wanting her to be sure of me in the aftermath as well as in the act itself. She ducks her head under my chin. In her silence, her fingers drift over the collar of my dressing gown.

"This isn't why—" she starts, and hesitates. "I haven't done anything for *you*."

"Don't worry yourself about that," I say, ignoring the ache in my groin. "I got plenty of enjoyment out of this interlude." Once she's left, another shower will *definitely* be in order.

Talia looks up and scoots against me to press her lips to mine. Her kiss is timid but so fond it leaves an ache not in my cock but somewhere in the vicinity of my heart. I brush my fingers over her hair and kiss her back with equal ardor.

I told her last night that nothing we did in this bed would affect her fate, but maybe I was lying to both myself and her. After this intimacy, after the trust she's shown me, the thought of handing her over to the arch-lords brings a growl into my throat.

And it's not even the greatest trust she's offered. I kiss her on the forehead next, and then say, "You stayed."

"I told you, I felt safer here than in my—"

"No, I mean the night before. After Kellan attacked you. You meant to leave, did you not?"

Talia's body tenses, but she doesn't push away. "I did. I thought *that* would be the safest thing—getting back home."

"But you changed your mind."

"When—when I saw how far you'd go to protect me... I don't know if there's anyone else in this world or the one I came from who'd care that much what happens to me. My real family is gone." She lapses into a momentary silence. "I know your people need me and the cure that comes from my blood. I know you can't promise anything. But at least here, I know where I stand."

I wouldn't have thought I could admire her resilience more than I already did, but she's proven me wrong again. I pull her a little closer against me in anticipation of letting her go. "I'll endeavor to ensure that's always true."

By my life, let me always be capable of that, regardless of what may come.

23

Talia

When I make it to the kitchen, changed from my nightie into jeans and a tee and with my hair combed into as neat a state as the waves will allow, at least half an hour has passed since I left Sylas's bed. Tingles still race across my skin at unexpected moments, with the graze of my shirt's fabric or the brush of my fingertips as I tuck an errant pink strand behind my ear.

Being with him was so exhilarating that I want to hole up with him in his bedroom and never leave, and that desire somehow makes the whole thing frightening at the same time. What I did with him and the affection he showed me hasn't really changed anything—about my status, anyway. My situation here is just as precarious.

But at least, if the days ahead are only one last short taste of freedom, I've experienced a lot more passion than I had before I came here. I've had more of a life.

August is already in the kitchen, grabbing baking dishes off the overhead racks. When he sees me, he shoots me one of his warmly enthusiastic grins, and an odd little wobble runs through my gut. August was the first man to help me discover the hidden pleasures of my body. I'm still not totally sure how to act around him.

He seems capable of acting as if nothing is at all different, though. He appeared downcast during Kellan's funeral, but he's back to his usual energy now. "I was thinking pancakes for breakfast," he says, pouring pale purple flour into a mixing bowl. "How does that sound to you?"

My stomach chooses that moment to gurgle its approval. August laughs. "Worked up an appetite in your dreaming, did you?"

More like after my dreaming, but I'm not going to mention that. I hop onto my usual stool. "Pancakes sound delicious."

"And you've never had them made with fallowrot flour before, I'll bet. Fluffy as clouds but full of flavor. Have a sniff."

He thrusts the bowl toward me, and I lean over it to inhale. A creamy, savory-sweet smell like hazelnuts fills my nose. My mouth starts to water. "Two thumbs up from me!"

"You can be my stirring assistant, then." He sprinkles a couple more powders over the flour and passes it to me along with a spoon. "All the dry components need to be evenly distributed to get the best effect."

"Aye, aye, chef." I grip the spoon, and he flashes me another grin. Even after the experience I just had with

Sylas, and as much as I wanted Sylas from the moment he loomed over me last night, that grin manages to wake up a familiar flutter in my chest.

Is it *normal* to be this attracted to two men at the same time? Maybe it's something about them being fae.

As I get to work stirring, a sense of loss creeps through my chest. I should have had friends I grew up with, or new ones I met at high school or college, who I'd be able to talk to about this sort of thing. Maybe I'd even have felt comfortable discussing men with Mom once I'd gotten older and out of the goofy puppy-love crush stage where I got the giggles after just locking eyes with a classmate I thought was cute.

August cracks several eggs into a different bowl and whips them into a froth with a whisk. I watch the muscles shift along his shoulders and chart the fall of his dark auburn hair against the nape of his neck.

Sylas has already had a proper mate—a fae woman. Maybe fae men only marry once and that's it. August must want to find someone he could really share *his* life with, which obviously can't be me.

Whitt strolls into the room with his usual languid nonchalance, glancing over both August and me as if the sight of us amuses him.

"Breakfast won't be for a little while yet," August tells him. "You're up early."

Whitt yawns. "I'm not really up. Just grabbing something to ease along the rest of my sleep. Pretend you never saw me."

He heads into the pantry. A clink here and a rustle there follows. August shakes his head, his mouth forming a crooked smile, and returns to his preparations. I do the same.

The flour mixture is giving off an even more powerful —and saliva-inducing—perfume now, which seems like a good sign that I'm doing my job right. August splashes a little liquid from one bottle and then another into his bowl, whisks it one last time, and leaves that to check on me.

"Let's see how you're doing, Sweetness," he says, leaning over by my shoulder.

The second I realize that's a nickname he's given me— and what a nickname it is—a deeper flutter shivers against my ribs. At the same moment, August stiffens beside me.

I glance down at the bowl, afraid I've screwed up the mix in my distraction, but he shifts closer—not to the bowl, but to me, with a sharp inhalation. A current of air tickles over my skin, and I realize he's taken a whiff of me, his nose nearly grazing my hair.

He yanks himself backward, his muscles tensed and his golden eyes fiercely bright. I stare at him, my own stance going rigid, utterly bewildered about what's going on.

"You… and Sylas…" he says, his voice hoarse. His hands flex at his sides as if he's trying to restrain himself from clenching them into fists.

Heat courses over my face. I washed myself before I got dressed, more thoroughly than I usually would, but I didn't have anything like a full bath. And the fae's wolfish noses are as keen as their ears. Sylas's scent could easily have lingered on my neck where he placed so many of those searing kisses.

"I—" I start, and don't know what to say. Should I

admit it? Deny it? Why should it matter to August anyway, when he made it clear he didn't think anything should happen between him and me?

Right now, it appears to matter to him quite a lot. He paces to the counter and back, his eyes still blazing. "It's fine. You have every right—*he* has every right—"

With a choked growl, he wheels toward the parlor. "I've got to—to look after something." He barges across the room and throws open the back door. It slams behind him. Through the window, I see his form hunch and lengthen, fur rippling over his brawn. In mere seconds, he's not a man but a massive ruddy-brown wolf tearing across the field toward the forest.

The mixing bowl teeters on my lap. I grip it before it can topple onto the floor, my pulse stuttering. Does he even want this anymore? Is he abandoning breakfast completely? I don't understand.

Was he *angry* with me, because I—

The joy this morning's encounter left me with drains away, leaving only a pinch of guilt. I don't know what's going through August's head, but he was obviously upset. I never wanted to hurt him.

"Quite the little drama you've decided to star in, mite," Whitt's voice drawls from the other end of the room.

I startle, nearly falling off my stool. This time, the bowl does slip from my grasp. It thumps on the ground, half the flour mixture jostling out of it in a purplish poof. I scramble to collect the bowl with its remaining contents and spin around. I'd forgotten the other man was in the room.

Whitt ambles by, casting a disparaging glance at the floor. "And what a mess you've made in the middle of it. Think you can manage to clean it up?"

I can tell he's not just talking about the flour. "I didn't mean— I wasn't trying to cause any trouble."

"It's starting to seem like the stuff follows you. Don't worry. I'm sure Sylas won't blame you." He turns toward the hall.

His tone has stayed light the whole time, somewhere between teasing and needling, but the impression pricks at me that he means his remarks more than he's showing. Is *he* angry with me too—because I upset August? Because of Kellan? They never appeared to like each other all that much, but what do I know from two weeks' observations?

If I'm going to keep any of the peace I've started to find in this place, I need all three of the men still ruling over it to at least accept my presence.

"Whitt," I say, setting the bowl down on the counter. "Wait."

He swivels partway around and cocks his head. "Why?"

"I—I'm sorry."

A frown curves his mouth. In that moment, he does look angry. Then it's gone again, and the breezy tone comes back. "Whatever for?"

I don't really know. I drag in a breath, searching for an answer, but I'm so uncertain of what he's bothered about in the first place that anything I say could just as easily be wrong as right. I don't want to piss him off *more*.

"Hmm," he says into my awkward hesitation, and

wags a finger at me. "Work on that too." Then he's sauntering away, leaving me in the kitchen alone.

There's still no sign of August. I wait for a few minutes, my stomach knotting, and then I poke around the room until I find a dustpan and a twiggy whisk-broom. I've finally managed to sweep the last bits of flour off the floor and am dumping it into the waste bin when footsteps thunder down the spiral staircase beyond the doorway.

"Sylas?" Whitt calls, the note of urgency in his voice so unusual that my nerves jitter. I creep over to the doorway. What's going on now?

The fae lord emerges from the dining room holding a steaming goblet he must have poured himself while waiting for the breakfast that now might never be coming. He looks as surprised as I am by Whitt's tone. As Whitt hurries over to him, Sylas studies the other man's face. "Bad news?"

"I'd call it a decidedly fraught combination," Whitt says, working in a little wryness despite the apparent emergency. "I've gotten word from one of my people that Tristan and his cadre mean to pay us an unexpected visit. At least now it's no longer unexpected."

Sylas raises his eyebrows. "Other than as much as we don't know why they'd mean to. What business do they have here—and why would they want to catch us unawares?"

"I'm not sure. My man wasn't even clear on when exactly they plan to come, only that it sounded as though it'd be fairly soon. It may be they simply want to check up on us, or it's possible—"

As Whitt speaks, he glances toward the kitchen and catches sight of me. His mouth snaps shut in mid-sentence. Sylas follows his gaze, his mismatched eyes pinning me in place before I can consider ducking out of sight.

I grip the doorframe tightly and decide to pretend I was part of the conversation all along. "Who's Tristan? Why would it be bad for him to come?"

Whitt frowns again, but Sylas answers me as if I asked a totally reasonable question. "He's a second-cousin to one of the arch-lords. Which means he has plenty of prestige and influence, and he can decide to use those for good or ill. And seeing as we've already lost rather a lot of favor that we're hoping to regain…" He grimaces and returns his attention to Whitt. "We'll need to begin preparing immediately."

"Are the three of us going to take on the entire task?"

I open my mouth to offer that I'll help in any way I can, but Sylas's gaze slides to me again, so abruptly solemn my voice dries up.

"No," he says. "We'll need to incorporate the pack. Talia, I'm afraid I'm going to have to ask you to confine yourself to your room until this matter is dealt with."

24

Talia

On the TV screen, a screeching woman leaps at the girl she's been berating, trips, and lands face-first in an icing-slathered cake. Not even a hint of a laugh tickles from my lungs at that or at the sight of the goopy mask of frosting covering her face when she straightens up, her eyes bulging.

I turn the movie off and flop onto my back on the sofa. I should be glad that after Sylas said I'd be confined to my room, he amended that to *two* rooms. I've spent most of the past few days in the keep's entertainment room, flipping through books I'm too distracted to really focus on and watching movies from the fae lord's collection—with headphones on, to make sure none of the pack members he's brought in to help prepare the keep catch on that I'm down here.

But now I'm bored out of my mind. I can't even

remember whether this is the fourth day or the fifth, they've blurred together so much—even more than before.

I've barely seen Sylas or his cadre. They knock when they leave meals outside the door and when it's time for me to move from my bedroom to the entertainment room or back again, and a couple of times Sylas has spoken to me briefly from the doorway to confirm I'm all right, but otherwise I've been totally isolated. They don't want to take the chance that the rest of the pack will smell me on their clothes if they've spent too much time around me, he explained.

If he's that intent on keeping my presence here a secret, then that's got to mean he isn't planning on offering me up to this second-cousin of an arch-lord dude, right? Or maybe he just wants it to be a big surprise. With every hour that passes since I cuddled against him in his bed, those intimate moments feel less real, less trustworthy.

Aren't faeries supposed to be tricksters? How can I trust *anything* any of them have said to me?

My stomach grumbles despite the tension wound through it. It must be getting on toward dinner. I've got even less sense of time than usual in this windowless basement room.

The knock comes as if on cue. But when I open the door, I find not a plate of food but August standing a few feet away, empty-handed.

He smiles at me, and I'm ridiculously relieved by the genuine warmth in his expression. I haven't seen him since he took off from the kitchen the other morning. However he felt about what he guessed about Sylas and me, at the very least he doesn't appear to hate me.

"Hanging in there?" he asks.

I shrug, feeling abruptly awkward. I'm not going to mention that earlier incident if he doesn't. "It hasn't been the time of my life, but it's still way better than an actual cage."

He winces at the reminder of how they found me and beckons me out, starting down the hall a couple of paces ahead of me. "A scout reported seeing Tristan and two from his cadre on their way into our domain. They should be here in less than an hour. Sylas thinks you'll be more secure in your bedroom. I've already brought up some food so you don't go hungry."

"Thank you." My gaze skims over the hall and the stairwell we head up. Every inch of surface area has been scrubbed and polished to gleaming. New artwork—fanciful paintings and twisted gold-and-bronze sculptures—hang on the walls on the main floor. Extra lantern orbs dangle from a winding branch that stretches along the ceiling. Every time I've come up, the keep has become fancier. I can only imagine how the other rooms have transformed.

"This guy is a pretty big deal, huh?" I say, continuing up the broader spiral staircase to the second floor. "I mean, I know he's related to one of these arch-lords and all…"

"Casting us off this far into the fringes is only one step up from total banishment," August says. "They'll be watching to see how we've handled the disgrace, and you can be sure he'll report back to his cousin. The higher we can hold our heads despite our situation, the more respect we'll earn. A real lord isn't diminished by his location."

That last bit sounds as if he's quoting Sylas. I can't help

thinking that anyone who puts conditions like this on their respect after casting people off is such a dick their respect shouldn't matter anyway, but I don't say that either.

August leaves me at my bedroom. It, at least, looks the same as it always has. Sylas obviously doesn't anticipate that the visitors will be examining it. I find a plate on the bedside table with a simple meal of bread, cheese, and a cold cut of meat, but since August prepared it, it's delicious in its simplicity.

I'm halfway through the sandwich I've assembled when a knock comes that I didn't expect. Are they moving me again?

"Yes?" I say from where I'm perched on the side of the bed.

The door eases open to reveal Sylas's imposing figure. He takes a couple of steps inside and then stops, studying me with both his unmarked eye and the scarred one. "All these restrictions should be over soon," he says. "It's unlikely our guests will want to spend the night, and if they do, we'll ensure they leave early in the morning."

I *am* looking forward to having full run of the keep again. I nod. "I guess I should just stay quiet up here?"

"Yes. If you can manage to sleep or at least attempt to, that would be best. Although I know how quietly you're capable of moving on your feet." He glances at my brace, which I've already taken off and set by the end of the bed. "Even if they stay over, we've set up a guest suite on the first floor. There's no reason for them to venture anywhere upstairs. You should be perfectly safe."

He doesn't intend to make a farewell gift out of me,

then. More tension than I knew I was holding unspools through my chest. I inhale deeply into my loosened lungs. "I'll make sure I don't do anything that'll tip them off that I'm up here."

"Good. I apologize for the stress this will have put you under."

He pauses, and like in other moments when he's stopped by to talk to me, I have the abrupt impression that he's going to step even closer, touch my face, maybe even kiss me again. Something smolders in the depths of his unmarked eye, and an answering flame sparks in me— but whatever he might have been considering doing, he holds himself back. If I didn't simply imagine the whole thing out of wishful thinking.

"Until tomorrow," he says with a slight dip of his head, and leaves.

Whitt must have been waiting in the hall. His voice travels through the door. "If they realize what we've been hiding—"

Sylas's answer is firm. "We've discussed this. It won't be a problem."

"You know we can't pretend her out of existence forever. It's not even a week until the next full moon."

"Which I haven't forgotten."

"The whole *point* of taking the risk of stealing from Aerik was—"

"I haven't forgotten that either," Sylas replies, a growl creeping into his voice, and they move beyond my hearing.

My stomach clenches, but I manage to put Whitt's complaints out of my mind and finish my sandwich. Then

I curl up on the bed, wishing I'd thought to bring one of the books from the entertainment room with me. After doing little more than lazing around on the sofa all day, I'm not remotely tired.

The thumping of hoofbeats tells me the visitors have arrived. I ease over to the window, which Sylas assured me has a "glamor" on it that makes it look from the outside as if the curtains are always drawn. To my frustration, no angle lets me see the front of the keep. Sylas's voice rings out in a greeting too muffled by the distance for me to make out the exact words.

A woman I vaguely recognize from Whitt's revels comes into view, leading three horses more elegant than any steed I ever saw in the human world: slim-legged and necked with gracefully sloping heads, hair and manes glinting with an opalescent sheen, one dusky gray, one pale bay, and one nearly white. They prance across the ground so light-footed I'd believe they were gliding above the grass.

She brings them around the other side of the keep to where the stable must be, and I see nothing more to do with the new arrivals. I sink back down on the bed and rub my foot absently. A trace of the rich smells from the extravagant dinner August will have whipped up—with help from pack members, presumably—trickles around my door. My stomach pinches even though it's full of a perfectly tasty sandwich.

I lie down and burrow my head into my pillow, but even with my eyes closed, my thoughts keep racing too quickly for me to have any hope of sleeping. I kick off the covers and then pull them back over me. What are they talking about downstairs? Why *did* this fancy-pants guy and part of his cadre come calling?

Even if they don't know I'm here, the outcome of this visit could still change how Sylas decides to deal with me.

Finally, curiosity niggles down too deep for me to ignore it. I *have* proven I can move silently through the halls. The shape of the spiral staircase means that even if someone approaches the second floor, I'll have plenty of warning before they can get a look at me. I need to know what's going on here and in the world around if *I'm* going to make the right decisions, as much as I'm able to decide anything at all about my fate.

Not bothering with my brace, I limp carefully to the door and open it only wide enough for me to slip by. With careful if uneven steps, I make my way to the bend in the hall and around it. My bare feet make no sound against the floorboards.

I don't even need to walk all the way to the top of the stairs. When I reach the lavatory door, the voices traveling up from the dining room sharpen enough for me to follow most of the conversation—at least on one side. The newcomers seem to enjoy talking in loud, sweeping voices, as if their volume makes them more impressive.

"From what I heard, the stuff didn't make it out this way very often," a deep male voice is saying.

"We managed without," Sylas replies. "After all, until recently, no one had it at all."

A female voice pipes up, throaty and strident. "True. And I suppose you can't blame Aerik for not wanting to bother sending his people right out to the fringes."

Aerik. They're talking about the tonic he made to cure

the fae of the full-moon wildness—the tonic he started making once he had access to my blood. Whitt mentioned that Aerik hadn't always shared that tonic with Sylas's pack, but I didn't realize the snub was major enough that the whole community would know about it. It sounds like he pretty much *never* let them have any.

With everything I know now of Sylas's ideas about honor and integrity, I have to think he must have been awfully desperate to have gone as far as breaking into Aerik's home.

Did this lord come all the way here himself because of the tonic—because he heard something that made him suspicious? I creep a tad closer, my ears pricked and my mouth bone dry.

It seems like the subject only came up so the visitors could needle their hosts, though. The man—Tristan?—starts rambling on about some quest he went on to slaughter an ivory boar, with occasional interjections from the woman. Then I think Whitt speaks—I can't fully make out his voice, but the laughter afterward sounds like the sort of response he'd be aiming for.

"When I last visited my cousin, he made some mention of you and your circumstances," the newcomer says eventually.

"He's welcome to call on us himself anytime he'd like to observe those circumstances firsthand," Sylas remarks, and I catch a snicker as if he's made a joke, though it didn't sound at all like one to me. I bristle on his behalf.

Whatever he did that forced him and his pack to move here, I can't imagine it was *that* horrible—only horrible by the standards of these stuck-up, pompous aristocrats who're clearly more interested in lording their power over those who have less than making anyone's lives better.

There's a span of quiet there I can't discern more than a word here and there. Kellan's name reaches my ears, and my back stiffens, but I miss whatever follows.

Then the voices get abruptly louder. The speakers are moving this way, I realize.

"Aren't you going to give us the full tour?" Tristan says, casually but with a hard edge that indicates he expects to be obliged.

Are they going to come upstairs after all? My pulse hiccups, and I scoot backward, spinning around. With one hand braced against the wall to help my balance, I scuttle back toward my bedroom as quickly as my legs will take me without betraying my steps.

I picked up on their intentions just in time. I'm barely two steps around the corner when I hear the bunch of them tramping up the steps. I limp onward, shaky with the rush of adrenaline and fear.

My bedroom door closes behind me with the softest of clicks. I stand on the other side, listening hard, but I can't even make out the visitors' voices anymore. Surely they're too far away still to have noticed that small sound? After wavering for a moment between eavesdropping and the comfort of the bed, I wobble over and clamber under the covers.

I assume the danger is past. My heartbeat evens out, and I slump deeper into the mattress, berating myself for risking leaving my room in the first place. If I'd been any less alert—

But I wasn't. I got out of the way in time. Everything's fine now.

Then Sylas's voice penetrates the wall, sounding as if he's just come around the corner. "There's not much down there other than spare rooms. We haven't bothered to do them up. I doubt they'd interest you."

He's talking a little louder than before. I shift upright, my fingers curling into the covers. Are they going to come down here—are they going to open up *my* room?

What the hell am I supposed to do if that happens?

"I'm impressed enough with what you've done with the rest of the space that I can't imagine they'll be a disappointment," Tristan says in the same demanding tone.

A chill floods my skin. He's going to insist on looking in here. Oh, hell.

Sylas laughs—again, louder than I'm used to. "Well, you'll see for yourself that there's nothing to look at other than a bit of furniture."

He *wants* me to hear him. He's warning me. The room needs to look as though no one's been living in it.

There are a few rooms between the bend and mine. I have a minute or two.

My head jerks around. The wardrobe—I can hide in there… and hope they don't smell me. It's farther from the door than the bed is. They won't walk right through the whole space, will they?

I don't have time to worry over that. I shove myself off the bed, remembering only at the last second to set my feet down gently, and tug the covers as smooth as I can make them. The dinner plate has to go too. I snatch it, set it as far under the bed as I can reach alongside my abandoned crutch, and whirl toward the wardrobe.

I'm nearly there when a jolt of horror wrenches through me. My foot brace—it's still leaning against the bedframe in easy view of the door. How could Sylas explain away *that*?

There was a pause in the voices, but they're on the move again, getting louder as they approach. I scramble back to the bed and accidentally set my bad foot down at an awkward angle that pinches the nerves. Clenching my jaw against a gasp at the sharper throbbing that forms between the misshapen bones, I bend down to grab the brace.

Every particle in me is hollering to dash to the wardrobe at top speed, but if they hear me running around, I'm toast anyway. I hobble over as nimbly as I can, cringe at the faint squeak of the hinges when I open the door, and crawl inside amid hanging quilts and folded sheets.

There's enough of a ridge on the inside of the door that I manage to pull it all the way shut. I crouch there, unable to see anything in the room beyond, unable to hear anything over the thunder of my pulse.

The bedroom door clicks open. Sylas's voice is brisk. "A simple guest room. We have more appropriate quarters prepared downstairs should you require them."

Someone chuckles. "I should certainly hope so."

There's a sniffing sound, and my throat aches with held breath. Then the woman from before says, "You've taken to keeping human servants again, I gather."

"It is difficult to do without any extra aid," Sylas says

smoothly. "And easy to bring them over while we're situated here. If the scent bothers you, I can assure you your rooms were seen to solely by my pack."

She hums to herself, and then the door thumps shut again. I press my hand against my mouth to hold in a sigh of relief.

Nestling deeper into the sheets, I lay down my head. I don't know if I'm going to be able to sleep a wink until they're gone, but if I do, I think I'll do it in here.

25

Talia

I wake up the next morning back in my bed—and realize after a few bleary blinks that it isn't actually morning at all. The angle of the light, only an indirect glow seeping through the window, means the sun has already passed from east to west. I've slept into the afternoon.

That's not much of a surprise. I'm not sure how late it was when I finally crept out of the wardrobe and crawled into bed after hearing the visitors' horses canter away, only that it was well into the early hours of the morning and my head was aching with nervous exhaustion.

The exhaustion has diminished, but my nerves are still jumpy. The past week may have brought new pleasures into my life, but it's also driven home just how easily any security I've found here can be shaken. Sylas couldn't even ensure his own cadre wouldn't try to hurt me. He couldn't prevent this other lord's visit either, despite the dangers of letting him in.

Within the keep, Sylas rules with an authority that feels so solid it's hard to imagine anyone not bowing to his commands. But there are people outside these walls—lots of people, apparently—who have more power than he does.

What happens to me may not be entirely up to him in the end, as much as he'd like it to be.

I fumble out of the bed, still groggy-headed, with those uneasy thoughts churning in my mind. Someone must have checked on me during the day: there's a new plate heaped with purplish pancakes on the side table. Seeing it, the hazelnutty scent reaching my nose, my heart squeezes. It feels like a peace offering, no words required.

Since I haven't eaten all day, it doesn't take long for me to wolf down the whole stack. My stomach no longer aches when I eat more than a bird-like portion of a meal, which I guess is some kind of progress. The pancakes leave a creamier hazelnut aftertaste on my tongue, so delicious I don't want to rinse my mouth and wash it away. I probably should, though, since my morning breath will have evolved into a higher level of blech by now.

I don't run into any of my captors in the hall. The view from the south-facing window suggests it's later than I assumed. Whitt is out on the field, his tall form casting a long shadow, the lowering sun searing off his bright brown hair. He appears to be directing a few of the pack members in setting up for one of his parties, one laying out cushions here, another arranging goblets on a table there.

As I watch, he produces the flask from his pocket and

takes a swig from it that I suspect is an early start to his reveling. Apparently last night's hosting wasn't enough festivity for him. Or maybe he needs this party to recover from that one.

When I make my way downstairs, the rooms on the first floor are all empty, the halls silent. I feel like a ghost walking through them—like maybe I'm not really here at all. After hiding for the better part of the last week, could I have faded away completely? It sounds absurd, but then, how can anything be more absurd than the fact that I'm living in a realm of faeries?

I venture down to the basement and gravitate toward the entertainment room at the lively music emanating from that direction. Peeking past the door, I find August braced at the edge of the sofa, his gaze intent on the TV as he jabs at his controller. On the screen, a digitized fighter whirls in the air with a spinning kick that knocks his opponent's head right off.

August lets out a whoop and lowers the controller with a grin. He looks so at ease that I convince myself it's perfectly fine to intrude.

"Hi," I say, slipping inside.

His grin widens at the sight of me, and there goes that damn flutter turning my insides all wobbly. When I was seeing him all the time, I must have started to get used to how handsome he is. Now it takes me a moment to catch my breath again.

He beckons me over to the sofa. "You're up! You looked pretty wiped out when I brought up your plate—I didn't want to wake you." A trace of shyness softens his expression. "How did you like the pancakes?"

"As delicious as you promised. I guess I lost most of the day."

"We all did. Tristan's bunch kept us up until it was almost dawn, and then Sylas wanted to go over everything they said before our memories had faded." He stifles a yawn. "We're all on Whitt time now. I'm not sure what's going to happen with dinner. Breakfast was already a late lunch. Sylas went out to check on something, and I don't know when he'll be back."

"Well, I won't be needing dinner anytime soon. I just stuffed myself with those pancakes." I step closer, halting by the sofa's arm. "I've had enough of my own company after the last few days. Do you mind if I watch you play?"

August waves off any concern I might have had about my welcome. "I've got some games you could even play with me."

I sink onto the sofa at the farthest end from him and grimace. "I haven't played anything in years. I don't even know what game system that is. I'm not sure I'll give you much competition."

August aims another grin at me. "I'll go easy on you. It'll still be fun for me. I can hardly ever convince Sylas to play, and Whitt only will when he's so loopy on whatever he's been drinking or eating that he spends more time shooting his mouth off than actually handling the controller."

He's so enthusiastic my hesitation melts. "All right. I can give it a try, anyway."

"Let's find something a little less violent for this…" He shuffles through his stack of games, makes a triumphant sound, and swaps out the discs. Then he hands me a second controller, pointing out the buttons. "This one's for jumping. This one for picking things up and then throwing. This one lets you run double-speed. You move around using this joystick. It's pretty simple. You'll get the hang of it fast."

I peer at the bright cartoony graphics on the screen. "What am I supposed to be doing?"

"We're competing to solve the puzzle first. The first levels are really straight-forward. It only gets complicated once you're warmed up." He gives me a playfully ominous look. "Just watch out for the beetles."

Even though it's been nearly a decade since I last faced off against my little brother on our old Playstation—which I guess is probably an antique by gaming standards at this point—my hands fall into the rhythm of button pushing and stick swiveling with just a few hitches. Apparently video games are like bikes, and once you've learned how to work them, your body remembers.

I direct my character through a maze and across a few obstacles to hit the goal at the end ahead of August—but I'm pretty sure he let me win. "Nicely done," he says, and I resolve that I'm going to win at least one level of this game fair and square.

The puzzles do get harder, but my fingers fly faster as I get used to the strategies. I can tell I'm actually putting up a decent fight when August starts aiming all of his attention at the screen rather than regularly checking in on me. He leans forward on the sofa, his golden eyes gleaming and intent. When I pull off a double jump and push a switch just in time to leap to the goal ahead of him, he rocks back with a little cheer. "You're a natural!"

I aim a teasing kick at his leg. "Don't go easy on me now."

He laughs. "Oh, I'll give you a run for your money."

He does, dashing through the next course so swiftly I'm breathless trying to keep up, even though the only part of my body that's moving is my hands. August wins that level, and we launch straight into the next.

As I sink into the flow, my mind creeps back to those long ago days when I played with Jamie—not this game, but plenty of others. He'd get so excited when he was winning that he'd hop right off the sofa in the living room and bounce up and down on his feet, as if he could propel his character faster that way.

I'm never going to see that gleeful smile again. Never going to trade joking challenges as we try to one-up each other.

The loss is nine years old, but the grief wallops me as if it's just happened. When have I really had space to grieve? I'm not sure I can even now, when I have no idea what happened to Jamie after Aerik wrenched me away, who found him, what was done with his body...

My hands shake where I'm clutching the controller, and my character collides with one of the chomping beetles. I'm sent back to the start of the course.

August glances over at me and presses pause. "Are you liking the game all right?" he asks, studying my expression.

I don't want to talk about what's really on my mind— about the carnage left in my wake, the blood spilled because of *me*. My throat has choked up, but I manage to swallow the emotions down. My stomach aches with them, but that's okay. I've had a lot of practice at tuning my discomforts out.

Instead, I focus on everything that's good about this moment I'm in right now. "Yeah, it's perfect for taking my mind off that Tristan guy and his 'surprise' visit."

August sets down his controller. "You must have been terrified last night. Sylas couldn't find a way to dissuade them from going upstairs without making them suspicious, which would have been even worse. You did a good job, hiding away as well as you did. As far as we could tell, they didn't catch on at all."

I'm glad I didn't screw anything up for them, at least. "Do you know why they came to see you? Was it really just a coincidence that they decided to after you brought me here?"

"Not exactly." August makes a face. "From the questions they asked, we got the impression Kellan must have said something that caught their attention. He handled most of our trade with the other packs when we needed anything we couldn't get or make in the domain, which is a lot more here on the fringes, and pretty much every lord has spies here and there listening for anything... interesting. I'd imagine the arch-lords have men scattered all through the domains keeping an eye on things too."

My shoulders have tensed. "He mentioned *me*?"

August shakes his head quickly. "No, nothing as specific as that, or I'm sure they'd have been asking a lot more pointed questions. Probably it was a more general discontented muttering... He might have given away that Sylas had some sort of plan in the works, one that Kellan thought he was handling badly, something along that line.

And as soon as an arch-lord catches a hint that there are plots afoot, they tend to be wary of the worst. Understandably, since there are plenty of lords who'd like to add 'arch' to their title. And—"

He cuts himself off and shakes his head again, more emphatically this time. "In any case, they seemed satisfied that we weren't in the process of preparing a coup and decently impressed by the state of the keep, so that's all good. Sylas came up with a story about why Kellan wasn't here that should also have hinted at a reason he would have been irritable for reasons unconnected to treason—or any thefts we've committed." He shoots me a smile.

Even dead, Kellan has left more trouble for Sylas and the others to deal with. I nibble at my lower lip. "Everyone's going to find out that Kellan is dead eventually, aren't they?"

"Of course. But Sylas will manage how that news comes out. He'll know the best way to frame it. And honestly, if he has to admit that he was the one to make it happen… Plenty of folk have seen what Kellan was like. It won't come as a surprise that he could have pushed his lord that far."

"But Sylas took him into his cadre anyway."

"There are expectations of duty…" August sighs. "I don't think any of us was really happy about it, including Kellan. But we hoped he'd settle in and adapt. Not so much."

It takes a little of the burden off me knowing that Kellan rubbed just about everyone the wrong way, that Sylas was telling the truth when he said his death was a long time coming. But I can see that even though he didn't like the guy, even though they fought, Kellan's death doesn't sit easy with him.

I can't say the thought of my own eventual death—sooner or later—doesn't horrify me, and I've been a lot closer to it than August likely ever has. How hard must it be to grapple with the idea when you should have centuries ahead of you?

August turns to me again, and I realize I've been staring at him, taking in the details of his face, which is even more stunning with that haunted expression over the boyishly handsome features. I jerk my gaze away, and it catches on the tattoo peeking from beneath his sleeve instead.

I motion at it, grasping onto that seemingly safe topic of conversation. "Do those mean anything? Your tattoos?" As far as I've been able to see from a distance, the regular pack members have a few here and there, but they aren't as inked up as Sylas and his cadre are—or Aerik and his. Maybe they're some sort of symbol of rulership?

August taps the one I pointed to, the arcing black lines twisting together like claws. "They're not exactly tattoos—not the way humans have them. We don't put them on ourselves. When we master a true name, the representation of it forms on our skin. The more true names you see a fae marked with, the more magic they can wield."

"True names?" I repeat. The term sounds vaguely familiar, maybe from faerie stories I read back home. With all the stealing of humans into the Mists, it makes sense that a little valid information about the fae would trickle back to our world.

"All things have true names tied into their essence. When you learn the true name of a substance or a plant or animal well enough, you can command it to your will." August gestures to the room around us. "We called up most of the keep from the trees that grew here, using their true names."

So they simply talked a bunch of trees into forming this massive building? Sounds like an awfully useful skill. "How do you learn them?"

"If you find someone willing to teach you who already knows, that gives you a huge step up. But most fae are protective of their knowledge. Otherwise, you work with whatever it is you're attempting to master in various ways until its true name reveals itself to you." He raises an eyebrow at me. "I wouldn't get any ideas, though. I've never heard of a human wielding magic."

I've wielded it, though. Once, anyway. Thinking of how I convinced the latch on my cage door to unlock, my pulse skips a beat. I'm not sure that's something I want August and the others knowing. Would it make me even more of a prize rather than a person?

"I think maybe Aerik used something like that to lock my cage," I say tentatively. The syllables are still burned into my memory. "What's 'fee-doom-ace-own'?"

August blinks at me. "You've got a good memory— your pronunciation is almost perfect. That's bronze. Your cage was made of it, wasn't it? There are other types of magic we can use, but true names are usually the most potent if you're not worried about someone else who knows them trying to counteract your spell."

And Aerik definitely wouldn't have worried that a

lowly human could manage that. *Did* I really? Maybe it was only that he didn't concentrate quite hard enough that time, and the spell broke on its own. I haven't noticed any unexpected tattoos springing into being on my body.

I'll have to find an opportunity to test it. Except I have no idea how to use it when I'm not specifically undoing a spell someone else made. Well, I'll just have to see what happens.

"How many true names do you know?" I ask, setting those thoughts aside.

"Fifty-four," August says with obvious pride. "Whitt has close to eighty, but he's had a lot longer than I have to learn. I think Sylas has over a hundred… He's always developed his spellwork whenever he can. That's a lot even for a lord. It gets harder once you've covered the simple ones and the areas you have the most affinity for."

Right. August said before that he had a knack for bodily magic like healing. Does he have symbols on him for skin and muscle and bones?

As I remember how he checked my foot, another possibility occurs to me, bringing a chill through my nerves. "Do *people* have true names?" Could the fae command me by knowing mine? Would "Talia" be enough or would they need middle and last name as well?

August nods. "Fae do. August is the name my father gave me, but we're all born knowing a deeper one that's bound to our soul. From what I understand, it's not the same with humans." He pauses. "But then, we have so many other kinds of magic that humans can't defend against, it wouldn't be necessary to go to the trouble of finding out."

Not exactly a comforting statement. "I guess you must keep your true names hidden most of the time," I say. Why would anyone want to give others that much power over them?

"All of the time is more like it," August says with a chuckle. "I've never shared mine. There are some lords who demand it of their cadre... I trust Sylas enough that I'd give him mine if he wanted it, but the reason I trust him that much is because he's *not* the kind of lord who'd rule that way, so it hasn't been an issue."

His admiration for Sylas reverberates through his voice. I think of the way he reacted when he smelled the fae lord's scent on my skin. My gut tightens, but August has been speaking freely and warmly enough that I find the courage to form the words.

"Were you... angry because Sylas and me—because we —" I can't figure out how to finish the question, both out of embarrassment and uncertainty about how to even describe what happened between the fae lord and me. We didn't have sex. Could you call what we did "making out"? That doesn't feel like the right phrase either—like something teenagers do in the back of a car, nowhere near the intensity of the energy created between the two of us in his bed.

Thankfully, what I have said is enough for August to catch my meaning. He drops his gaze, his shoulders tensing, but he looks more awkward than upset.

"I'm sorry about my reaction," he says. "I had no claim —it just took me by surprise. But it isn't as if I could compete with him."

It takes a few seconds for that comment to sink in. I

knit my brow. "I didn't think it was a competition. I didn't think— You said we shouldn't do anything together."

His laugh comes out hoarse. "Not because I don't want to. Skies above, Talia, you have no idea— But I've seen what happens to humans who're taken in with the fae that way. It doesn't often end well. I'm not sure, even if I *mean* well… It matters more to me to protect you than to take you as a lover. But Sylas can protect you better than I can, so he can probably manage both. I can't resent him—or you—for that."

A jumble of emotion fills my chest, confusion and longing and frustration and more that I can't easily label. "It's not as if I've married him or something. It was just one night." So far. I also can't say I wouldn't want another, given the chance. But I couldn't say that about August either. Argh.

I bring my hands to my face. "I like you a lot too, okay?" I go on, my voice partly muffled by my palms. "I don't think he's… better than you, or whatever. This is all just really overwhelming. I don't know how I'm supposed to act."

August's tone softens. "You're doing just fine. I really wasn't angry with you. If I was angry with anyone, it was myself—and I've dealt with that."

He reaches out to stroke his hand over my hair, and a quiver runs across my skin that's both eager and anxious. I want to kiss him, but I'm also terrified of screwing this whole thing up.

Maybe it's better if I don't get too intimate with any of the fae men while my future is still so uncertain. But that doesn't mean I can't allow myself a little closeness, does it?

I swallow hard and lower my hands. Then, carefully and deliberately, I shift my body over on the sofa so I can lean my head against August's shoulder.

He hesitates for a moment, and then he presses a whisper of a kiss to my forehead. His arm tucks around mine. A sense of peace I haven't experienced since Whitt first announced that Tristan was coming wraps around me with the warmth emanating from his side.

In this moment, being nestled against him feels perfectly *right*. This is all I need, and I don't want to risk it by experimenting with more.

"Do you want to keep playing, or are you chickening out in the face of my immense skills?" August asks, lightly teasing.

A smile crosses my lips. "No chickens here. Bring it on."

After a couple more losses, I manage to beat him at a level, bringing our points to a near tie. "Maybe I'm the one who should be worried," August jokes, nudging me with his elbow where I'm still leaning against him, and the door swings open.

Sylas looks in at us. For the first instant, he looks weary but contented, maybe expecting to find only August in here playing alone.

At the sight of me cuddled up to the other man, the fae lord's jaw clenches and his unscarred eye blazes like it did when I told him about August guiding me in the pool. He barrels into the room with an aggressive energy so potent it seems to lift the dark waves of his hair with a rising wind. His voice is little more than a growl. "I told you—"

He's looking at August, not at me, and August is already jerking away from me as if burned. Guilt stabs through me—and then something even sharper, a blaze of my own it takes me a second to recognize.

It's anger. I've forgotten what it's like to be angry myself.

"Stop it!" I snap. My voice squeaks, but the reprimand is firm enough that Sylas actually does halt in his tracks.

I catch August's hand and twine my fingers with his before meeting the fae lord's eyes again. "He wasn't hurting me. We were just sitting together. What's wrong with that?"

Sylas's gaze is still searing, but it's dampened from a full-out inferno to a more subdued smolder. "He did more than that with you before," he says.

"So what?" My pulse is rattling through my veins, so fast I'd almost think it's going to burst free of my body, but all of a sudden I am *so* angry. I'm not sure I've ever been quite this furious in my life. About the way Sylas is acting right now, about how he ordered me shut away for so many days before. About all this time waiting to find out whether I'm even going to have any kind of life beyond the next full moon. About all the moons that passed before I came here, while I was tortured and bled by the whims of the fae.

I've been terrified and anguished and despairing and grieving, but whatever anger started to rise up before, I must have bottled it away. Now it's overflowing, swelling through my chest and spilling from my mouth.

I cling onto the rush of power that reverberates through the anger. "You can force me to stay here and take my blood if you decide to, and I can't do anything about that. But I don't *belong* to you. I don't belong to either of you. So don't treat me like I'm a toy for you to fight over."

Sylas inhales slowly. The smolder retreats, although it'd be hard to say he looks *happy* about the situation. His shoulders come down too, his arms folding loosely over his chest. He eyes me for a moment as if waiting to see if anything else is going to burst out of me.

"That's fair," he says finally. "It wasn't my intention to treat you that callously, and I apologize. Your affections are yours to do with as you see fit. If this is your choice, I—"

A growl of my own escapes me, and he's so taken aback he shuts his mouth.

"I haven't made any choice," I say, more irritated than angry now. "I don't know if I'm *going* to make a choice. Like I said, we're just sitting together. I think that's about as much as I'm interested in for the time being. I'd be happy to sit with you too. There's plenty of room on the sofa. Why does it have to be such a big deal?"

August has been sitting rigid with tension through the whole conversation, but at that question, he gives my hand a gentle squeeze that soothes some of the terror that's coursing through me beneath the anger.

Sylas blinks, apparently lost for words. His gaze slides to the younger man and back to me. Then, to my enormous relief, the corner of his mouth twitches upward.

He lowers himself onto the sofa at my other side and gives my knee a light squeeze. "I suppose it doesn't."

"There. The world didn't end." Now that my fury is fading, I'm a bit dizzy from the sudden surge of emotion. And maybe also from being tucked between the two sexiest men I've ever met, the heat of their bodies enveloping mine.

I drag in a breath, composing myself. "Is there another controller? You've got to have at least one three-player game, right?"

August's grin comes back, wary and then widening. "I can scrounge something up." He glances at Sylas. "If you're not afraid of getting your ass whooped by a human girl."

Sylas glowers at him but without any real rancor. "I don't know about her, but you can count on being thoroughly whooped yourself."

"I accept that."

He gets up to switch games and comes back with a third controller. Sylas accepts it happily enough, and the tension in the room ebbs.

As the game starts up, I snuggle deeper between the two men, resting my feet against August's thigh, leaning my head on Sylas's shoulder. I don't know what's going to come out of any of this, but I'm struck by the sense that as long as this moment lasts, I'm exactly where I want to be.

26

Whitt

The berries burst between my teeth, their sweet-and-sour juice trickling down my throat and vibrating through my senses. I let the dizzying rush consume me, knowing from a multitude of experience that the initial tsunami of a high will temper into a milder exhilaration if I give myself over to it.

The stars that dot the night sky sparkle brighter. The three-quarters moon glows so starkly it burns my eyes. Music and buoyant voices surround me. I turn on my heel, ingesting it all like a decadent feast.

I don't ever lose myself for very long. I'm exorbitantly familiar with my limits and how to avoid crossing certain lines. But these fleeting moments when nothing exists but the glittering sensations of the present are the only times the constant tautness wound through my chest ever dissipates completely. Without them, I might find myself stretched so far I'd break right in half.

And that wouldn't do, now would it?

The dark thought signals the dwindling of the high. I exhale in a careless huff and return my attention to the business at hand. Because these revels are as much business as they are entertainment—for me, at least.

Brigit drifts closer to me, peachy smoke wafting snake-like from her lips. A stoned haze clouds her eyes. She offers me a lopsided smile as if she can't quite remember how to curve her mouth into the right shape and then giggles at herself.

"You've outdone yourself tonight, cadre-man," she says. "Such a celebration for the pack."

"Such a pack to celebrate," I return, the play on her words slipping glibly off my tongue. "I thought you deserved every pleasure we could afford after the work you all put into preparing for our visitors."

"Stuffy lordly ones," she mutters, and I immediately perk up to a sharper alertness I don't show. The first rule of success is to never be more than half as inebriated as you appear to be. Already I'm filing away the knowledge that Brigit is definitely not someone we should be including in any revels that include visiting lords or their cadres. If her tongue can slide into disrespect around me, it could around anyone.

But I was *hoping* to hear that disrespect from a few of my pack-fellows. I'll get the most truth from those bold enough to show their true feelings.

"Well, they didn't stay all that long," I say, carefully not approving of her choice of words while tacitly encouraging them.

"I'd say they wore out their welcome." She takes

another gulp of smoke from the spindly pipe she's holding and lets it stream from her arched nostrils. "Coming back around to poke at us."

I study her from the corner of my eye. No one else mentioned Tristan lingering, but after the show Sylas made of how important it was to give the intruders a spectacular welcome, it's no wonder they'd feel hesitant voicing any criticism. They may respect Sylas as their leader, but they have a healthy dose of apprehension mixed in as well, as it should be with any lord.

"All three of them?" I ask.

"Just that woman. Bad enough. Stares at everyone like she's considering how their heads would look mounted on pikes." Brigit's voice starts to slur. "I was just getting up to pick thistledew—you know it's best if you catch it just before dawn—and spotted her lurking by the outer homes, writing something on paper like she was making a report."

Perhaps that was exactly what Jax, the female cadre member Tristan brought with him, had been doing. It would have been beneath any lord, let alone one of Tristan's stature, to admit to an interest in the lives of the faded folk of our pack. Apparently he took one anyway and sent one of his cadre back to indulge it.

They were sly enough to escape the notice of our official sentries. If this ordinary pack woman hadn't been headed out for some pre-dawn dew-gathering, we would never have known that their concerns weren't fully resolved.

A prickle condenses in my gut through my light-headedness. What would Tristan have wanted Jax to look for? What did that bastard Kellan say that made them so concerned?

It wouldn't have mattered a month ago. A month ago we had nothing to hide. Now, we've just spent days covering up the presence of a girl who could solve the arch-lords' greatest problem. The longer Sylas lets this insanity go on, the worse it'll be for us if some small misstep reveals our secret.

Brigit's chosen mate weaves through the revelers to her side and plants a sloppy kiss on her cheek. From the dilation of his pupils, he's indulged at least as much as she has in the recreational substances on offer.

He casts his bleary gaze toward me. "I hope our lord will rest easy now that the visit is over."

I keep my voice light, even though that remark turns the prickle inside me into a deeper jab. "Lord Sylas wanted the best for our honored guests, but I'm sure he wasn't overly troubled."

The man hums. "So it should be. He did seem rather —" He cuts himself off, focusing more clearly on me for an instant and remembering I'm more than a fellow reveler.

Brigit sways in his arms. "Our lord has a lot on his mind these days."

They drift away, leaving me with a hole in the pit of my stomach that seems to drain away the lingering effects of the berries and the wine I drank before.

The folk of the pack have picked up on Sylas's distraction. He would never want to present anything to them but total assurance and attentiveness. The problem of the girl is affecting him more than he must realize.

We're lucky even this many have stuck with us so long —and none of us can pretend it's entirely out of loyalty. If the risks of staying under Sylas's rule began to appear greater than the risks of searching out a place in another pack, one better situated as well… We wouldn't have a mass exodus on our hands, but our numbers would dwindle more than they already have. And the fewer are left, the less secure our position becomes, as well as our chances of bettering it.

I laugh and eat and dance with a couple of the women, but all the while that knowledge stews inside me. When the revel peters out, some of the folk sprawling under the stars to sleep and others ambling away to their homes, I head back to the keep far more sober than anyone—least of all me—should ever have to be.

I need to speak to Sylas. When I make it clear how precarious our position may have gotten, he'll *have* to see he can't keep delaying the inevitable. Lovely as the mite is to look at, damaged though she may be through no fault of her own, at the same time she's a ticking bomb that could explode at any moment, taking all of us down with her.

I won't pretend not to see why he might hesitate. That moment after he felled Kellan when she crept to his side and offered her regrets, even after the way the bastard meant to savage her… The way she apologized to *me* after August stormed off on her…

A soft twinge passes through my chest, but I dismiss it as quickly as it rose up. She puts on a good show of honor and compassion, as if any being could really be that benevolent—and Sylas buys into it just like that. This despite the fact that her presence has caused more turmoil in and around this keep than we've faced since we were exiled here. Despite the fact that she has far less reason to consider our welfare than Kellan ever did.

It's hard to believe those gestures weren't actually strategic. How could she possibly truly care that much about any of us? Even Isleen—

I cut off that line of thinking with a jerk of my head and stalk onward. I don't have to convince our lord that the mite is playing to his sympathies. I only need him to see the bigger picture. Nothing and no one could make him shirk from his duty.

Sylas isn't in his study or his bed chamber—he isn't one to ignore an insistent knock. Frowning, I prowl through the main floor and then down to the basement.

A murmur of voices and the jangle of modern human music carries from the entertainment room. He must be watching one of those absurd movies.

The door stands a few inches ajar, so I can see into the room before I reach it. I jerk to a halt within arm's reach, my body stiffening.

I've approached quietly out of habit with the stealth it's my nature to fall into when I'm alert enough. None of the figures in the room have noted my arrival. They *are* watching a movie, the shifting lights of the screen playing across their faces in the semi-darkness: Sylas, August, and the human girl tucked between them.

Her eyes have closed, her features even more delicate in sleep. Her head is tipped against Sylas's shoulder, and his hand rests on her leg. By her other thigh, her fingers lie interlaced with August's. As I watch, he glances at her with unmistakeable tenderness.

When he shifts his attention to Sylas, his expression tightens. Our lord glowers in return, his thumb tracing a gentle line across the girl's knee.

What's left of my stomach balls into a knot. Before I'm aware of the motion, my jaw has clenched. I have to tense my legs against the urge to storm in there and demand to know whether they're out of their minds.

She's wormed her way even further into their affections than I suspected. *Both* of their affections. And whatever truce they've come to tonight, that look exchanged tells me it's far from settled. There will be a reckoning—there will be *several* reckonings, between them and within themselves.

August, I can understand. He's got a soft heart under all that muscle, especially for vulnerable things. But Sylas —by all that is dust, I thought he was wiser than this.

Neither of those facts justifies the rage boiling up inside me, the grating of my teeth against each other. Of course she would turn to both of them and not to me. The one who's buttered her up with his chumminess and his cooking, and the one who's protected her at the risk of everything else he holds dear. What have I done other than offer her a few wry remarks and a spectacular high? Oh, and a panic attack, let's not forget that.

That shouldn't be a problem. It *can't* be. I want nothing to do with her, this treasure of Sylas's. I learned my lesson far too well for that.

Yet against my will, my mind slips back to fragments of a dream a few nights back—of a slip of a girl dancing naked in starlight, her pink hair flying wild and her arms stretched out with the uninhibited joy she took to so easily when I gave her the cavaral syrup. Of her bright eyes gleaming with abandon… and then glowing with a more wanton vitality as she reached for me.

My fingers twitch. Would her skin feel as smooth, her body move as lithely against mine as it did in that delusion? Or would I rather have her crouched in my bedroom like the other morning, shaking and then unexpectedly shrewd—

Whirling, I yank my eyes away from the actual scene before me. I stalk back to the staircase, groping for my flask as I go. The first gulp—duskapple wine tonight— burns the edge off my frustration. The second clouds over the images I wanted to banish. The third brings me back to that glimmering plateau where my wits fly free of any hindrance of emotion but I haven't quite tipped over into unsteadiness. I stop there.

It's no good talking to Sylas. I can see that much. If he's already allowed himself to stake that much of a claim over the girl, there's nothing this situation can end in but an absolute mess, no matter how well I master my… curiosity, no matter that Kellan's no longer spurring the tensions onward. As long as she's with us, the fissures that were already forming will only widen.

As long as she's with us.

I pause in the hallway outside the kitchen, the fermented spirits fizzing through my veins. My gaze lifts to the door at the far end of the parlor.

Wouldn't our lives be so much simpler if she'd made her escape as she intended to a week ago?

What of it if we lose our "cure"? She could never have been a permanent solution anyway, as Sylas himself admitted. We're only delaying the inevitable. We are wolves—we're meant to be wild. Why shouldn't the rest of my folk accept that?

There are other ways we can win back the arch-lords' favor. Ways that won't mean fracturing the bonds between lord and cadre even more. Ways that won't require me to watch my brothers—

I shove off that thought and the memory of her striking, pink-haired head tucked between them. It *isn't* about me. I was weak once and nearly destroyed us myself. This time...

This time I can save us.

And to do that, the girl must go.

27

Talia

While I bathe in the pool, August keeps up a steady stream of seemingly aimless conversation, chatting about everything from human sports—it seems he's a football fan; big surprise—to what exercises I might try to strengthen the muscles around the warped part of my foot. I don't think his rambling straight from one subject to another really is so aimless, though. The aim is to avoid any mention of what happened between us here several days ago.

I'm okay with that. For a little while last night, everything seemed so simple and right. But it's been impossible not to notice throughout the day how the energy between August and Sylas has changed.

They haven't argued—they haven't said anything directly about their interest in me or mine in them at all—but there are pauses where there didn't used to be before, glances that give me the impression of sizing up rather than comradery.

I'd rather not fuel whatever tensions are lurking unspoken any more than I already have inadvertently. In the pool, I stay away from the jets, and when I get out, I dry off and pull my clothes back on quickly. August smiles at me as he emerges from behind the folding screen, but he leaves a few feet between us as we walk down the hall to the stairs.

In less than a week's time, I might have much bigger problems. I thought getting closer to the fae lord would make it harder for him to give me up, but with the way things are going, maybe he'll decide it's better for his cadre if he hands me over to the arch-lords and lets them work out how to best make use of my blood's inexplicable power. I'm sure he'll try to arrange things so that they'll treat me kindly, but he won't really have any say once I'm in their keeping, will he?

Every step I take here, every decision *I* make, feels so precarious. I can't even predict all the consequences that might ripple out from a single word or act.

I shrug off those worries as well as I can—nothing's happened *yet*, and I don't know what I could do right now that would definitely make my situation better rather than worse anyway—but it's hard to ignore them when we reach the top of the stairs to find Sylas waiting for us. Or rather, for me. He gives August a nod of acknowledgment with another of those brooding looks and waves the younger man off before turning to me.

"I'm still attempting to work out what's causing the

effect you have over our 'curse'," he says. "Would you allow me to take a few of your hairs to test?"

The request eases my nerves a little. My wellbeing matters enough to him that he's asking even when he could probably have snatched a few without my noticing. And he hasn't given up his search to find a way to free me from his people's needs.

"Of course." I swivel to offer him the full array of my hair, damp but not outright wet after the recent toweling. "I hope the dye won't interfere with testing it."

"I'll take that into account. Close to the root, there'll be an unaffected section. It's better that I waited until it had time to grow."

He plucks the hairs so deftly that I only feel the faintest twinge in my scalp, careful not to touch me otherwise. The nape of my neck still tingles with the awareness of him standing so close, his hands mere inches from my skin.

We walk up to the second floor together, my foot brace tap-tap-tapping against the floor since I can't keep up with him even at his slowed-down pace if I aim for silence. At the branch in the hall, Sylas brushes his fingers over my shoulder in the lightest of caresses and heads in the opposite direction, presumably to his study.

Even that brief touch sends a wash of heat through me. It's like I've been starved after all this time without the slightest affection, and now my body is ravenous for whatever contact I can get.

I'll just have to keep a close eye on myself until I have a better idea where I stand now—and how Sylas and August are going to work out their uneasiness.

In my bedroom, I curl up in the armchair August recently brought up and open a book I borrowed from the entertainment room in recollection of how much I wished I had reading material up here the evening of Tristan's visit. The sky beyond the window is darkening, but the amber orb mounted over the chair wakes up with its wavering glow. This is some kind of life, at least. It could be so much worse.

I've sunk deeper into the chair, my legs slung over one of its arms and my mind sucked well into the story, when my bedroom door swings open. My head snaps up with a flinch, my pulse skittering in alarm. Sylas and August always knock—unless maybe it's an emergency…

But it isn't either of the fae men who've come to my bedroom before. Whitt stalks inside, shutting the door behind him and coming to a halt halfway to my chair. His sun-kissed hair looks even more wildly ruffled than usual, his blue eyes stormy, his jaw firmly set. He's so fiercely stunning that my heart stutters again in both awe and fear.

I scramble to straighten myself, clutching the book tightly as if it'll defend me from whatever he's come to demand. "Is everything all right?"

He cocks his head and considers me. "You've proven yourself decently observant, mite, even when you shouldn't be observing. Do *you* really think everything is 'all right'?"

I blink at him, my stomach twisting even in my confusion. "I don't know what you're talking about."

"Oh, no? So it's truly escaped your notice that your two paramours aren't quite as at ease with each other as they used to be—as they're meant to be?"

My face flushes at the clear insinuation of the word "paramours" before I've even processed the rest. How does he know—did Sylas or August tell him what's happened between us? Has it been obvious without anyone needing to mention it?

How *much* does he know?

Enough to realize the tensions he's picked up on are my fault. I tuck my legs up, hugging my knees with the urge to shrink in on myself. "I didn't mean for anything like this to happen."

Whitt waves an erratic hand through the air. "Of course you didn't. Why would it even occur to you to consider it?"

"Have they been fighting about it when I'm not around?" How bad have things gotten?

"From the looks of them, it's only a matter of time. And believe me, you won't want to find yourself in the middle of *that* squabble."

I grip my knees harder. "I don't know what to do. I tried to tell them— I haven't let anything happen since I realized— Me being here has already caused so much trouble with all of you. The last thing I want is for them to be at each other's throats."

Whitt pauses, studying me with his scowl shifting into a frown that's more puzzled than foreboding. What reaction was he expecting?

Whatever threw him off, he recovers quickly. "There's an easy solution," he says, brusquer than before. "They're riled up over you, so we take you out of the equation."

My body stiffens. I knew this might happen, and still

— "Sylas is going to send me to the arch-lords now?" I ask, my voice thinning.

"No. I think you'll like this solution much better. You can head right back home."

This time I'm so startled I outright gape at him. "*Home?*"

He smiles, but it has none of August's warmth. "Yes, exactly. That's what you've wanted all along, isn't it?"

It is, but I didn't expect to have the opportunity handed to me like this by one of the cadre. I never anticipated getting an offer like this at all. It's a second before I can wrangle my words into order again. "You're saying Sylas would let me—"

"No," Whitt interrupts. "Sylas doesn't know about this. *I'm* arranging it. It'll be better for him and August— for all of us. Obviously it's better for you too. But you'll need to get on with it. Sylas is holed up in his study now, and August's taking out his frustrations on that long-suffering punching bag of his, but the window when they'll both be distracted is relatively short."

He wants me to go *right now*. My mouth opens and closes again. I ease my legs down, scanning his face for any hint that this is a trick or a trap. I wouldn't have thought Whitt would mess with my head like that—he's never seemed outright cruel—but I don't really know him.

"What—what about my blood? The cure? It's not much longer until the full moon."

"That won't be your problem anymore. This is your ticket out of the whole mess."

"But—" The twisting in my gut spreads through the

rest of my body. "It'll still be *your* problem. All of yours. If I'm gone, you won't have any way of making the tonic."

Whitt pauses again, the frenetic energy that appeared to have gripped him faltering. "Why should that matter to *you*?" he asks abruptly.

I guess that's a reasonable question. I give the best answer I can. "You rescued me from Aerik. Sylas has protected me—you've all been… kind." Well, maybe that's not the best word for Whitt's behavior. "You've been counting on me to help you in return."

And honestly, I want to. I wouldn't hesitate for an instant if there was a way I could help that didn't require me to remain a prisoner for the rest of my life.

What will Sylas think when he realizes I'm gone—that I've run off on him after all?

Whitt seems to be rolling over my explanation in his head. His fingers flex at his sides as if he's grasping for a response. He takes a slow breath, and then says, "Your freedom matters more than that, doesn't it? We'll make do. We always have before. We *won't* make do if having you around tears our cadre apart."

Maybe he's right. I don't know Sylas or August all that well either—I don't know how fae in general act when they're vying over a potential lover. Whitt would have a much better idea about the potential for disaster than I do, wouldn't he?

And he's offering me a way out that will help me too. How *can* I say no to my freedom?

I push myself to my feet, tensing my thighs so my legs don't wobble. A lump has risen in my throat, but I force my voice past it. "Okay. I can see that. But the magic on the doors—and I don't know where to go even once I'm out…"

Whitt nods, his expression relaxing. "Go now. I've left the parlor door unlocked for you. Walk straight ahead from there across the fields and through the woods. You'll know you've reached the very edge of the Mists when the actual mist thickens. Watch for a thicker patch—by twilight, it'll look like a puddle turned sideways, deeper and darker, almost liquid. Walk through that, and you'll be back where you belong."

This is happening so fast, my head is spinning. I don't like running out on Sylas or August, but would *they* let me go like this? I can't imagine it.

But if I exist, then there have to be other cures out there somewhere, right? They'll find another way, and I won't stir up any more animosity between the two of them.

"Okay," I say, psyching myself up. "Okay." I raise my head to meet Whitt's gaze as directly as I can, letting all the gratitude in me color my voice. "I'm sorry for—for all the trouble I've already brought down on you. Thank you for this. And thank Sylas and August for me too, when they realize—tell them I know they tried to do right by me, and I really was happy here some of the time."

Whitt stares at me for a long moment. Has his face paled? Maybe he's thinking forward to when the others discover my disappearance and how they'll react. I can't imagine they'll be pleased, even if it's for the best.

"Yes," he says. The word comes out strained. He clears his throat and goes on. "Yes, I'll do that. Go on now. If we're lucky, they won't notice you're missing until morning when you'll be well away from here."

I nod. He steps into the hall ahead of me, checking that the coast is clear, and motions me out.

"It's for the best," he mutters, so low I'm not sure whether he's talking to me or to himself. "It's all for the best."

And that's why I have to do this. I hustle down the hall, setting down my foot in its brace as lightly as I can manage without sacrificing too much speed. Whitt meanders off toward his room.

Down the stairs, through the kitchen, my heart thumps faster. I'm still half-expecting to find out this is some hugely elaborate joke.

It isn't. The handle on the parlor door turns smoothly in my hand. I push the door open.

A light wind tickles over me. The long sprawl of the field lies ahead, the forest thick with shadow beyond it. My legs momentarily lock. Then I propel myself forward with a sharper skip of my pulse.

For the first time in more than nine years, I emerge into the outside world. The scents of hay and wildflowers that lace the warm evening air are familiar from the breezes that've carried through my bedroom window. They fill my lungs more swiftly out here, though, wrapping around me, teasing through my clothes and hair.

It's overwhelming to the point of dizzying me, but I can't let myself linger. As long as I'm in view of the keep and the pack's houses, someone could spot me and raise an alarm. Training my gaze on the dark stretch of the forest, I hurry toward it as fast as my limp allows, worrying less about stealth on the soft grass that muffles most of the sound of the brace.

I'm going home. I'm really going *home*. Whatever that might look like after all these years. A giddy tremor shoots through me. I can't tell whether I'm excited or petrified.

Once I've slipped between the trees, the tension in my chest loosens a little. The air licks cooler over my skin but stays warm enough that I don't regret my tee's short sleeves. I pick my way across the uneven terrain more carefully now, squinting through the dimness as I watch for rocks and jutting roots on the forest floor.

How far is it until I reach the edge of the Mists? Will I find it in the forest or somewhere on the other side?

I should have asked Whitt more questions. But he sent me off so urgently… He must have been concerned I wouldn't get another chance—or that even one more night with me around would push Sylas and August into a fight they couldn't come back from.

I won't think about how disappointed or worried or—being realistic—*angry* Sylas will be when he notices my empty room. I won't think about all the uncertainties that await in the world I was stolen from. Better not to think at all.

Just keep walking. Just keep going forward, and somehow this insane scenario will sort itself out. It has to.

An ache starts to creep through my warped foot despite the brace. It wasn't meant to support me on a hike through the wilderness. But ahead of me, through the twilight, I can see the trees are thinning. Strands of mist trail around them, glowing in the moonlight.

My spirits leap. I'm almost there.

I take several hasty steps and stub my toe on a fallen branch. As I catch myself against a tree trunk, hissing at the pain, a rustling sound from somewhere to my right makes me freeze. I hold totally still, listening, straining to see through the thickening darkness.

Nothing moves in my view. It must have been a deer or a squirrel or some faerie equivalent.

I move to keep walking, and a figure materializes out of the shadows just a few yards away.

A long hooded cloak covers her from head to knee, but I can make out enough of her face to know she's a stranger. Heavy-lidded eyes skim over me as an amused smile curves full lips.

"Well, well," she says, and with a jolt, I realize she's not a *complete* stranger. It's the female voice I heard carrying from the dining room two nights ago—the woman from Tristan's cadre.

She stalks a few steps closer with predatory grace, her lips pulling back to reveal her gleaming teeth. "Where do you think you're going so far from your master, little human runaway?"

28

Sylas

The tincture I drip onto the root end of Talia's hair shows no reaction whatsoever—not a hiss or a gleam or even a wobble. I lean back in my chair with a growl of frustration.

There's magic in her somewhere—there has to be. So why does the source and nature of it elude every attempt I make to understand it?

Humans aren't meant to possess magic at all, and I've seen no indication that she's anything other than human besides the effect of her blood during the full moon. Whatever causes it, it must be with her at all other times as well. If Aerik discovered some spell that would bring out that power in any human's blood on command, he wouldn't have needed this particular human so badly.

My sense of the waxing moon beyond the keep weighs on me. It's merely days now before the full moon is on us again. I may find a few other tactics to use, but those will be last-ditch efforts rather than anything I believe has a solid chance of unraveling this mystery.

At some point, sooner rather than later, I'm going to have to accept that I *won't* unravel this mystery before the wildness takes us again. I've let myself hold off on making any broader decisions while hoping my tests would reveal answers that would guide me, but that hardly seems likely now.

None of my possible solutions will let my conscience rest easy. If I offer Talia to the arch-lords as the solution to our curse, I betray a woman I've come to care about more deeply than I'd willingly admit even to my cadre—a woman who's earned that affection with the strength and generosity she shows at every turn. By handing her over, I might fracture my cadre as well, knowing how August feels about her.

Even forcing her to give up her blood to myself and my pack would be betraying the trust she's put in me, and I doubt word could fail to reach Aerik that somehow only my pack resisted the wildness during the first full moon after his treasure was stolen. As soon as he's aware we stole her, we'll have a battle on our hands, one that could ravage those who've stood by me and depend on me.

And if I require nothing of Talia at all, I betray all those folk—I fail the pack I've sworn to serve and shield in every way I can. They deserve my loyalty above all others.

Will I run more of my tests and grasp at straws for weeks longer until some misstep gives us away after all, and instead of being celebrated, we're reviled for withholding the "cure" from the rest of our Seelie brethren?

No, there are no good answers at all. And I have seen the consequences that can come when I fail to tackle an uncomfortable situation head on. My pack has paid for my reluctance once before in spades.

That acknowledgment provokes a resolve that stabs through me as brutal as a blunt dagger, but I can't avoid the realization as much as it pains me. I must bring Talia to the arch-lords. For my pack, for my people, I cannot let my selfish desires undermine my responsibilities to those I rule over.

There's no more time for dallying. If I'm going to make proper arrangements to ensure the transition will be as safe as possible, to fulfill my promises to her as well as I can, I need to begin now. I can still do *some* right by her, even if not as much as I'd wish to.

With a heavy heart, I stand up and head into the hall.

She deserves to know my decision. She deserves to be heard, to be given a chance to speak, even if I can't imagine what she could say that would sway the balance. She's surprised me more than once before, after all. I'll tell her she has a few days to prepare to leave and that I'll see to it she finds herself in the care of the arch-lord most benevolent to humankind. With the strength and tenacity she's shown, who's to say she won't carve out a *better* place for herself there?

And I'll back off on any attempt to claim her. If she and August should wish to seek each other out in those remaining days, they can proceed without fear of reprisal.

By the Heart, let that be enough.

As I walk to Talia's bedroom, the burning sensation in my chest doesn't fade. Even my final act of charity digs into me like a wound. Last night, I meant to claim her for myself for as long as I could have her with me. And she refused to be claimed at all—by myself or by August.

I want her. She wanted me. I'm not used to contending with the possibility that a potential lover might want another man as well, let alone one of my cadre-chosen. But I doubt she'll have much affection left for me after our conversation tonight. She'll be better off with him in what time they have, if she wishes it. Even if the thought stirs a denial in me so furious it sears through my ribs.

How ridiculous is it to be worrying over that when I'll be quite literally casting her to the wolves in a few days' time?

I steel myself and knock on her door.

No answer comes, not even the sound of movement from the other side. I knock again, listening closely. Even if she has fallen deeply enough asleep that she wouldn't rouse at the rapping on the door, my sharp ears will make out her breathing.

They don't. There's no indication of any living being in the room beyond.

Frowning, I ease the door open. It's as empty as it sounded. The only sign of Talia's presence is the book lying haphazardly on the seat of the armchair by the window.

The moment my gaze catches on it, an afterimage floats through my vision from my dead eye: Talia sitting up with a jolt of her spine, her mouth tensing, her eyes startled and... sad? The book falls from her hand to the cushion—and then I'm seeing only the chair before me again, that fragment of what I have to assume was the recent past vanishing.

My hand tightens on the side of the door. Why would she have looked upset just now? What drew her from her reading and her room?

There could be a perfectly simple explanation. It might be as innocuous as that the book reminded her of some uncomfortable event in her own life, and she went to find another activity to distract herself. But as I stride down the hall, a thread of uneasiness weaves through my gut.

Both the shared lavatory and the privy are vacant. Talia isn't in the kitchen, the dining room, or the entrance room, but those weren't likely possibilities at this time of night anyway.

I barrel down the stairs to the basement, checking the entertainment room, the sauna, and then heading toward the gym. She could have gone to August before I even gave my blessings—

No. August emerges before I've reached the room, rubbing his dampened hair with a towel, his face flushed from the exertion he's just put his body through. The wary look he gives me sets my teeth on edge, as annoyed with myself as with him. He is my brother-by-father, my cadre-chosen—it isn't right that he should mistrust me.

But that is a hurdle we'll need to overcome another day.

"Has Talia been down here?" I ask.

His wariness falls away behind a flash of concern. "I haven't seen her, not since she went upstairs with you."

By all that is dust, that's not the answer I wished to hear. "She headed to her room, but she isn't there now.

Nor any of the other places I might have expected. I haven't checked *every* room in the building yet, though."

Perhaps she's gone to one of our bed chambers. I've already covered the lower two floors thoroughly.

We lope to the upper floor together, veering in separate directions at the split in the hall without needing to consult one another. All of the bed chambers are empty other than Whitt's. As I come up on his door, his voice carries through it in a dull mumble. "…the best."

Is he talking to Talia? The idea that she's in his chamber with him—for what purpose?—sparks a clash of relief and possessiveness. I shove the door open.

She isn't with him, though. Whitt sits slumped against the footboard of his bed alone, his head tipped back as he drains the dregs from a goblet. A large bottle of absinthe sits beside him, only a thin ring left in the bottom. Its heady, sour scent fills the room.

Has he gone through that entire thing tonight? It's not like my older half-brother to get drunk to the point of stinking, especially on his own.

As he glances up at me, the swaying of his torso while he repositions himself not giving me much confidence that he'll be any help at all, I rein in my annoyance. He couldn't have known we might need him.

"Looking awfully serious, li'l brother," he slurs. "Have some of this to ease your spirits." He waggles the bottle in my direction and then focuses blearily on it, his face falling as he must realize there's none left to share.

Skies above, I can't remember the last time I saw him so inebriated he couldn't even talk straight. He hasn't been far gone enough to call me "little brother" rather than "my lord" or at least "Sylas" since I took Hearthshire. What's gotten into him?

I don't have time to try to shake him out of it. "Have you seen Talia?" I ask.

His gaze sharpens then, the haze clearing for an instant. His mouth forms a grimace, and he sets the bottle down with a thump. "Why would I have?"

August comes up beside me, his unusually grim expression giving away the bad news before he speaks. "There's no sign of her anywhere."

I exhale slowly, willing the turmoil inside me to settle. She couldn't have left the keep. I set the spells on the doors myself before I came upstairs with her. I didn't even think I *needed* them after she decided to stay rather than go through with her first escape attempt.

"Maybe we've just missed her," I say. "Let's go through the keep from top to bottom together. Call her name as well as looking into each room. She'll be here somewhere. You take the rooms to the left, and I'll take the right."

August nods without a moment's hesitation. Whatever tensions had risen between us, they've fallen away now that we face a shared concern. I can't forget that he earned his spot as a trusted member of my cadre.

As I turn from the doorway, Whitt lurches to his feet. From his bedroom doorway, he watches us begin our sweep. The ruddiness of intoxication still colors his face and neck, and his gaze veers at odd moments, but he's holding himself up steadily enough.

He wouldn't be a trusted member of my cadre if I didn't know he's rarely as soused as he lets himself appear to be.

"You lost the mite?" he says, and chuckles hoarsely. "One slip of a human girl giving two big bad fae quite the run-around."

I don't need his snarky remarks. "Help us look, or keep quiet," I bark at him.

We head downstairs, and he shuffles after us, seemingly more out of curiosity than with any intention of assisting.

"Did you check the pantry?" August asks. When I shake my head, hope lights his face. I head into the kitchen after him, scanning the space between the counters and the islands, the chairs in the parlor—

My deadened eye prickles. A ghostly figure swims into my vision. The specter of Talia grasps the back door, her expression so miserable it makes my throat constrict. She tugs, and it opens.

I stop in my tracks, staring, but the image is gone. It can't be from her first escape attempt—she was at the front door then. And how can I imagine it's from some future moment when she's missing right now?

My voice comes out rough. "She isn't in the pantry, is she?"

August emerges, the hope that kindled in him faded but not gone. "No. There's still a lot more—"

I cut him off. "She's gone. Out that door." I stride up to it and can sense before I even reach it that the magic in the lock has dispersed.

Nothing moves on the starlit field beyond the windows. How long ago did she take flight?

August sucks in a startled breath. "How? I swear she didn't have salt this time."

"I know." He gave me his word when I laid into him over that indiscretion before, and I have enough faith in him that I wouldn't have asked. "She must have discovered some other trick. Maybe her blood gave her the ability to crack the spell." Who can say when I can't discern the slightest thing about how that power of hers works?

"But—*why*?"

The same question twisting through my thoughts. The immediate impression may be gone, but the memory of the filmy image of her, of the misery on her face, has etched itself in my memory.

She didn't even look as if she wanted to leave. Why now? She couldn't have known what I was going to say to her tonight. What changed since she told me she felt safest by my side?

That question has barely crossed my mind before the obvious answer strikes me. I felt her gaze on me every time August and I interacted over the past day. I know she was taking in the friction between us. And she made it quite clear how she felt about any show of animosity to stake a claim over her.

"Perhaps she no longer felt secure while there was tension between us over her affections," I say. "She'll have picked up on it, as much as we held it back. She's a sensitive one."

August pales. "That would be just like her, wouldn't it? To leave because she didn't want to cause problems for *us*?"

My hands clench at my sides. I resist the urge to drive one of them into the wretched door that released her. "I should have heeded what she said last night more. She couldn't have been clearer that any aggression to compete for her favor made her uncomfortable."

Whitt coughs where he's leaning against one of the islands. I'd almost forgotten he'd trailed in behind us. His forehead has furrowed. "She told you *not* to fight over her?"

August lets out a laugh, short and humorless. "She put us right in our places. But I didn't think— We've kept the peace, even if we can't completely control our feelings. What could have pushed her to this point so quickly?"

Whitt glances from one of us to the other, looking rather green all of a sudden. I'm about to shove a bowl in front of him in case he's about to vomit all that absinthe up when he appears to shake the queasiness off. "It's better for her in the long run if she's rid of us, isn't it? Puts us in a bit of a bind to be sure, but we've managed in the past well enough. She wanted to get home."

My gaze travels back to the window. Another memory hits me—an observation that unsettled me at the time and now chills me straight through to the bones.

"*If* she makes it out of the Mists. If she's not caught by folk worse than us. I saw evidence of trespass in the woods during my evening run. Someone's been lurking in our domain." I march forward, jerking my hand for my cadre to follow. "We have to go after her and hope we find her before our enemies do."

In Whitt's current state, I'm not sure he'll come, but he hustles out alongside August, his eyes clearing with a gleam that looks almost frantic. "They wouldn't dare—to attack what could be one of our servants in our domain…"

"Are you sure enough of that to gamble on it? We went right into another lord's *home* to steal her in the first place, didn't we?"

He doesn't speak again—and then none of us can, because we've released our wolves. We all know we'll cover ground much faster in lupine form.

We sprint toward the forest at the fastest pace we're capable of on all fours, knowing we'll have to slow as soon as we reach the trees. I drag the cooling summer air into my lungs, tasting every breath for a trace of her scent, training my ears to pick up whatever sounds they can over the thump of our paws. As we pass between the trees, we slow to a trot that won't throw us headlong into a stump or boulder, but I keep going as quickly as I dare.

There—a scuff in the dirt with her smell and the imprint of the bottom of her brace. She made it this far unhindered. I run onward.

I could lose her—I could lose all the hopes I had for my pack. If this goes wrong, I will have failed everyone, and I'll have no one to blame but myself. I delayed too long in my selfishness when I should have taken decisive action.

If we find her, I can't let this incident become another excuse. I have to do what's right, as hard as it may be. I have to be the lord my pack put their faith in.

I push myself faster still, the brush scraping at my shoulders and haunches. And then a sound reaches my ears that makes my blood run cold: a cry of fear, so faint in the distance I don't know if we can possibly reach its source in time.

29

Talia

The woman from Tristan's cadre draws a dagger from a sheath at her hip. She stays where she is, braced to spring, her dark eyes fixed on me. "I asked you, where are you going?"

My whole body has frozen, including my vocal cords. I'm not remotely prepared for a fight. I have no weapons, nowhere to take shelter. There's no sign of any of those thicker patches Whitt mentioned that should lead me to the human world—and even if I found one, I wouldn't be surprised if this fae woman followed me through to continue her interrogation.

My gaze focuses in on the gleam of the moonlight catching on her dagger. Bronze. One of my last conversations with August wavers up from my memories —true names and the magic that comes with them.

I don't know if there's a hope of working magic, but it might have happened once before, and I haven't got anything better. *Fee-doom-ace-own*, I repeat in my head. *Fee-doom-ace-own*. Like a mantra, like a shield.

"I'm taking a walk," I say aloud. For once, despite my fear, my voice comes out clearly—not booming by any means, but more than a whisper. My heart is thudding, panic twisting through my veins, but holding me steady against the terror is that new emotion I've discovered. I'm scared, but I'm also *angry*.

Every faerie in this realm seems to think they have the right to demand things from me and order me around, if not outright torment me, even this woman I've never met face-to-face before. If I don't belong to Sylas, I sure as hell don't belong to her.

"A walk so far from home?" the woman says, spinning the dagger between her fingers. "Does your master know you've come all this way?"

"Of course he does. He told me to come." There are other stories I could spin, lies I could tell, but I stop there. I don't know what magic *she* might cast on me, what secrets she might force me to reveal, but I suspect the less I say, the better. What I have told her could even be presented as true if I count Whitt as one of my "masters."

"Somehow, having watched you for a while, I doubt that." Her eyes narrow. "And what have they done with your hair? That can't be its true shade."

"They thought I looked nicer this way."

"And for all they care about prettying you up, they didn't allow you to make any appearance during our recent visit to your keep." She cocks her head, her grip on the dagger tightening. "I think there's more to this than you're saying, but that's easily fixed. I think you'll find that if you don't volunteer the truth, I can cut it out of you quickly enough."

A deeper shiver runs through me. Panic is gaining ground over the solid foundation of my anger. It's a struggle to get my next sentence out. "I don't think Sylas would appreciate that."

"Oh, he'll have to understand when I explain how uncooperative you were."

Without any more warning than that, she launches herself at me, snatching at my wrist and yanking me toward her and her blade. The painful jolt through my arm shocks a yelp from my throat.

I kick out instinctively, and the foot brace gives me one small advantage. The wooden slats smack into her shin harder than my foot could have on its own, throwing her off balance. As I try to wrench away from her, I stumble, and we both topple over.

The fae woman throws herself onto me a second later, pinning my arms, her knife flashing toward my neck. A snarl reverberates from her chest. At the same moment, the syllables spill from my lips in a ragged gasp. "*Fee-doom-ace-own.*"

The dagger slams down toward me and droops as if melting. When it hits my shoulder—she wasn't trying to kill me after all, only wound me into submission—the sharp tip has folded in on itself into a blunt end that jabs me hard enough to bruise but doesn't slice into my flesh.

The fae woman spits out a curse and yanks her dagger back to stare at the collapsed blade. I stare at it too, my pulse skittering, hardly able to wrap my head around the fact that *I* did that.

I don't think even my attacker realizes that. Why would she even imagine I could have when it's supposedly impossible for a human to use fae magic? I said the true name so raggedly she might not have heard it at all over her snarl.

She mutters a few more curses aimed specifically at Sylas and tosses the apparently useless weapon away before glowering at me. "What protective charms has he put on you? Why is he so concerned about one feeble human girl?"

"I—I don't know," I stammer. Squashed beneath her, I can't fend off the panic anymore. It floods my mind and stiffens my body. If I could just grab the ruined dagger myself—or a stick—something— But I can hardly breathe, my lungs closing in on themselves.

"One more answer I'll have to discover for myself," she snaps, and flicks her wolfish claws free from her fingertips.

The immediate surge of fear sends a sharp enough spike of adrenaline through me to break me from the vise of panic. I flail out with another cry, so abruptly and wildly I must take her by surprise. My knee slams into her gut. She reels backward with a wince, and I shove myself out from under her. Where's the dagger? I have nothing, nothing but a word that can't do a thing against her claws or fangs, or her magic if she turns to that instead—

Recovering in an instant, the fae woman hurls herself at me again—and a massive, furred shape charges out of the shadows with a roar.

The wolf rams into my attacker, sending her rolling across the forest floor. She shifts as she spins and leaps onto her feet in her own wolfish form. My rescuer is already leaping at her, fangs bared, eyes glinting with fury —one dark, one scarred through and ghostly white.

My pulse stutters, grateful for Sylas's arrival but also terrified of how he'll react once he turns his attention on me. I fled; I abandoned him and his pack. He might be furious with me too.

Watching the immense beasts tussle and growl in the darkness sends me spiraling back to the night Aerik and his cadre found me—to the slashing of claws and the splatter of blood...

Another wolfish form bursts from the depths of the forest to join the fight. The pale wolf of the fae woman wheels, bringing her dangerously close to where I'm sprawled.

A sound like a whine seeps from my clenched throat. I try to scramble backward, my fingers fumbling against the dry earth, and strong arms grasp me from behind.

I've lost so much of my breath that what would have been a scream comes out as only a squeak. But then the hands that have grabbed me tug me partway around, and I catch a glimpse of Whitt's face, his ocean-blue eyes focused on the skirmish beyond me.

He pulls me with him a few feet back through the trees, putting the broad trunk of an oak between us and the fighting. Then he tucks me close against his chest. I gulp for air, feeling like a fish tossed into the open air of a beach.

It should be fine. Sylas could probably have overpowered that woman on his own, and now it's two against one. But all I can see now, flooding my mind and drowning me in terror, is Jamie's body the way it lay mangled on the grass the last time I saw him under trees like these, the vicious paw cracking open his skull, the teeth flecked with scarlet—

My fault. And Mom and Dad and— They came after me. It was all my fault.

Whitt's voice penetrates the icy fog in my head, his breath coursing over my forehead. "I've got you. Sylas and August can take her. You're safe now."

My cheek is pressed against his shoulder. His scent washes over me, warmer than I would have expected, like sun-baked sand tossed by the summer wind. Between that and his melodic voice, the suffocating sensation begins to ease.

I manage to drag in a breath, catching a strong alcoholic tang as I do. Either he was drinking quite a lot before he showed up here, or he spilled a sizeable portion on his shirt.

As the muddle in my head clears, confusion creeps in. This doesn't make any sense. I thought he wanted me gone. He could be hauling me off to one of those passages to the human world right now while Sylas is distracted.

Instead, he's hugging me to him so tightly you'd think he's afraid to let me go.

"There," he says. "That's better."

Is it? I twist my head to see as much of his face as I can. "Why are you protecting me?" I say, my voice still wobbly. "Shouldn't you be telling me to get going?"

He gazes down at me as if it's taking him a moment to remember who I am. Then he makes a sound somewhere between a laugh and a huff. "It's become clear I owe better to my brothers."

He's looking after me for their benefit? That makes even less sense. "You said they'd be better off if I left."

His head lists to one side. He's definitely not totally sober. "They refused to accept as much. And perhaps, having now experienced your absence, I've drawn new conclusions."

"I kind of wish you'd figured that out before I nearly got mauled," I can't help saying.

Whitt snorts. "My apologies," he says, in a tone that's not apologetic at all. He pauses, and his arms adjust around me, his nose grazing the top of my head. When he speaks again, his voice has softened. "I *am* sorry for the way I talked to you. And not just because of the distress it caused those two. I was... I was mistaken. We all gain something from your presence. Please, stay."

As if I could go anywhere right now while I'm gathered in his embrace. But there's an actual pleading note to those last two words, like he really means them, for himself as well as his brothers. I don't know what to make of that, and before I need to, he's straightening up, helping me stand with him.

Sylas and August are tramping over to join us, back in human-esque form. Blood seeps along Sylas's jaw from a thin scratch mark, and teeth marks stand out against August's forearm, but those appear to be their worst injuries.

"Are you all right?" Sylas asks the moment our eyes meet.

"Just shaken up," I say. "She hadn't managed to actually hurt me yet, just scare me."

He glances over my head to Whitt as if needing

secondary confirmation, and his shoulders relax incrementally. "That's one relief. She can't know what you are—what powers you hold—if she hasn't drawn your blood to smell or taste it."

"Are you saying you let her *get away*?" Whitt says, so incredulous it's as much a compliment to their skill as a complaint.

August grimaces. "She was fast, I'll give her that. Tristan wouldn't have picked wimps for cadre, would he?"

"We had to moderate ourselves so as not to damage *her* more than could be seen as warranted in trying to force a yield," Sylas adds. "She could obviously tell the odds weren't in her favor. The first chance she got, she was off like a shot."

"Does it matter if she didn't yield as long as she's gone?" I ask.

Sylas swipes his hand across his jaw and eyes the streak of blood on his palm as if it's no more concerning than a smear of paint. "If she'd yielded, I could have required that she not speak of you or what went on here again. I could have formally banned her from our domain. As it is, she's faced no consequences, and she can tell her lord whatever she likes." His eyes fix on me again. "Did she say anything to you before she attacked?"

I grope to remember what happened before the real chaos began. "She wanted to know where I was going— whether you'd sent me out here." My muscles tense up again at the thought of just how far I've gone *against* what Sylas would have wanted, and I hurry onward. "And she thought it was strange that my hair was dyed and that she hadn't seen me when they visited. I didn't say much to her. I don't think I mentioned anything that would have given the truth away. That was why she attacked me—because I wasn't cooperating as much as she wanted."

"Then she's only left with whatever suspicions she and Tristan must already have had for him to have tasked her with patrolling our domain." Sylas frowns. "I still don't like that she was here at all or that she encountered you." He peers down at me, his gaze abruptly twice as intent. "Why *are* you out here? How did you even get out of the keep?"

Behind me, his hand still resting against my back, Whitt stiffens. I hesitate. I could say he told me to go and opened the way, but that'll only stir up even more conflict between Sylas and his cadre, won't it? Whitt didn't force me to leave. I made that decision on my own, and I can take responsibility for it.

"I—I was worried about how upset the two of you seemed to be with each other because of me," I say, tucking my arms around my chest to hug myself. "It seemed like I was making things worse for you, not better. I found the door unlocked—I realized I could just leave— it seemed like the right thing at the time."

I can't see Whitt's reaction to my partial lie, but Sylas's makes my heart ache. He lowers his gaze, his mouth twisting. "I'd like to think my cadre and I are made of stronger stuff than could be broken that easily," he says. "And it shames me that it would have appeared otherwise to you. Whatever tensions arise between us, those are our duty to manage, not yours."

"Okay." The breeze licks over my shoulders, cooler

with the deepening night. "I'm sorry. I should have talked to you first. I didn't know that woman would be out here."

"I can't blame you for taking the opportunity that presented itself." Sylas squares his shoulders. "Are you ready to return to the keep?"

Not "Do you want to" or "Are you willing to"? Just a given that I will go back. Because their rescue was never just about defending me as a person but protecting the power my blood represents as well.

August makes a soft sound of consternation, but the thought of him arguing on my behalf sends a different sort of ache through me. Even if I was sure I'd be better off in the human world, which I'm not, I can't fight or outrun Sylas. If I was leaving to avoid drawing them into an even greater conflict, then I can return for the same reason.

"Yes," I say, raising my head as if it was completely my decision. "Let's go."

30

August

When Talia doesn't join me in the kitchen at the typical breakfast-making time, I take a detour upstairs to stand outside her door. I don't knock, not wanting to wake her, but the whisper of her breath reassures me that she *is* still here.

But is this really where she should be?

Normally I get so wrapped up in the bustle of meal preparation that just about everything else falls away. Today, that question keeps nagging at me. I crack an egg too hard and have to fish bits of turquoise shell out of the bowl. I fold the pastry dough so vigorously it turns stiff in my hands and I have to start over again. Before I can ruin anything else, I go off in search of Sylas.

We'll all survive a slightly late breakfast. I'd like to be sure Talia's going to survive the next week, and in a state I can sit easy with.

A quick prowl and traces of scent lead me to the

orchard. The summer heat is already expanding over the fields, the potent rays of the rising sun baking the leaves on the fruit trees. As I venture between them, their dry, green smell fills my nose.

Sylas is standing under a duskapple tree, his hand on the trunk, his gaze scanning the branches. This one and a couple of its neighbors developed patches of sickliness over the past few months. Baking with their fruits might be my area of expertise, but the magic of all types of plants comes most naturally to our lord. They've started to thrive again with his coaxing.

He turns at the sound of my footsteps, regarding me with typical composure. It's easy for him to criticize me for getting riled up when keeping a rein on his fiercer emotions seems to come naturally to him too. Does that pale eye of his tell him what I'm here to talk about before I've even opened my mouth?

Or maybe he knows me well enough not to need any Mist-borne awareness to figure it out. My half-brother has been a constant presence from the moment of my birth. He remembers more of my life than *I* do.

"Come to harvest some fruit?" he asks in a tone that suggests he does already know the answer.

Might as well get straight to the point. I sniff the air to confirm there's no one else nearby and then meet his gaze head on even though the deferential part of me wants to dip my head in recognition of his authority. I pitch my voice low. "I want to talk about Talia."

Sylas's jaw tenses. He steps away from the tree, letting his hand fall to his side. With one word, the breeze ripples around us, and I know he's persuaded the air to muffle our conversation as an extra precaution.

He returns his attention to me. "What's there to talk about?"

He thinks he can still sidestep the issue, does he? A prickle of frustration wears at my sense of respect. This kind of evasion isn't like the brother who guided so much of my upbringing or the lord I swore to serve—at least, I don't want to believe it's like him. The loss of our former domain and the shattering of his mate-bond and his pack have taken their toll, possibly to a greater extent than I've seen.

I keep my stance firm. "We brought her back last night. You didn't even give her the option of continuing on to make her way home. It's almost the full moon. What are we going to do with her?"

Sylas sighs. My heart starts to sink, preparing for him to dodge the subject even more blatantly, but instead he says, "What do you think, August? It isn't really a choice even for us, especially now that we have Tristan's cadre sniffing around more than they should. We must turn her over to the arch-lords."

I wanted a straight answer, but now that I have it, everything in me resists. "We *can't*. They might throw her into a cage no better than the one Aerik shut her away in. They won't care about anything but keeping her alive enough so they can harvest her blood."

"Skies above, don't let yourself ever talk about them so carelessly in anyone else's company." Sylas frowns. He isn't happy with the decision, but that doesn't change the fact that he's made it. "You think too little of our overlords.

Celia isn't known for unnecessary violence, and Donovan has some kindness for humans—his servants have always been well-treated when I've visited his domain. I intend to approach him, to see that she goes into his care."

"But none of them will see her as worthy of having an actual *life*, not when she's the answer to this unsolvable problem all our kin are facing. And if they let Ambrose take the lead regardless…"

Tristan's second-cousin has never made a secret of his disdain for all things mortal. He might lack Kellan's concentrated hostility, but I saw plenty of casual cruelty when we were held in high enough esteem to call on the arch courts.

He'll probably *insist* on taking lead when he finds out it's us offering up this gift. He was the one who spoke the most harshly against Sylas when the judgment was laid down. *Not surprising*, Whitt said at the time. *Those who usurp their way to a throne are always the most offended by any whiff of treason from anyone else.*

"Do you think I wouldn't send her off to live in peace in her own world if I could?" Sylas demands. "She lost that chance the moment Aerik tasted her blood. Even if we returned her and gave up what she offers us, how long would it take before he tracked her down again and she was even worse off than before? He found her once without even meaning to. You know he'll never give up."

I do, and the knowledge angers me more than the pronouncement Sylas made. But Sylas is the one in front of me—Sylas is the only one I can argue with.

"Then we keep her here where she's protected and we figure out the rest from there."

"I can't see any way to protect our *pack* and keep word from getting back to the arch-lords—and she'll be treated much more harshly if she's taken through force."

"Then we don't use her at all. Whatever caused this curse, it's ours to bear, not hers. She deserves better."

"We can't *offer* any better." Sylas motions for me to head back toward the keep. "Enough, August. You've said your piece. I've made my decision, and believe me, I wasn't hasty in it."

I should stand down. The instincts honed through decades of service wrench at me. But this once, something stronger holds me in place: the memory of Talia's mouth against mine, her taste on my lips, her body both delicate and unimaginably strong pressed to mine.

I swore to myself that I wouldn't let her down.

When I don't budge, Sylas moves to walk past me. I step into his path, blocking my way. "I'm not done."

A hint of a growl creeps into Sylas's voice. "*We* are done, because I've said we are. Move aside, son-of-my-father."

His tone dredges up another memory—of his expression when he came to the entertainment-room doorway and found me with Talia. So sure he had a right to claim her. The possessive heat that rushed through me when I smelled him on her skin surges up again.

I clench my jaw, my fangs itching to emerge. "What kind of man are you to take her into your bed and then cast her aside so callously? I never thought I'd see you model yourself after our father."

Sylas can't quite suppress his wince. He bares his teeth. "If you can't see the difference between—"

I push on before he can continue, driven by that roiling anger. He might know me better than anyone, but I know him pretty well too. I'm aware of exactly how to best wound him. "You treated *Isleen* with more leniency, after everything she—"

"Do *not* bring her into this." Sylas takes a step toward me, drawing himself even straighter to emphasize the few inches of height he has over me. His unmarked eye burns. "This is nothing like that."

"No, it's not. Because Talia has done nothing at all to prompt this outcome, and you're punishing her anyway."

Sylas advances farther, nearly close enough to shove me. "I'll say it one more time, August. We're done talking about this. Get out of my way."

He starts to shoulder by me, and the fury that's been swelling inside me boils over. Adrenaline and the horror of defying him hitting me at the same time, I push him backward.

Sylas snarls and tries to cuff me in the head. I dodge the blow and sock him in the jaw. He lunges at me then, looking as shocked as he does enraged, and I release my wolf without any conscious thought, all my senses shifting into combat mode.

As I whip around on all fours, my claws digging into the rich soil of the orchard, Sylas transforms in mid-leap. He's larger than me in wolf form just as he is as a man. I manage to roll under him, raking my claws across his foreleg and spinning around to face him again.

He doesn't give me a chance to go on the offensive. I've barely found my footing when he's slamming into me, sending me toppling onto my side. I slash out with all four legs, gnashing my teeth, watching for an opportunity to bite, to gouge, anything to get the upper hand.

The instant I began this battle, it became a matter of who could overpower who the fastest. I might not have much of a chance, but I can't surrender.

Sylas snaps at my neck, but I yank my body to the side at the last second. With all my strength, I heave him off me and spring at him. He smacks my muzzle hard enough to make my head reel.

I throw myself to the side, bound off the trunk of a tree, and hurtle toward my lord. He swivels, just barely escaping the lash of my claws, and clamps his jaws around my leg.

One hard jerk sends me tumbling. Before I can scramble up again, he's on me, his full weight jamming me into the ground. His paw presses against my throat, claws digging in only enough to prick my skin. His hindlegs are braced against the most vulnerable part of my belly.

Even knowing it's pointless, I struggle, forcing him to jab his claws deeper in warning. He presses me into the dirt until I start to choke. Then he swipes his paw across the underside of my chin, opening four stinging welts through my fur, and pushes himself off me. Not even bothering to demand a full yield. Just enforcing his power and rebuking me with a superficial wound, like a parent chastening a pup.

Shame ripples through me, stinging sharper than the scratches of his mark. He shifts back into his usual form, standing over me, his scarred brown face intense with an emotion I can't read.

I rein in my wolf and sit up with the transformation.

Without meeting Sylas's eyes, I lean back against a tree trunk, grappling with my own frayed emotions. The air is so warm I only faintly feel the blood trickling down my neck.

"She means that much to you?" Sylas says. I can't read his tone either.

"I've trusted you in so many things, but you're wrong about this one," I reply. "I'll fight for her again if I have to."

"It shouldn't come to that. It shouldn't have come to *this*." Sylas makes a rough, wordless sound and lowers himself to the ground across from me.

We sit there for several minutes in silence. When I dare to look at him, he's staring into the distance, his expression gone pensive.

"I will not rule like our father," he says finally. "I made that decision so long ago that maybe I didn't remember it well enough. It's no kind of lord to be, staying on top by browbeating everyone less powerful than you. I intend to be worthy of every bit of loyalty shown to me. That's why the pack has stayed with us, as many of them as could—because they knew I *wouldn't* compromise my convictions and stoop to baser methods to get ahead."

I'm not completely sure where he's going with this. "You never have," I venture.

His gaze comes back to me. "But I almost did. Those convictions should apply to this girl as much as they do any other being. The moment we found her and saw what Aerik had done to her, she came into our care. It should be beneath me to turn my back on her or look the other way knowing how others might treat her."

Hope flickers into being within my ribs. This—this is why I would lay down my life for this man, why seeking another lord has never occurred to me. "What will you do, then?"

The muscles in his jaw flex. "We've survived the curse this long. We'll continue to survive it until we find our own way to overcome it, permanently. What kind of fae would we be if we find ourselves dependent on a single human girl to save the whole of the Seelie race?" He considers me. "Would you also fight to see her returned to her own world?"

I hesitate, uncertain of how much my answer will sway his judgment regardless of what it is, wanting to be certain of my answer in case he does take it into account. Some of the impulses that jolt through me at that question are selfish, but I think I get the same result even when I separate those out.

"You were right before when you said Aerik will keep hunting her. She's safest with us, as long as no one else discovers the power her blood holds."

"I'm glad to hear I won't have to grapple with you over that point as well." Sylas's tone is dry enough to be a gesture of forgiveness. "It will be… complicated. But following what is right often is. I'm sure we can work out a strategy that minimizes the potential damage."

"You'll talk to her?" I ask. "It's been weighing on her— the uncertainty. I can tell. She should know as soon as—"

"I'll talk to her this morning," Sylas says, gruffly amused. "Give me a moment or two to get my thoughts together first, whelp."

The wolfish part of me wants to lay down in the dirt

belly-up in prostration, to say I recognize his authority and that I'm sorry for challenging it. But the marks on my chin are enough of a chiding—and maybe if I hadn't fought, he wouldn't have recognized his miscalculation in time. I won't regret it.

I might regret what I'm about to say next, but the words tumble out anyway. They've been jostling around in my head too forcefully since the other night.

"Many other cadres have shared lovers between them. Maybe the lord wasn't generally involved in those cases... but it could happen."

The corner of Sylas's mouth twitches upward. "I'm aware of that. But perhaps you should enjoy your first victory before chomping after the next."

He brushes his hands on his slacks and stands. As he strides toward the keep, I can't help noting that while that wasn't a *Yes*, it definitely wasn't a *No* either.

31

Talia

The next time I wake up in my bedroom in the keep, it feels almost like the first morning. I don't remember reaching the building or getting into bed. But the dissonance of finding myself there unexpectedly doesn't come with anywhere near as many fears this time.

Somewhere along the hike back here, fatigue and the ache in my foot caught up with me, and Sylas scooped me into his arms. I must have fallen asleep there. He carried me the whole rest of the way and tucked me in afterward. A tender warmth unfurls in my chest at the thought.

When I kick off the covers, my foot still throbs dully from all the walking. I massage it, careful of the malformed ridge of bone where the broken bits fused wrong, and other memories from the rest of the evening begin to surface. The tension between Sylas and August. Whitt's insistence that I leave. The woman from Tristan's cadre, so suspicious of me and determined to get answers.

I shiver. Are we all in even more danger now? This world scares me, but at the same time, I hate that so much is happening that I can't play a part in. I'm here now. I wish I had more say in my future. I wish I could be more of a participant in the conflicts going on around me instead of an object to be fought over.

I wish my life in the realm of the fae could be as simple as resting nestled against Sylas's chest, but fat chance of that. Even cuddling against him doesn't seem all that simple when I think of how August must have felt, watching us.

The sun is bright beyond my window. I've slept in after that late night, but from the smells seeping under my door, I don't think I've completely missed breakfast. There's definitely a whiff of bacon in that mix. While I'm filling my stomach with deliciousness, it'll be easier not to worry about all the things I can't control.

I've pulled on my clothes and am just fitting the brace around my ankle when there's a knock on the door. Sylas's voice filters through. "Talia?"

"Come in." I pull the last strap tight and straighten up where I'm perched on the seat of the armchair.

As the fae lord steps into the room, my pulse stutters. He didn't chastise me for running away last night, but maybe he didn't want to lay into me while I was exhausted and recently attacked. The full reprisal might be coming now.

Sylas doesn't look angry, though. His unscarred eye gleams bright with an energy I haven't seen in him before, his expression both determined and I want to think a little hopeful. He holds his head high, his massive frame as imposing as ever, but there's something oddly hesitant in the way he stops partway between the doorway and the chair.

I don't know what to make of it. A quiver of anticipation tickles over my skin.

"I've made a decision about your place here," he says, and my heart outright stops.

I curl my fingers around the edge of the seat cushion to steady myself. "Okay."

The corner of his mouth curves upward into a hint of a bittersweet smile. "Don't look like that, little scrap. It isn't bad news—at least, I'd like to believe it isn't. We won't be turning you over to the arch-lords or anyone else."

The shock of the reprieve hits me so hard it's a second before I can breathe again. "What?"

He doesn't wait for me to produce more than that single started word. "You can stay here with us. And I won't demand blood from you either. We *do* believe you're safest if you stay in our domain rather than returning to your own world while Aerik is still searching for you."

I grope for words, still stunned. "Won't you get in trouble for hiding me here?"

"I don't intend for anyone to discover what we're hiding. While you're with us, we can shield you from anyone who might prowl by. And if they should put the pieces together regardless, we can protect you in ways no one in the human world could."

"But—you don't even want a cure for your own pack—?"

His smile widens and tightens at the same time. "I do, but not like this. Whatever has afflicted us these past decades, you aren't a real solution, only a stop-gap that might very well lull us into a false sense of security when we should be seeking out a full cure. We've weathered the wildness plenty of times already, and we can weather it again."

I can stay here, and I won't have to bleed to earn that kindness. A smile of my own splits my face so suddenly my cheeks ache with it.

"We can't keep you cooped up in the keep for all eternity," Sylas goes on. "And now at least one fae beyond these walls knows there's a pink-haired human in our midst. August's bit of frivolity works in our favor, though, since Aerik isn't looking for a girl so brightly colored. Your face and your figure have filled out some since you started getting regular meals, too. We can put a glamour on you to make your limp slip others' notice, and there'll be nothing at all to identify you as his stolen captive. You could go out into the lands around the keep with us, even meet the rest of the pack."

That thought sends a jitter through my nerves. I haven't done a regular "getting to know you" with anyone since I was a kid. What will the regular fae think of me? "Won't they wonder why I'm here?" I ask. "You don't have any other human servants."

He studies me, probably reading my anxiety in my stance. "We don't need to rush that part of things. You might be best off waiting until after the full moon, as everyone gets more tense in the last few days leading up to it. But after... I thought we'd simply tell them that a human girl caught August's fancy keenly enough that he insisted on bringing her home."

Like I'm a kitten the fae man spotted in a pet shop window. The picture that forms in my mind brings back my smile, but it's a little shier than before. "Only *August's* fancy?"

Those three words are all it takes to spark the smolder in Sylas's eyes, hot enough to warm my skin even from a few feet away. His voice drops. "I suppose what happens in that tale next depends on who you bestow *your* fancy on, if anyone."

The heat trickles into my chest with a giddy flutter that's tempered by just one question. "Having me here— it's not going to cause problems between you two, is it?"

"I think we've worked that out," he says, and pauses. "Cadres frequently enjoy the affections of the same woman—or man, as the case may be. When their first loyalty is to their lord, they can't fully devote themselves the way a regular mate would, and sharing a lover can be a way of... offsetting the potential deficiencies in their attentions. If that can be so, then there's nothing to say a lord and his cadre-chosen couldn't have the same arrangement, even if it isn't typically done."

"So, no more fighting?"

The smolder in his unmarked eye darkens, and the memory of his touch the other morning teases over my skin. "You've shown qualities I've found to be rare in fae and humans alike, Talia, so perhaps it's not startling that you've affected both August and me as much as you have. I won't pretend it would be easy for me to share you. Every instinct in me wants to possess you for myself alone. But you *don't* belong to any of us, and if you want us both...

I'm willing to suppress those instincts and see what we can make of it."

The giddiness spreads through my whole body. "Okay. That's fair."

Sylas steps closer, his gaze never leaving my face. "Can you accept the life I'm offering you? All I ask for is honesty. If you still feel caged, and you'll try to run off again—"

I shake my head vehemently, willing the relief that's flooded me to color my voice. "I won't. I'm sorry about yesterday—I… I didn't really want to leave, as crazy as that might sound. I don't have *anything* back in my world. It hardly feels real at this point. My family is gone; my friends will have moved on. And to live with the constant fear that Aerik or some other fae might stumble on me and realize what my blood can do… I think I can be happy here. For now, at least."

Maybe in the future, if the fae find some other cure and I'm no longer such a commodity, I'll want to see what kind of a life I could make back there. The keep already feels more like a home than the house that's faded into fragments of memories, though. And that house wouldn't still be mine anyway.

Sylas's voice drops even lower, washing over me like a caress. "I'm glad to hear that." He touches my face in an actual caress, his fingers brushing over my hair and down across my cheek, and all the heat in me seems to pool deep in my belly.

I do want him—I want so much more with him than we've already done, more than I know how to put into words. But I find there's also something I need to know before I can totally come to terms with that desire.

"You had a mate," I say. "Before. Kellan's half-sister?"

Sylas inclines his head, his smile falling away. "I did. She died before we came here."

I wet my lips, measuring out the question carefully. "Will you tell me what happened to her?"

With a slow exhalation, he sinks onto the edge of the bed across from the chair. His eyes focus on the distance beyond the window. "She was always very… ambitious. And not always in ways I agreed with. Some aspects of temperament ran in her family that you'll have seen in Kellan—stubbornness and a certain ruthlessness." He lets out a rough laugh. "She attempted an incredibly risky move that brought the wrath of the arch-lords down on her. In the ensuing battle, she was cut down. She fought until her death was inevitable, like he did."

The wrath of the arch-lords. A lump rises in my throat. "Is that why you lost your original domain—why you had to come all the way out to the fringes? They punished you too?"

"And also why we have arch-lord's second-cousins concerned enough at the slightest whiff of malcontent to come investigating and leave sentries skulking about."

"But—you've been here for *decades*, haven't you? And if it was all her fault to begin with—"

Sylas makes a dismissive gesture, bringing his gaze back to me. "Her faults were mine. Soul-twined mates are essentially considered one being, reasonably so. You're simply born with something about the essence of your being that resonates with that one other person, and once you complete the bond, your souls *are* literally intertwined. You're aware of each other's thoughts and emotions… I knew what she meant to do. I tried to persuade her otherwise, but I didn't manage to stop her. In that, I share responsibility for her actions."

That still doesn't seem fair to me, but obviously the fae have different ideas of justice. And this whole "soul-twined" thing sounds pretty intense. Maybe I don't understand well enough.

I look at his hand, resting next to his thigh on the bed —wanting to reach for it, not sure if the gesture would be welcome while we're discussing this subject. "It must have been hard, losing her."

"It was. But it was a long time ago. And in some ways it was hard *having* her too. There's a reason only true-blooded fae can make a soul-twined match, and only once in a lifetime. Even the most powerful of us can't always find a way to a happy equilibrium."

True-blooded—I've heard August use that term. Fae who don't have all that much human heritage, the only ones who are considered "pure" enough to rule as lords. I glance up at Sylas's face. "Then August and Whitt—they won't ever have a mate like that?"

Sylas shakes his head. "They could form a mate bond if they and a partner decided to, but it would be voluntary and not so all-consuming. But Whitt has generally preferred not to tie himself down in any area of his life other than his role in the cadre, and August hasn't had a great deal of opportunity… None of us are considered ideal prospects in our current situation."

His tone has become wry. I don't get the impression

he's all that bothered about a lack of consistent female company. And I can't say I'm exactly *sad* to hear that fae women aren't lining up at the keep's doorstep to offer themselves as mates. Maybe August mourns that lost opportunity, though.

As I study Sylas's face, a swell of emotion that's much more than just desire reverberates through me. He's giving me as much freedom as he believes he can without risking someone stealing it away, he's shown more patience and passion than I ever could have hoped for, and it's all been while carrying more responsibilities and regrets than I can imagine. Responsibilities and regrets he shoulders without complaint or letting them weigh his spirits down.

If all those fae women think someone like *Aerik* is a better "prospect," they should have their heads checked.

In my silence, he pushes himself off the bed and moves to go, his demeanor business-like now. "Well then, everything is settled for the time being. I'll determine the best way to construct the glamor around your foot and gait, and there'll be measures to take to ensure your safety during the full moon, but we have a few days for that." He takes a sniff of the air and aims one more smile at me. "There's no rush, as August had a bit of a… delay in getting started on his cooking, but I expect you'll be welcome down for breakfast in a half hour or so."

"Okay. And—wait."

Driven by that rush of emotion, I scramble to follow him, but when I reach his side I find I don't know what to say. The only way I know how to express everything I want to is to grip his shirt and rise up on my toes, seeking out his lips.

Thankfully, Sylas recognizes what I'm attempting, because there's no way I'd reach high enough on my own. He bends to meet my kiss with a fervent rumble that carries from his chest into mine.

For a few seconds, as our mouths meld together and his arms wrap around me, I can't think about anything but the hot, heady thrill of being caught in his embrace. The earthy, smoky smell of him, rich and wild, overwhelms all my senses. I kiss him harder, feeling as if, as long as we're locked together like this, nothing could harm either of us.

Sadly, we can't kiss forever. Sylas lifts his head, and I ease down on my feet reluctantly, still clutching his shirt.

"Thank you," I say.

He leans in again, just long enough for his forehead to graze mine. "And here I feel as if I should be the one thanking you. If I didn't have other matters to attend to…" He makes a frustrated growl. "Well, there is plenty of time ahead of us."

I wait a minute after he's left the room to catch my breath and let the flush fade from my cheeks. Then I limp down the hall to the lavatory for a quick wash and to dampen down the twisted bits of my slept-on hair. A stronger smell of breakfast cooking wafts up the stairs. With a gurgle of my stomach, I emerge, only to find Whitt standing in the hall outside.

Not just standing—waiting for me. As I step past the door, his pose shifts from an aimlessly nonchalant stance to sharper attention. A glint dances in his blue eyes over unfathomable depths that could rival the ocean they stole their color from.

I halt where I am, uncertain. Yesterday, he went from

coldly accusing to protective and repentant in the course of a few hours. How much of either of those states can be blamed on wine or drugged syrups or whatever else he's ingested?

Which side of him am I going to get today?

His gaze is clear enough, his posture steady as he tips his head to me. The suspicion prickles over me that he's sizing *me* up as much as I am him.

"You didn't rat me out to our glorious leader about my role in last night's escapades," he says, his dryly melodic voice quieter than usual. Because he doesn't want Sylas overhearing, presumably.

I can't tell whether that's a statement of gratitude or accusation. Does he think I should have?

I will my posture to stay as straight as his. I'm so tired of being scared. And after last night, after the way Whitt held me... I don't think I need to be. "You said it was a mistake. Unless you've changed your mind about that?"

"Not at all. May you remain our honored guest." The glint in his eye is more a twinkle now. "I still wouldn't have expected you to shoulder the blame."

I shrug. "I made the decision. And I can't see that anything good would have come out of bringing the rest of it up."

Whitt's lips quirk upward into a slanted grin. "Too true, too true." He runs his hand along his broad jaw. "It would have been an awful shame if this beautiful fae face of mine had ended up getting bashed about."

A renewed flush creeps over my face. He's teasing me about the comments I made after drinking that faerie syrup of his and nearly losing my head. The joke doesn't entirely sit right with me, though. "Would Sylas really have attacked you?"

Whitt gives me a shrug of his own, so purposefully casual that I don't believe his indifference. "Probably not. My lord brother has always been more generous than I truly deserve."

A little too much truth carries through in his tone and the momentary flick of his gaze away from me. Did he seek me out not because he wanted to make sure that I wasn't planning on tattling on him later but because he feels guilty... about this? Or more than that?

Without thinking, I step toward him, drawn by the urge to meet that trace of vulnerability with some fraction of the gentleness he showed me pulling me from the fray last night. But the moment I move, something in the fae man's expression shutters. He dips into a mocking little bow and sweeps his arm toward the staircase. "I believe our breakfast awaits. Ladies first?"

I can't see anything good coming out of pushing him either. I turn toward the staircase and drag in a breath, ready to begin my first day here as an actual guest rather than a prisoner.

32

Talia

Sylas tests the uppermost sliding bolt on the door for what must be the hundredth time, giving it a tug with the full heft of his massive shoulders. It doesn't budge, but he still doesn't look entirely satisfied, even though there are three of those bolts now ready to lock my bedroom door from the inside. Watching the fae lord, August frowns, unusually serious himself.

I shift on my feet as if I can squirm away from my anxiety. "Is this necessary? You wouldn't really..." I can't bring myself to finish that question.

Sylas glances from me to the open window. Light glows through it, but it's turned an orange-gold hue as the sun sinks to the west. Soon the day will dwindle into evening. And then most of the light that shines over the keep will be that of the full moon.

"I wish I could say no," he says gravely. "But when the wildness takes over, it clouds our minds completely. We won't remember in the morning, won't have any idea where it took us other than what we can piece together from the evidence around us and on us. Often there's blood. We have a solid enough strategy here that no one's been gravely injured so far, but you are a new factor."

A vulnerable human factor. I restrain a shudder. "But if you taste my blood, that should snap you out of it."

"Any of us could do an awful lot of damage on the way to that tasting." Sylas's gaze falls to my shoulder, the ragged ends of the scars peeking from beneath the short sleeve of my shirt where Aerik or one of his cadre mauled me.

"But if you took it before the moon—"

He cuts me off with a sharp shake of his head. "I will not ask that of you," he says emphatically. "This affliction is our responsibility to deal with, not yours. You've already given up far more for my Seelie brethren than you should ever have had to."

I can tell there's no point in trying to argue. Since the other morning when he told me he wouldn't require me to offer up my blood to the pack, he's stubbornly avoided the subject of my cure and what it could mean for him, as if allowing me to make that offering would injure me in some way far greater than a few drops pricked from my finger.

Still, I can't let it go completely. "Will *you* be all right?"

"As I've said, we have a solid strategy. The one saving grace of the wildness is that we can't work magic or useful things like doorknobs while we're in that form. We lock ourselves in separate areas of the keep so there's no chance we'll injure anyone. The pack members who are most vulnerable stay shut in their homes while the others roam far before the moon has fully risen so there's less chance of them meeting up and savaging one another."

"We've had to patch up wounds here and there the morning after," August puts in. "But nothing serious so far. The furniture and the lesser beasts in the forests are in much more danger than any of us."

Sylas pats my door, grim but apparently satisfied. "This should hold. You'll be fine as long as you stay inside with the bolts drawn. So do that." He glowers at me as if he can force me to follow his command with a stare.

I'm not in any hurry to seek out the company of the fae in murderous wolf form. Just the thought stirs up too many memories, ones that send a chill over my skin. When I've seen Sylas and the others as wolves before, they were always still in control, even when they were fighting. In the grips of the uncontrollable rage the full moon brings out in them, they might be just as vicious as Aerik and his cadre all those years ago.

Whitt's voice steals in from the hallway. "Let's hope all the packs who've had the benefit of Aerik's tonic these past years manage to prepare at least half as well as we do after all this time resting on their laurels." He appears in the doorway, eyebrows arched. "Or, on the other hand, perhaps let's not."

"We shouldn't wish the wildness on anyone," Sylas mutters at him, but it's a mild rebuke.

August motions to the plate he brought up with him, now sitting on my bedside table covered with a silver lid to keep in the heat. "You have your dinner whenever you want it. Did you grab a new book so you don't get bored?"

I motion to the armchair. "I picked out a couple." Though I suspect I won't be able to concentrate on either of them.

Sylas comes over to give my arm a gentle squeeze. "We should check with the pack and then get ourselves situated. As soon as we leave this room, engage the bolts and don't open them until after sunrise, no matter what you hear from the keep or outside. Even if one of us throws ourselves at the door, you should be safe in here." He's checked over the hinges too.

I square my shoulders, trying to sound much calmer than I feel. "I understand. I'll be fine. You just… look after yourselves, as well as you can."

August shoots me a soft smile, Whitt a thinner one, and the three of them tramp back out, Sylas shutting the door behind them. His footsteps stop in the hall, waiting for the sound of the bolts. I hurry over and shove them into place.

For a while, as the glow deepens from gold to amber and then fades into a mere haze, nothing disturbs my sort-of vigil. I spend an hour or so trying to read one of the books, finding myself gazing at the page unsure of what I've just read and having to backtrack more often than not. Then I bring the dinner plate over to the armchair and eat with it balanced on my lap as I peer out the window at the darkening sky.

I can't see the moon from here, but I can feel it coming in the apprehensive tingling that creeps through my body.

The natural light dwindles completely, my orb-like lamp gleaming on beside the chair. The last of the blue in the sky vanishes into blackness speckled with stars. A warm breeze drifts through the window, wildflower-sweet, but with it comes a distant snarl. The hairs on my arms stand on end.

As if that sound has set off a chain reaction, there's a sudden thumping from somewhere below me. A rattle as if the windows in one of the lower rooms are shaking. A howl erupts through the night, followed by the scrabbling of claws and gnashing of teeth from the direction of the pack village. Then a wooden groaning reaches my ears—a door straining with the weight of a heavy wolfish body attempting to thrust it open?

I curl up in the chair, my pulse skittering. More bangs and scuffling sounds carry through the floor. I don't know exactly where Sylas and the others have shut themselves away, only that Sylas intended to keep them all out of this section of hallway. The fact that he put those bolts on my door despite those other precautions shows how wary he feels he needs to be of their potential for violence. Have they broken down barriers they set up before?

How can he be completely sure *my* door will hold?

The creaking groan starts up again outside—or maybe it's a different beast in a different building attempting the same escape. Something crashes through the brush near the edge of the forest. A roar of rage splits the air from some distant spot, followed by a vicious snarl, and I suspect two of the pack members didn't manage to steer totally clear of each other.

The thought of them tearing into each other makes me cringe. I get up and yank the window shut to block out most of the sound.

The sound from *outside*, anyway. Without that distraction, the noises within the keep come into sharper focus. The smack of a body ramming into a wooden surface reverberates through the walls. Claws scrape against the boards. A strangled growl reaches my ears, angry but also... anguished.

I know how much Sylas and his cadre hate falling into this state, and it doesn't sound as if the wolves they've become are enjoying the wildness either.

I get to my feet, a twisting sensation in my gut driving me to pace the floor in my hobbled way, worrying my lip under my teeth.

How can I sit here when the men who've sheltered me, cared for me, and fought to the death for me struggle in the grips of this curse? I don't know what caused it or who might be responsible, but they don't deserve it. No one deserves to be forced into becoming the thing they hate most.

Thunk. Thunk. One of them is hurling himself into a door or perhaps a wall over and over again. Oh, God. How bruised will his body be when he comes back to himself? Will they tear into themselves when they can't find anyone else to take out their rage on?

I can't let it come to that. I wanted to have more say in everything going on around me; I wanted to be a participant rather than an object. Well, this is the one time I definitely can intervene in a way that'll make a real difference, isn't it?

The second that thought crosses through my head, a strange stillness fills my chest. I stop by the door, the tension in my gut easing. My heart is thudding faster, but not with fear—or at least, not only fear. There's resolve in there too. Resolve and hope and a sense of power like the moment I let myself become furious for the first time. Except this calm certainty is more potent than the chaotic surge of anger.

Sylas wouldn't let himself ask me. He wouldn't take my blood even when I offered. He probably didn't trust that I was doing it freely and not because I felt I owed him.

The wolf he's turned into won't refuse me, though. If I can bring him and August and Whitt out of this wild state, no one will find out. It won't hurt any of us, and it'll release them from this horror.

I can make this one small offering of help after everything they've done for me. I'm the *only* one who can help them through this.

The resolve spreads through my limbs, bolstering my courage. It isn't a question of whether I'll do it. It's only a matter of how.

If I'm not careful, if I end up getting hurt, they'll come out of the wild state only to be wracked with guilt. There's got to be a way to avoid their jaws. All they need is a tiny bit of blood. Aerik never took more than would leave me a little light-headed, and that was enough to make tonics for dozens, maybe hundreds of fae.

I lean close to the door. A savage bark reaches my ears, then a sound like glass smashing, but it's definitely not *close*. There's at least one more door between my room and wherever the fae men have shut themselves away.

I have to go out and see what I'm working with before I can come up with a plan.

My throat tightening, I push the bolts aside and ease open the bedroom door. I keep my hand clamped on the knob as I peek outside, but the hall is empty as I expected, nothing but the dim glow of the single lantern orb halfway down its length.

Creeping out, I can discern the violent noises more clearly. As far as I can tell, they're all coming from below— I don't think any of my protectors are on this floor. They'll have wanted to keep themselves as far from me as possible.

Sylas is going to be pissed off about how I risked myself even if I *don't* get injured in the process. Oh well. I raise my chin and limp onward. I belong to me, and this is my life to risk or not. He'll just have to get over it.

I've reached the top of the staircase when a roar loud enough to make the floor tremble tears through the keep. My legs lock, my pulse lurching.

An icy wave of panic races through me. The images flicker up: blood and grass and twilight shadows, cries and snarls, pain searing through my shoulder—

I close my eyes and grit my teeth, my hands clenched so tight my fingernails dig into my palms. That night was horrible and brutal, and maybe I'll never make up for the devastation I caused, but it's been nearly ten years now. I'll definitely never make up for it if I let the horror overwhelm me every time I'm faced with a vivid reminder.

If that moment stops me from doing what I think is right, what I *want* to do, then I don't belong to myself after all. I'm letting the fear and the vicious fae who triggered it own me.

The fae in this keep aren't vicious, not like Aerik and his men. They might be lost in their wildness right now, but I know they're different. I know that even if they do hurt me, they'll make it right.

The terror doesn't leave. It stays tangled through my ribs and stomach. But with a few gulps of air, I manage to master it enough to move my feet. One and then the other, the soft padding of my bare sole and the tapping of the brace forming an uneven tempo, I slip down the steps slowly but surely.

33

Talia

The first stretch of the main-floor hallway looks as normal as the hall upstairs, but when I reach the bottom, I'm met by even more unnerving sounds. Thuds echo up from the basement along with ragged grunts and then an inhuman moan. At least one of the fae men has locked himself away down there.

But the clearest noises carry from up ahead. I propel myself onward to where the hall splits.

A solid wooden barrier stands toward the end of the passage to my right, where the entrance room should begin. Now I know exactly where one of these crazed wolves is. As I approach the barrier, racing animal footsteps pound across the floor on the other side. With a harsher *thump*, the wooden surface shudders. The beast on the other side must have thrown himself against it.

It's holding—but I can't do anything for the man it's holding back while it's in place. My breath coming shakily,

I walk down the hall until I'm only a few feet from the barrier. At the snarls and snapping of teeth on the other side, my whole body shivers with the urge to flee as fast as I can. I tense my muscles, willing myself still so I can examine this new door.

It fills the entire width and height of the hall, which is substantial. As far as I can tell, it's constructed so that it slides out from behind a panel in the wall, which must be why I never noticed it before. The thick bronze hinges barely quiver when the body in the room beyond slams into the barrier again. The thumbturns for five deadbolts form a line up the other edge, securing it in place.

Did one of the others lock him in from here? Or maybe it's safer having access to the locks from both sides of the door in case whoever's trapped beyond injures himself in his wildness and can't release them himself the next morning. Either way, I can get to him. The question is how I do that without being halfway devoured.

While I stand there, gathering my nerve and grasping at my options, the savage noises from the front hall travel farther away. A few distant thumps, rattles, and scrapes suggest the beast is grappling with the front door now. Then there's the sound of tearing fabric and a feral growl.

Fabric—maybe I could work with that. I hurry back through the halls to the kitchen and jerk open the drawers until I find the rags August uses to wipe the counters. Gripping one against my palm, I scan the glinting metal handles of the knives in their sharpening block. As I pull the smallest one free, my mouth goes dry.

No big deal. Just make a little cut, dab a bit of blood on the cloth, and make sure the wolf gets it in his mouth.

Aerik cut me open enough times. I should be able to handle it when I'm the one holding the blade.

Sitting on my regular stool, I brace myself against the island behind me and bring the cutting edge to my thumb. My hands shake. The knife glides through my flesh like I'm made of butter, slicing deeper than I meant to with a lance of pain that shoots right through the joints to my wrist.

Hissing through my teeth, I press the rag to the wound. A crimson splotch blooms across the cream-colored fabric faster than I was prepared for. As I stare at it, my head swims. I close my eyes, clamping my pressure around my thumb and breathing in slow, soothing breaths, imaging sparkling ponds and serene forests.

I can't stay in the peaceful images conjured in my head, though. Not if I want to see this task through.

The pain eases but doesn't disappear. As I fumble for another rag to tie around my thumb as a bandage, stinging jolts keep radiating through my hand. The rag I'll use to offer the wolf his cure is streaked with plenty of blood now, so at least I've got that part of the plan thoroughly covered. I can't imagine it won't be enough.

I just have to get the cloth into the creature's mouth. A raging, ravenous creature that sounds ready to slaughter the walls themselves if it could. No big deal.

A slightly hysterical laugh spills from my lips. It's either that or give in to the urge to sob.

My pulse races faster with each step I take toward the front hall. Halfway there, I have to stop and catch my breath, fighting the terror constricting my lungs.

I can do this. Just one taste of the blood on this rag,

and the beast on the other side of the door will be himself again.

I stop at the sliding barrier and listen. A low growl reverberates through the room beyond. The grating sound of claws against wood paints a picture of the massive wolf stalking back and forth, pacing with frustration.

If I simply toss the rag in there, will he even bother with it? One little scrap of cloth isn't likely to interest or enrage him. In this wild state, he's seeking out a real fight.

A sense of understanding settles over me. I have to make sure he sees me. That he comes this way with enough aggression that he'll snap up the cloth when I throw it. Once it's in his mouth, I'll be safe again. There's no reason that tactic shouldn't work.

But there's no reason to assume I'll pull it off exactly as I'm picturing it either.

At the thought of the ferocious monster in the hall charging at me, another wave of panic smacks into me, leaving me dizzy. My fingers curl around the bloody rag. I brace myself against the door, gulping for air and willing back the images flooding my mind, the shivers wracking my limbs.

It would be so easy to scurry back up to my bedroom, throw the bolts, and curl up in bed until morning. No one expects anything more than that from me; no one would blame me for it.

No, that's not true. *I* expect more. I would blame me.

I'm here. I've done everything I need to except face the beast. How many battles have these men already fought for me?

If they're going to keep me safe, nurture me, and stand up for me, then I've got to find a way to stand *with* them.

As the seconds slip by, I drag breath after breath into my lungs. When the images from my attack flash through my mind, I train all my awareness not on landscapes I've never visited outside of my imagination but on the very real times when the men I mean to help kept me safe. August offering me the pouch of salt. Sylas nestling me against his chest. Whitt hugging me to him, murmuring soothing words to drown out the snarls of a fight.

Gradually, my chest loosens. Each breath courses deeper than the last. The violent images of the past dwindle, and then it's just me in the hall, one hand flat against the wooden barrier and the other clutched around a bloody rag.

Despite everything my former captors put me through, I haven't been broken. I'm still alive. I'm still living. Nothing they did can stop me now.

My heart continues pounding against my ribs, but I focus on the movement of my free hand: raising it to twist the highest lock open, and then dropping it to the next, and the next, and the next. As I reach the last one at the bottom, my arm trembles. I inhale once more, long and steady, and turn the tumbler over.

There's no sound on the other side of the barrier. Has the wolf heard the click of the locks? What's it doing now?

Only one way to find out.

Before my fear can paralyze me again, I give the sliding door a forceful yank. It's heavy enough that even that effort opens a gap of mere inches. But inches is enough.

Orbs glow amber in the hall on the other side—except

for one that lies shattered on the floorboards. Floorboards mottled with gouges from brutal claws. And the source of those claws, the hulking wolf whose dark fur glints with that hazy light, whirls to face me at the rasp of the door.

That instant is all it takes for me to recognize it as Sylas—the scarred white eye reveals him at once. An instant is all I really have, because the next second his wolf has pitched toward me, barreling across the hall like a speeding Mack truck, a snarl tearing up his throat.

My spine stiffens, and panic blanks my mind. My hand gropes to heave the door shut again, but I've readied myself for this act well enough that the rest of me moves automatically. I resist the terrified impulse and tense my other hand. Sylas's wolf hurtles toward me, faster with every stride, jaws yawning open—and I whip my arm forward.

The bloody rag flies through the air. The wolf lunges at it, close enough that the momentum of his charge ripples through the air and over my skin. His fangs snatch the cloth out of the air, the bloody folds falling into his open mouth.

He skids to a halt, claws scrabbling against the floor, so close that if I stretched, I could touch his thick fur from where I'm standing. I don't, because I'm gasping and shaking, renewed tremors shooting through my limbs just at being this close to the beastly form.

The wolf shakes his huge head. He spits out the rag and looks up at me. And those eyes...

Those eyes are Sylas in every way, not just by the color and the scar. For the first time, I'm close enough to see *him* in the wolf. To realize that the other times I panicked, the other skirmishes I witnessed—it was always my men fighting for me. Not monsters, not even really animals. Except for this night with the full moon's curse, they've always been themselves, just in a different skin.

Sylas hunches, and then all of him transforms into the man I'm used to, kneeling there on the floor. He's wearing a simple short-sleeved shirt and loose slacks for tonight, barefoot, with the waves of his hair falling riotously around his face. Still, he looks every inch a lord.

"Talia," he says, his voice so hoarse I suspect even saying my name took some effort. "You—what are you *doing*? I told you—"

I grip the side of the sliding door and stare right back at him with a flare of defiance that cuts through my dwindling fear. "You told me to stay in my room. I know. But *I* decided it mattered more to me to snap you out of the curse." My throat closes up all over again, but this time it's not out of terror. "You broke me out of a prison I never deserved to be in. Why can't I do the same for you?"

That wildness trapped him in his wolfish body and the feral rage even more soundly than the bars of my cage had trapped me.

His mouth slants as if he wants to argue but can't quite bring himself to. "We talked about this."

"We talked about why it wouldn't be safe for me to help the whole pack and why you didn't want to ask me to help just you. You didn't ask. This was totally my decision, made freely. And no one will know you came out of the wildness early, will they? Right now, every other fae in this realm is mad with it."

He glances down at the crimson-splotched rag by his

knee and then at the cloth wrapped around my thumb. "I could have hurt you."

"But you didn't. So there's nothing to complain about."

His lips twitch. I think that time he might have suppressed a smile. "I suppose this is what I get for stealing away a little scrap of a woman who's got more mettle than anyone would give her credit for."

The corners of my own mouth curl upward, and the last lingering traces of panic melt away. I set my hands on my hips. "Yes, it is. Now come on. You can help make sure I take care of August and Whitt without getting torn to bits."

"Taking orders from a human," Sylas mutters to himself, but he gets up, grabbing the rag as he does. He eyes the damp fabric. "I think this should do the trick, no more bloodletting on your part required. I doubt you needed half this much."

"Well, I didn't want to take any chances. And also, the knife slipped." At the darkening of his eye, I wave off his impending objections. "I'm *fine*. But August and Whitt aren't. Are they both in the basement?"

"Yes." Despite my insistence about my wellbeing, he slips his hand around my wrist and mutters a magically-charged word. My skin prickles beneath my makeshift bandage, the ache in my thumb fading as his power must seal the wound. Then he pulls ahead of me, stalking toward the basement stairs as if either of the other wolves might come barging up right this minute to attack me. If taking the lead makes him happier about the situation, he's welcome to it.

The basement hall has been barricaded at both ends with sliding barriers like the one upstairs, the first by the gym and the second just beyond the entertainment room. Having seen the smashed lantern orb in the front hall, I have to guess the TV and game systems wouldn't survive a full moon night intact if one of the beasts got at it.

The wolf behind the barrier at that end is clawing at it, letting out a sharp howl when I pause.

"That's Whitt," Sylas says. "As much as it actually is him in this state."

I turn toward the other end. "Let's start with August." I'd rather save whatever snarky remarks Whitt is going to make for after I'm finished with this ordeal.

It's less of an ordeal with the fae lord by my side, though. I insist on standing by the door, but he unlocks it and shoves it aside, braced to shield me if the gambit doesn't work. August's ruddy-furred wolf wheels from where he was wrestling with the high, narrow window frame and springs toward us. I barely have time for my stomach to flip over before Sylas has tossed the rag and my blood has touched the wolf's tongue.

When August shifts back into his usual form, he scrambles to his feet at once, blinking at us. "What— I thought—"

"So did I," Sylas says, a trace of amusement lightening his baritone. "Our lady had other ideas." He grazes his hand over the top of my head, rumpling my hair.

Our lady. Not "the girl" or even "our guest." As if I'm an actual part of this household now. I beam at August, afloat on the pleasure of those words and of seeing him freed, and he grins right back at me. "You're a marvel," he says.

"I'm not done yet. Let's get Whitt."

I've got even less to worry about with two immense fae warriors flanking me, but somehow the sight of Whitt's wolfish form still sends a jolt of panic through me. Tawny furred and as muscular as his half-brothers, he tears toward us with fangs gleaming. His own blood darkens one side of his muzzle where he must have scraped his flesh raw in his attempts to break free.

When he snatches the tossed rag out of the air and falters, the ocean-blue eyes gleaming in his wolfish face look dazed. He seems to gather himself as a wolf, dipping his head and rubbing his wounded muzzle against his foreleg, before he transforms with a dog-like shake of his frame.

He cocks an eyebrow as he pushes himself upright, ignoring the abrasion still seeping blood over the edge of his jaw. "Change of plans?" His gaze lingers on me.

I smile at him, a little nervously. "We're all in this together."

August steps toward him, and after a half-hearted protest, Whitt lets him speak a few words that transform the shallow wound into a patch of solid if pinkish skin. Afterward, the younger man glances in the direction of the outside houses, the muscles in his arms flexing with restless energy. "What about the rest of the pack? They'll be so scattered by now—and it'd still raise all kinds of questions if we bring them out of the wildness."

"We'll have to let them ride out the moon," Sylas says, and touches my head again. "But don't think you haven't given them a gift as well. Now that we have our heads, we can go out and keep some kind of order between them. Fewer injuries to treat in the morning."

Whitt rolls his shoulders. "Good. I could use a run after being cooped up down here."

Sylas nudges me around so I'm fully facing the fae lord. "*You* will remain inside behind locked doors—and actually *stay* this time. We won't be able to protect you out there with so many fae roaming around. Understood?"

I nod emphatically. I don't have a death wish. "I'll stay inside. I swear it."

"And I accept your oath." His fingers skim down my arm and back up again, and a tingle travels over my skin at his touch. "I can only imagine how difficult coming to us in this state must have been for you, Talia. You will never owe it to us to do so. And I won't forget your bravery on our behalf."

"It was the least I could do after everything you've given me." I glance at the other two men standing around me. "All of you."

Sylas hums low in his throat. When I turn back to him, his hand glides up to my jaw. He tips my head back and claims my mouth with the hot brand of his lips. The earlier tingle blazes with a rush of heat.

A rough sound like a choked-down growl emanates from August's chest. When Sylas releases me, I don't let myself hesitate. I reach for the other man who's made my heart and body sing and rise up to kiss him too, ignoring the very definite growl that escapes Sylas before he bites it back.

August meets my kiss tenderly but determinedly,

unleashing a torrent of passion with the press of his mouth. I could get drunk on this. I *feel* a little drunk as I sink back down, which must be why when my gaze reaches Whitt, I bob up without thinking and kiss him on the cheek.

It's only a peck, and I barely even reach his cheek, my mouth skimming the uninjured side of his jaw, but Whitt stiffens. I swivel toward Sylas, my face flushed. I don't want to witness the other man's rejection of even that small gesture of affection.

The fae lord's gaze smolders down at me, but he keeps any possessive emotions he's grappling with under wraps. "We'll likely be out until dawn. Don't wait up for us."

Even with Whitt's reaction, the sense of being part of this household hasn't left me. I balk at the thought of losing it, even for a moment. "What if I want to?"

Sylas chuckles softly. "Then I suppose that's up to you, as you've well proven." He nods to the others. "We'd best get moving."

34

Talia

True to my word, I don't venture outside the keep. Instead, I settle into one of the parlor armchairs and watch from the windows as Sylas and his cadre shepherd their pack.

They've shifted back into their wolfish forms to do it, as makes sense when they're contending with beasts in the grips of the full-moon ferocity. Sylas, the most massive creature of them all, lopes across the field emanating feral power and shoulders apart two wolves who've started snapping at each other. August clamps his jaws on one's neck, just tightly enough to hold and not wound, and tugs it in one direction while Whitt shoves the second wolf in another.

I've heard them refer to the pack so many times, but I've never grasped just what that means until now, witnessing them working together as leaders over their people, watching the other wolfish fae respond even in their wild state. Seeing it, the glimpses of fangs and claws no longer spark the fear they used to.

Those aren't the marks of monsters. They're tools to be used as their owners see fit. And Sylas and his cadre bring them to bear with care and conviction.

When the first rays of the sun peek over the horizon, my head is muggy but my eyes still open, if starting to ache. The three wolves of the keep come trotting around the side of the building as one being. I push myself out of the chair and head to the entrance room to meet them.

The gouges from Sylas's raging claws still scar the floorboards. I guess he must use his magic to fix them once he's recovered from the night's horrors. Now, the fae lord bobs his head to me and sprawls on the floor with a wolfish yawn as if too tired to move any farther, to even shift into his typical body.

I hesitate and then, my heart beating only a little faster than usual, walk up to him. As I sink down on the rug next to him, I stroke a tentative hand over his fur.

It's a mix of coarse and silky, so thick I could bury my fingers in it and barely make out my knuckles. The wolf lets out a pleased thrum and nuzzles me closer to his side. As I rest my head on his body, his chest rising and falling with slowing breaths beneath me, August and Whitt join us.

The other two wolves recline on the floor, forming a circle around me. I stretch my arm to rub the spot between August's ears, and he gives me an eager pant with a flash of his tongue before tucking his muzzle over my knee and closing his eyes.

My eyelids slip shut too. It's been a long night, and the

rhythm of Sylas's breaths within that ring of warmth lulls me right to sleep.

I wake up late enough that the sun shines brightly through the skylights, and find not fur beneath my head but the fabric of Sylas's shirt. Sometime as they slept, the fae lord and his cadre have transformed back into men.

Sylas's arm rests protectively against my back. Fingers are stroking over my ankle. Glancing down, I'm surprised to see they belong to Whitt. His head is cushioned on his arm just inches from my heel, his other hand drifting idly as it rests against my calf, maybe caught up in some dream. From their relaxed expressions and the slackness of their bodies, all three appear to still be asleep.

I suppose they tired themselves out a lot more than I did last night. My part of the work was over pretty quickly. And maybe they're more used to sleeping on floors. When I ease myself into a sitting position, my back protests, an ache running from my shoulder blade to my hip.

A yawn stretches my jaw, but my bladder pinches at the same time, demanding release before I try to get any more rest myself. August stirs but doesn't wake as I step carefully over his legs. I slip down the hall, setting my foot brace down as quietly as I can given the stiffness of my joints. Once I reach the staircase, I let myself move a little faster.

When I emerge from the second-floor privy, the brilliant gleam of the sunlight catches my eye. I meander over to the big window where weeks ago I watched Whitt host a revel and realized there was more to him than wry remarks and artful carelessness.

A few of the pack members have gone to sleep in the field, finally at peace after that long, horrible night. No one is moving around the houses that I can see. My eyes travel beyond them, over the wider plains and the distant forest, and then across to the rolling hills at the southeast end of Sylas's domain.

My gaze stalls on a lupine form poised at the top of one of those hills. A fae still embracing his wolf.

There's nothing so odd about that. It could have been that one of the pack members woke up early and went for a run to shake off uneasiness leftover from last night. But what's frozen me in place isn't the fact that there's a wolf at all, but the color of its fur catching in the sunlight.

It's a blueish white like a thick layer of ice over open water. Like icicles reflecting a clear winter sky.

Like the hair of the sharp-edged man from Aerik's cadre.

The wolf is watching the keep just as I'm watching the wolf. It tilts its head at a devious angle so like my most vicious former captor that the bottom drops out of my stomach, taking any doubt I'd held onto with it.

Then the creature whips around and vanishes down the back of the hill, leaving me clutching the window frame and wondering how long I have before the home I just won is wrenched from me.

ABOUT THE AUTHOR

Eva Chase lives in Canada with her family. She loves stories both swoony and supernatural, and strong women and the men who appreciate them. Along with the Bound to the Fae series, she is the author of the Flirting with Monsters series, the Cursed Studies trilogy, the Royals of Villain Academy series, the Moriarty's Men series, the Looking Glass Curse trilogy, the Their Dark Valkyrie series, the Witch's Consorts series, the Dragon Shifter's Mates series, the Demons of Fame Romance series, the Legends Reborn trilogy, and the Alpha Project Psychic Romance series.

Connect with Eva online:
www.evachase.com
eva@evachase.com

.

Printed in Great Britain
by Amazon

40721497R00209